The Wrong Lover

Contact Nancy at:
www.NancyBrophy.com
NancyBrophy@gmail.com

Other books Published by Nancy Brophy:

Plotting Your Story Arc, Workbook for Fiction Writers, Plotters and Pantsers

Fiction:

Hell On The Heart
The Wrong Brother
The Wrong Hero
The Wrong Cop

The Wrong Lover
Bonus Book 3.5

The Wrong Lover is the only book in the series in which the hero was not a SEAL. It is the prequel to The Wrong Cop, book 3.

Lily Carmichael and Dori Conners were business partners, co-owning Luscious Foods. I love smart hard-working women who aren't waiting for a man to save them. This is where Dori's story begins.

Marshall and Lily are too old, too busy, and much too clever to fall in love. The oceanographer Marshall views women as a wonderful recreational pastime. Lily the successful caterer seeks a fantasy man for one steamy, passionate night.

This was the perfect arrangement. What could possibly go wrong?

Book 1 –
The Wrong Brother
Zack and Chloe

This is what lying got you – the wrong brother.

Book 2 –
The Wrong Hero
Travis and Abby

"If this is a chess game, the one thing you should have been able to predict is that the queen always protects the king.

Book 3 –
The Wrong Cop
Grant and Dori

"It pisses me off I'm attracted to you." His erection betrayed his words.
He was lying, but so was she. "You're like the wad of gum on the sole of my shoe. Only worth as much consideration as it takes to get rid of you."

Book 3.5 - Bonus book –
The Wrong Lover
Marshall and Lily

Her brown eyes and raspy voice stayed with him. Her taste lingered on his lips. After this fiasco was over, he'd find her. All he knew was that her name was Lily, but it wasn't her name he was after.

Book 4 –
THE WRONG HUSBAND
Austin and Nicole

"It's a vacation and we are going to have a fabulous time."

Book 5 –
THE WRONG SEAL
Sam and Imogene

She had no idea how lucky she'd been to be raised in a place where crazy people weren't running the circus.

Dedication

This book is dedicated to all the women who are adept at finding the one guy in a large group who is absolutely toxic for them.

I am such a woman. Not only can I find that guy, but then I devote all my resources to making a doomed relationship work. Recently I read less women are marrying now than ever before.

Scientists wonder why.
(Waves hand)
I know. Call on me. I can tell you.

And this book is for Lily who risk everything to give love one more chance - just like you and I would.

Someone once said: When love happens, hope triumphs experience.

The Wrong Lover

Nancy Brophy

Chapter One

Lily Carmichael, co-owner of Luscious Foods, stepped into the white canvas tent housing the buffet tables, still hearing the bride's screeching words in her ears.

"No sides." The tall brunette with up-swept lacquered hair, perfect makeup and elaborate nail polish, referred to the tent walls. "Let the beauty of the Gorge come through." She threw back her hand in a gesture worthy of a Broadway show and spun on a spiky heel.

Lily smiled. Brides should be happy on their wedding day, but a decision needed to be made and every choice had a consequence. "The food will be cold because the Sternos won't hold a flame in this wind."

The bride stopped in mid-swing and pondered that statement for a brief moment. "Bruce, what do you think?" She turned toward the groom, seated at a table for ten, his face tilted toward the mini IPad in his hand.

Nuts. Lily could predict his answer without a crystal ball. "Will it cost less if we don't use sides?" Bruce didn't even raise his head.

That had been three hours ago – before the tent workers had left. Before the wind had gotten serious.

A dentist wrestling with a stubborn tooth hadn't worked any harder to extract a compromise from the couple. Two clear plastic walls were set on the riverside. The rest would remain open.

All had been calm. Now the walls snapped, and the nylon cords tugged at the metal poles. The blustery weather, angry at being thwarted, set up a pitiful mourning wail.

The caterers scrambled as the guests arrived for the ceremony held further up the hill.

The bride's mother came to inspect, clutching a hat. "Can't you do anything about this weather?"

Acorn. Tree. Lily bit her lower lip to prevent errant thoughts from escaping.

The sun was shining. In Oregon in April that was a blessing in itself. What did the family think would happen when they chose a venue on the cliffs high above the Columbia River, mere miles from Hood River, the windsurfing capital of the world?

"Light the Sternos," she directed two of her catering staff. "The ceremony is well underway. There is a receiving line, so we've got fifteen to twenty minutes before guests head for the food."

The women flicked their wands, clicking the stubborn triggers four or five times until the flames appeared. The row of silver-plated food chafers held two Sterno burners each to keep the food hot. Despite the sunshine, spring was still jacket weather and today was no exception.

Guest tables surrounded the stage where the band instruments waited. Lily's business partner, Dori crawled on hands and knees stapling the linens to the tables. Following on her heels and crouched even lower was Dori's niece and sometime employee, Allyn, taping tablecloths to the ground.

She returned her attention to the staff. "When you're finished, light the centerpiece candles. If they don't stay lit, it's not our problem, we told the bride candles would be a mistake."

The women headed toward the guest tables to complete the task. Lily laughed for no particular reason. She loved being outdoors, she loved catering, and while she hated the venue, the majestic view of the mountains overlooking the Columbia River was a sight worth seeing.

For a brief fanciful moment, she saw herself in a dirndl skirt singing, *The hills are alive with…"*

She snorted.

Wheeling the hot boxes closer to the buffet table, Lily elevated the salads, tilting the bowls and cascading the fruits and vegetables.

Luscious Foods was renowned for their attractive food displays. Pristine yellow roses sparkled against black linens like gemstones in a jeweler's showcase. The stunning effect set in a garden of blooming pink and purple azaleas was photo-op perfect. Only the intermittent blasts of breeze roaring through the cracks in the tent siding interfered.

Her partner's shoulder-length blonde hair had been secured at the nape of her neck by a black bow, maintaining a professional look in her crisp uniform. Lily admired her resilience. The wind had a personal vendetta with Lily and had whipped her short dark curly hair into a wild frenzy as if the Bride-of-Frankenstein underwent electric shock therapy. Despite the matching uniform, Lily's professional appearance sucked.

Opening a hot box, Lily breathed in the smell of succulent chicken edged with the tangy bite of citrus. She hoisted the first of the scalding insert pans. Her flying hair stung her cheeks and blocked her vision, but not her hearing. The nylon cord had given up the battle. Gale force currents of air charged through the ever-increasing opening like shoppers on Black Friday.

She braced her feet as a series of metallic pings warned of impending disaster. At the end of the buffet line, a chafer toppled. The wind upended not one can of Sterno, but two. Pink goo oozed across the table. Flames followed the accelerant's path igniting the linens.

With her hands full, Lily stared in horror. The yell caught in her throat. In seconds, the entire table was ablaze. Hungry fingers of fire reached for her.

The pan of chicken tilted when she jumped, slopping lemon caper sauce onto her skin. Burning pain seared as the hot liquid skated over her hands. Her fingers opened, and the hot pan plummeted to the table's edge, catching a chafer before crashing to the ground.

Boiling water and hot chicken sauce splashed against her pants. Lily yelped and stumbled backward hitting the corner pole of the tent. She scraped the tender skin from her arm as she lost her balance and collapsed against the brick edge of the flowerbed. Pain cut like a knife across her back.

As she scrambled to her feet as another gust lifted the lightweight Sternos. Like a flaming Frisbee game, the wind tossed the gelatinous incendiary fuel and ignited areas previously untouched.

Lily ripped off her jacket to beat at the flames, leaping out of control. Somewhere in the disaster she found her voice, but the stress from the impending doom had her swearing like a sailor in a sinking boat.

Marshall Caudill arrived at the wedding, in time to hear the minister say, "Who gives this woman…" The couple along with the bride's father stood beneath the arched trellis doubling as an altar.

Heavy traffic on the long drive from the coast slowed his car and soured his attitude. Rather than being seated late, he lounged against the stone pillar of the lodge porch and watched from a distance. Absently he searched the guests for Muffy.

Why would anyone want to be married here? Not only was it off the beaten path, this place was a wind tunnel. The bride's veil was plastered to her. The minister used a microphone, but his words disappeared in the air.

The grounds were well-groomed, a touch overly floral for his taste, but this sorry excuse for a lodge looked like an abandoned miner's shaft. The oversized padlock on the door probably was designed to protect the owner from lawsuits.

Since these were Muffy's friends he bet it cost a bundle to use the grounds. Marshall shifted against the pillar and glanced at his watch. "C'mon. Say 'I do.' Let's get on with this."

Work piled up on his desk. He'd brought his computer and the most pressing files with him. Had he not had a weekend of activities scheduled he wouldn't have come at all. He groaned inwardly.

His sister had begged him to participate in the Cancer Fund Raiser tomorrow evening. Reluctantly, he'd agreed two months ago when his calendar had been fairly clear.

This was followed by Muffy's coy invitation. He frowned. The woman was a one-woman train wreck. After only a few dates, she acted like their names had been etched in concrete forever and all time. She dangled sex like a carrot but backed away with every move he made.

"Marshall, this wedding is important to me. You must come. There will be a reward in it for you."

What? Another kiss? And another admonishment not to mess her hair?

Ice water ran in the woman's veins, not passion.

As he aged, dating became trickier. With some dates, a man could walk away. Others required finesse. He'd tried both with her. Nothing had worked.

The groom's back was toward him, but the bride beamed as the music faded. He shook his head reminded of the old joke about the reason a woman smiled at her wedding because she knew she'd never have to give another blow job again.

Yeah, hard to believe he hadn't rushed into that delightful trap.

He pushed himself from the pole and took two steps closer to see if he could spot Muffy before he became entrenched in the entire mass exodus.

In that tranquil moment, the distinct sound of a female swearing ripped away the silence.

He took a few steps to the left to the see the patio farther down the hill. Under a scorched white canopy, flames boogied with a passion that threatened to take the tent and most of the wedding reception with it.

A dark-haired woman wearing black pants and white bra emptied pans of water onto the table before throwing them to the ground.

Great balls of fire. Literally.

Marshall's heart leaped into his throat. With this remote location, the place would burn to the ground before a volunteer fire department could get anywhere near the property. He grabbed a bucket stuck up against the porch in a decorative display. Somewhere there had to be a water spigot and if he was lucky – a hose. The spigot was an easy find. No hose.

Moving quickly, he shoved the pail under the too-short faucet and spun the dial to full blast. With the tub almost full, he maneuvered the sloshing water from under the hardware and hot-footed it down the incline.

The caterers danced in a stomping frenzy across burning fabric on the grass. Others pushed over tables, scattering their burdens across the debris, adding fuel to the fire. The topless brunette's jacket was half-burned, but she still beat at the flames furiously. Among all the panicked cries from the caterers, her cursing was a curious note of sanity.

"Stand back."

Five pairs of eyes looked at him. No one spoke, but each scrambled out of the way. Marshall poured the water carefully over the charred mess dousing the final flames.

Burned linens and miscellaneous pieces of service ware littered the lawn. Overturned tables, a smoke-blackened canopy, discarded food and a half-naked woman made it the most interesting wedding reception he'd ever attended.

Then as though a silent bell rang, without a word spoken, four of the women sprang into action. Two righted the tables, another reassembled the metal pans, and a fourth gathered the ruined tablecloths. The brunette, whose fast action saved the tent, now stood stunned. It was impossible not to notice her idle in a group of busy women.

He almost laughed. Talk about an inaccurate understatement. He'd already noticed her – a woman in singed clothing and a bra smudged with soot covering a pair of the nicest breasts he'd seen in a while. A woman, whose command of gutter language impressed him, amused him. And even shocked him a bit.

The rounded curves represented a lushness he seldom saw. Not the bountiful abundance of a fertility goddess, but sensual curves that made his fingers curl.

He studied her face. Maybe forty, but pretty skin. Pale with rosy cheeks. A milkmaid? No, something more exotic. A seductive nymph.

Marshall wanted to slap his forehead. A seductive nymph? Man, it was time to get laid if this was where his mind was going. The disarray of her short curly hair soaked at the ends by sweat appealed to him in a tawdry way. His lips curled. This was how she would look after a rousing afternoon spent between his sheets.

Interesting. Since it was tall, blonde Nordic types that usually drew his interest like Muffy, the model for the statuesque ice princesses he selected in the past. Funny, she wasn't nearly as arousing as this little topless wood sprite.

"Shit!" Lily murmured unable to repress one

last cuss word. The man whose presence of mind had finished off the blaze stalked toward her. Rugged face, spellbinding blue eyes and laugh lines bracketing a full-lipped mouth. Oh, lord, he was gorgeous.

The laugh lines gave him away. He might not have been wearing a ring, but he was married. Or gay. Single men did not look like him.

A weakness in her knees threatened her ability to stand. The man was better looking than George Clooney. If he had a Scottish accent, like Sean Connery, she'd go down like a soggy graham cracker.

The wind, which had taken time out to have a good laugh, picked back up, chilling her skin. Lily glanced down at her state of undress and quickly looked back up again. At least it was a fairly new, pretty bra. His gaze had followed hers, and a definite look of interest lit his blue eyes. Well, he wasn't gay.

A blush burned down her arms, and her fingers tingled. She held up her hands and saw blisters forming on her fingers. "I need — "

"Get those hands in ice water."

Good thinking.

She hurried to the beverage table on the far side of the bandstand and plunged her hands into the icy beer tub. A low cry escaped her as the pain intensified before receding. She squeezed her eyes closed.

What a mess this day turned out to be.

The sound of glass clinking against glass forced her to peak though her lashes. Mr. Gorgeous pulled beers out of the tub to give her arms more room.

She could smell his cologne.

Would it look bad if she leaned over and inhaled deeply?

His tailored suit with a monogram shirtsleeve that peeked out from under the cuff, an alluring scent, and an expensive haircut screamed Mr. G had some bucks. It was truly a shame he was married because she bet he was a guy who got a lot of action.

Not with her, of course. She wasn't that type.

Across the patio, Dori snapped out orders. "Get fresh linens out of the van. Someone hide this bucket behind the tent. No need to light the chafers, we've had enough fun with flames. Hurry."

As the staff scurried to follow her commands, Dori sprinted to her side, "You okay?"

Lily pulled her attention away from the stranger and did her best to ignore the pain in her hands. "I've got to get burn spray and another jacket from the van. Can you handle things here?"

Automatically Dori straightened the table. "We're fine. Take care of yourself."

As Lily pulled her hands out of the ice bath, her partner surveyed the reception area. "Your quick action saved the tent. Take a few minutes and catch your breath. You look like you've been run over by a Mack Truck."

Lily grimaced, hating to hear the words she knew were true. With a nod, she lifted her hands from the ice bath, flailed them in the air to dry as she hurried across the patio toward the parking lot.

Action swirled around Marshall, but when the brunette hurried toward the parking lot, he was compelled to follow her to make sure that she was okay. Before he could escape, the blonde caught his arm. "We appreciate your help. Not many would have jumped in like that."

"No problem," he said. "With this wind it could have happened to anybody."

"Still," she said. "Thank you."

Not knowing what else to do, he reached out and patted her awkwardly on the shoulder as she groaned.

She pointed. "The guests…"

Marshall's gaze followed the direction of her hand. A hundred or so guests thundered down the hill as though scurrying to avoid the bulls of Pamplona.

He started to say something but stopped. The woman beside him was a professional. She'd swung into full action mode. He cast one lingering glance toward the parking lot. Going after the brunette now would be a waste of time.

Another staff member, this one a young woman with short spiky red hair positioned herself between the reception area and the wedding guests. Like she was directing a 747 to a docking gate, she systematically waved her arms to direct the stampeding crowd off to the right into an orderly reception line.

Bracing himself, he studied the crowd, searching for his date. She would not be part of the stampeding mob. Muffy never merely appeared. She created an entrance – usually a dramatic one.

The crowds parted. Heads swiveled. Marshall restrained a smile as she stepped into the spotlight like a model on the runway. True to form, she was perfect. He'd come to expect nothing less. Her hair, too blonde to be a gift of nature, pulled back into a tight chignon, highlighted her angelic face. The full-length lynx fur draped artistically across one shoulder not hiding the expensive designer dress. She strode, her chin held high, with just the proper amount of disdain in her eyes.

She was a head-turner. It was what had

attracted Marshall in the first place, but after only a few evenings together, Marshall had discovered an ugly little secret.

Muffy was without a doubt the most mind-numbingly boring person he'd ever met. His dates were rarely interested in his career, but they could usually find a common subject of interest to discuss. But she was the first woman he'd met who spent twenty minutes discussing the shade of her nail polish.

Chapter Two

Lily had always been in control of her life and even in times of great stress refused to operate on automatic pilot. Time was valuable, and she didn't have it to waste.

Today, after the disaster of the fire, she'd spent hours covertly searching for the attractive dark haired man, who had already left.

Nor had he been alone. Dori's description of his wife as beauty-contestant Barbie, complete with an out-of-season fur coat, had been sadly funny.

On the drive home, Dori informed her that Blue Eyes had been among the first to leave. "You should have seen this woman. She'd give beauty-contestant Barbie a run for the money."

Lily found herself staring out the window.

"Oh, for the Pete's sakes, Lily, you've got to find this funny. The woman wore a lynx coat. The temperature's barely above fifty degrees."

Lily forced herself to laugh encouraging her partner to continue.

"And her dress. I'll bet it would have cost me a month's salary."

She hadn't wanted to ask, but she couldn't help herself. "Was she pretty?"

Dori let out a low whistle. "Stunning, but

she was one of those women, like Kim Kardashian, who won't smile, because they are afraid of wrinkles in later life. Sad, really."

Now, hours later, Lily lay in her bed unable to sleep. The adrenaline rush from their fire still had her thoughts tumbling.

The blisters on her hands were minor and by tomorrow wouldn't even be noticeable.

Unable to sleep, she rolled onto her side and stared at the open sliding glass door to her patio. The spring air carried the scent of freshly turned earth from her backyard garden. Sheer drapes fluttered. The hours she'd wasted tossing and turning were gone forever. She had to get some sleep.

Concentrating on deep breathing, she relaxed each muscle group from her toes to her head. Gradually, her mind shut off, and she drifted toward sleep, hovering between fantasy and reality -– on the edge of the abyss. The cool sheets cocooned her, lulling her deeper into a world where dreams and reality intertwined.

The air snapped, crisp with anticipation. Hairs on her arm lifted. He was here. The black-clad figure stepped out of the shadows, outlined by the moonlight streaming into her room. The drapes swirled around him obscuring his face. A smile quivered on her lips. Through half-closed eyes, she willed the man closer.

Wanting him. Needed him to touch her, stroke her and make her shiver with anticipation.

Silently his feet glided over the hardwood floors, face hidden, concentration palpable. Certain she was the target, she lay motionless. Movement disrupted him. How many nights had he entered her bedroom, only to abandon her? To leave before she was ready. Tonight, she would outwait him.

The caress of his warm breath against her neck drew her from muddled sleep to skate the surface of desire. Even in her foggy state, she fought waking, tried to sink lower into the delicious erotic haze the faceless, dark-haired man brought with him.

He hovered, his hands strumming her body, playing it like a violin that had sat too long upon the shelf. Taking his time to bring out her sweet music. The sheet drifted, freeing her body, allowing his touch her arms, hips and thighs.

Her nipples pouted, vying for attention before his callused fingers offered relief. She longed to pull off the hindering gown and tug his head to her breasts and let him suckle his fill.

Fingers circled her nipples until the teasing drove her over the edge. Unable to wait another second, she arched her back, and a moan escaped her lips. Moisture dampened her inner thighs. Exhilaration pounded in her pulse. The heat raging through her body kept her warm even in the cool room.

Shadows concealed his eyes, but lips curled upward, pleased with her reaction. The man who lived in the night, without a face, without a name, was the most familiar man she had ever known and the hottest relationship of her life.

His tongue traced the upper curve of her breasts leaving her strangling for air as her excitement increased. Tonight would be the night.

He would bring her to fulfillment – beyond her wildest dreams, beyond her experience. He shifted. His face came into view, but not the features she expected.

Intense blue eyes stared at her – the man from the fire. Her eyes flew open. Reality slammed to the forefront. Completely awake, Lily stared at the ceiling. The room was empty. Her fantasy, which had sustained her for months, was shot to hell.

The door flung open. Dori loaded down with files slammed the folders on the adjacent desk. Lily didn't look up.

"The newspaper's conducting a survey," Lily challenged. "What questions does a caterer hate to hear from clients?"

Dori paused halfway to the burgundy

leather chair in front of Lily and fired off an answer. "'How much does a wedding cost?' I never can answer that. Why do brides ask it? Every wedding's different."

Lily grinned at her quick-thinking partner.

Encouraged, Dori continued. "Then there's the 'You wanted to be paid today?' I wonder if they ever read those contracts they sign. But the number one question I personally hate is, 'Can we use our volunteers, instead of paying for service labor?'" Dori sighed. "Save us from fifteen people standing around watching us work, unable to do anything, because they're too busy socializing or just had their nails done."

Lily laughed and nodded in agreement. "If we use that answer, they'll quote us and we'll look mean-spirited."

"We're not mean-spirited. We're mean." Dori admitted, shrugging. "Any one of our employees would be happy to confirm that fact."

Lily nodded, disregarding her partner's callousness. "Call me foolish, but I'd prefer all of Portland didn't know it."

Dori smiled, her green eyes dancing. The sprinkling of freckles across her nose and her apple cheeks gave her the appearance of an animated fairy, missing only gossamer wings and a sizzling wand. "So what'd you do last night?"

Why did she ask? Last night was like all her nights – not special.

"A good book, the hot tub and a perky Merlot with just a hint of pretentiousness," Lily squeezed her fingers together to demonstrate how little attitude her wine had held. The sunlight shifted, leaving streaks across her computer screen. She reached behind her to adjust the window blinds.

"Only a hint? You need to get out more."

Lily hoped to change the subject. "Why, because my wines aren't pompous enough?"

She almost groaned when her partner kicked back and folded her arms behind her head. "When was the last time you had a date?"

"It's been a while."

Dori could be tenacious once she got rolling on a subject.

"Can you name the President in office during that year or is it too far back?"

"Rutherford B. Hayes." Lily shot back. "And where would you suggest I meet men? Online? A bar? Please don't tell me a grocery store -- even though I know it's supposed to be a hot meeting place. I spend more time in grocery stores than any single woman I know, and I've never been approached by a man offering to squeeze my melons."

As Dori burst into laughter, Lily changed the subject. "Are we set for tonight?"

Her partner faltered with the sudden switch

of topics. "Yes. We've got twenty-two wait-staff arriving at three."

Lily did the math in her head. "We'll need that many to pass hors d'oeuvres for four hundred. Do we have an agenda from the committee, yet?"

"Your copy's in your e-mail."

Six hours later, Luscious Food's staff hit the floor running. The rentals for the Cancer League Fundraiser arrived late. As quickly as the tables rolled into the large auditorium, waiters covered them with linens and dishware.

Dori erected elevation to create the tiered Viennese dessert table. "Beer and wine, ready to go?" she asked when Lily whizzed by with additional linens.

"Just about. Hors d'oeuvres are trayed. How close are you?" Lily's attention was diverted from the answer when she noticed a waiter kicking spilled ice under the table. "Pick it up. We don't need a lawsuit because someone slips and falls."

Twenty minutes later the door swung open to admit the first guest. No one would have guessed at the last frantic hour. Uniformed waiters passed hors d'oeuvres and smiled invitingly. The dessert table sparkled. The bar pumped out beer and wine.

Lily paced the floor in the staging area, pushing her staff to keep to the timeline. Waiters scrambled in and out of a crowded backstage dressing room, packed with racks of costumes from a previous college production, rolling hot boxes, and worktable. She'd asked for an empty room, but there were none to give her. All the spare rooms were needed for the bachelor's' dressing rooms.

Adding to the packing conditions, the staff had shoved two bicycles into a corner. With the cost of bikes, waiters refused to leave them outside, even chained.

Hors d'oeuvres faded into a three-course dinner as the madhouse drew to a close. Lights dimmed in anticipation of the bachelor auction. Dori and the rest of the crew bussed dishes onto the loading dock.

Lily tackled the staging area cleanup. Tables loaded with pans and serving trays needed to be re-packed for the vans. Random hors d'oeuvres lay scattered on almost empty trays and food cast aside during the hastily assembled dinner service stood ready to be tossed. It was a one-person mindless task, but the appeal lay in the few minutes of uninterrupted solitude.

Behind the racks of costumes, Lily sank onto a short hot box, slipped off her shoes and let her tired feet rest for a brief respite. The unadorned institutional beige walls were boring. Her mind drifted.

Behind her, a door opened and closed. When

no one spoke, she chose not to call attention to herself. If her staff wanted her, thanks to modern technology, they could reach her on her cell phone.

Giving into the temptation, she fantasized about the blue-eyed stranger. She closed her eyes and felt his long fingers curling into the skin of her hips, as he pulled her to him. The warmth of his chest, the beat of his heart, the curl of his lips…

"Hell and damnation." A very real, very loud masculine voice jarred her from her reverie.

The swearing didn't faze her, but the unknown male voice surprised her. *What idiot on her staff invited complaints from the guests?* She hurried from behind the racks of costumes.

As she emerged into the larger room, her feet stopped, bringing her body to an abrupt, jarring halt. Five feet in front of her was the muscular back of the nearly naked man, wearing only a miniscule blue and white striped bathing suit and black socks.

What was he doing in the caterer's staging area?

He wasn't dressed for any occasion she could imagine. They were nowhere near the swimming pool. And why the mystery of the socks?

While her mind rattled off unacceptable reasons for him to be here, her eyes ignored every rule of manners and decency and continued to stare. Had someone asked her to define a cute butt, she could have pointed to the one in front of her.

Things like this did not happen to her.

He leaned forward, allowing her to see his face in the mirror. Lily closed her mouth and blinked hard in rapid succession.

Oh, my. The blue-eyed stranger from the fire with an angry scowl across his face.

Had she conjured him up from her fantasies? Was this a waking dream?

Truth be told, it was better than her fantasies. He was flesh and blood. And extremely well put together flesh and blood at that.

She squirmed. Her skin tightened. Certain body parts demanded her attention. Her lips were too dry, her nipples were so hard they ached, and she refused to acknowledge what was going on below her waist. He shouldn't affect her like this. He was just another man. Not to mention married.

Chapter Three

Marshall glared at his image in the dressing room mirror. This weekend was a disaster.

Muffy was first and foremost a problem. His plan to ease out of any future relationship with her was thwarted. He'd broken up with enough women over the years, he had gotten pretty good at it, but honestly, she was better.

Every time he'd broached the topic, she'd changed the subject. By the time he took her home, he'd vowed not to call her again. In a month or so, she'd figure it out. And yet his voice mail had recorded three calls from her today.

He'd agreed to do this bachelor auction only to placate his sister, Caroline. "Please, please, Marshall. I'll do anything you ask. Just do this for me," she'd begged. "Cancer killed our mother. This will pay for research that may save others."

How could he refuse?

Except his sister had failed to mention, bachelors were required to wear a sporting outfit. Maybe it hadn't been her fault. He deleted a wealth of email every day, he could have overlooked it. But he'd talked to her as late as yesterday and the topic hadn't been discussed.

He owned all manner of sports clothes none of which was with him. Instead, he was forced to wear another man's clothes. An irritated shudder shot through him.

He studied himself in the cheval glass and gritted his teeth. He couldn't do it. He couldn't stand on a stage in this skimpy bathing suit and not feel like a fool. Or worse.

Maybe the wetsuit would be a better bet. It hung on the wall on the far side of the mirror. Closing his eyes, he visualized how he'd look on stage and shook his head. Better to be out of step than to see a camera photo of himself going viral on the internet complete with snarky comments. He reached for his shirt and stopped.

A crawling sensation along his spine told him he wasn't alone. Slowly he turned his head, the hair on his neck rising along with his temper. His eyes narrowed in disbelief. A woman, dressed totally in black, pressed against the rack of costumes, stared mutely at him. Something was familiar about her. He looked closer. Recognition hit. The woman from yesterday's fire? She catered the auction?

"Hello," he said, working to keep the annoyance out of his voice. For a woman whose fast thinking he'd previously admired, she appeared disoriented. No… not disoriented…

Her warm chocolate eyes gazed at him with

a combination of innocence and desire hard to resist. Her tousled hair and deep rose cheeks enhanced by pouty red lips reminded him of how powerfully he'd been attracted. His body's reaction assured him nothing in that arena had changed.

The black double-breasted uniform hid her shape, but her bare feet and ruby polished toes taunted him in a game of hide and seek.

She cleared her throat. "Uh...," she cleared her throat again. "What… um… are you doing here?" Her voice was a hoarse whisper.

The scenario was straight out of some masculine fantasy -- alone with a flustered woman, gazing at him like a mirage in a desert. Wasn't this why he'd let Caroline pressure him into being an auctioned bachelor? He'd viewed it as an opportunity to lie back and let a woman have her way with him. Perhaps not a caterer in the dressing room, but other than that, this was precisely how he imagined it.

However, now was not the time, he still had to find acceptable clothes, face a live audience and murder his sister.

Before he had time to act, her appearance drew him in again. Raw desire pooled in her deep brown eyes, not a calculated gleam, but pure unadulterated lust. He almost chuckled.

A hundred good reasons raced through his mind as to why he should send her away, but the yearning in her eyes and the flush on her cheeks held back the words. Without a moment's hesitation, he closed the gap between them, grabbed her partially raised arm and pulled her to him. His wood sprite offered no resistance.

That's right, darling. Dinner is served.

Expecting her to fight, slap him or pull away, he tightened his grip. Instead, she floated in a dream state into his arms. Her unfocused eyes worried him and overwhelmed his better judgment as his mouth covered hers.

Her soft, pliable lips parted to welcome him, assuring him that the hunger he'd seen was not an illusion. A low moan escaped. He pulled back to study her face. Her heavily lidded eyes flickered open briefly before she wrapped her arms around his neck and drew him closer.

He adjusted his head and deepened the kiss. She squirmed closer. Her body molded to his as if they were long-time lovers instead of total strangers. Any resistance he possessed vanished.

Lily swam in desire. Real? Fantasy? Who cared? Her body trembled under the force of it. The hands stroking her back and squeezing her buttocks assured her this was true.

After years of lonely nights, her secret fantasy had sprung to life. A handsome man with no name and no past came to reawaken her from the dead. Even she didn't believe it, but she couldn't stop herself.

She ached. One of her legs wrapped around his hip in an attempt to place pressure where she needed it most. His hand inched between their bodies.

Yes. Yes, oh, please. Yes.

The loud pounding on the door took her already pounding heart rate to near attack status. Her entire body jumped. Her eyes flew open to a reality illuminated by florescent lights. Harsh words penetrated the fog surrounding her brain.

"Five more minutes."

What was she doing?

Her hands dropped from his neck to his chest and pushed him away. He let her go. She stumbled back out of his grasp.

His hand reached out again, but she slapped at the questing fingers.

This time she'd completely lost her mind. Kissing a stranger. Kissing? Hell, she'd practically given him a tonsillectomy. Forty-four years old and acting like a slutty high school girl. And at work.

Mortification flamed her cheeks, followed quickly by the twins – shame and guilt.

Her panting was, to say the least, embarrassing, but at least his breathing was equally ragged, and he sported an erection. She

stifled a giggle as a feeling of giddy relief swept
through her.

Her dream man may have wanted her.
However, he'd never demonstrated the evidence
that this man did. But dream or reality, the
ending was the same. Both of them had left her
on an edge, fighting for release.

However, in his defense the dream man had
the courtesy to disappear, and not stand there
staring. She couldn't imagine how she pissed the
gods off so much that they teased her with this
offering.

Marshall exercised all his control not to
lower her to the floor. In his present condition,
he could take care of business and still be ready
for the stage. Five minutes might well be long
enough. Hard and fast could be good. It had
been a long time since he had allowed himself
such as tasty indulgence. For some reason, she
not only triggered an impassioned response
from him, but also instilled confidence that she'd
be willing and eager.

He needed to say something, but the only
words he could think of were, "Screw the
auction. Let's get out of here." His fingers
reached to stroke her cheek, as an inducement
for her to sneak away.

She stepped out of his reach, shaking her head. "I'm working." Her husky voice rekindled his flame.

Marshall shortened the distance between them. No, was not an acceptable answer. He simply had to have her. Without thinking, he put his hand on her neck and massaged her jawline with his thumb. "I'll pay you."

Two pink spots appeared on her cheeks. Her chocolate eyes, which had seemed hazy before, were now focused and distinctly hostile.

"Wait. Wait. Wait." He cursed himself for his stupidity. "That didn't come out right. I thought that if you needed the money, I'd pay you for your time."

Now, the look she gave him threatened violence.

"That didn't come out the way I meant either." This woman made him behave like an idiot.

"I know what you meant." She snapped, jerking her body away from his. "You've been clear enough!" Her husky voice reflected her antagonism and something deeper. Hurt?

Before he could read her expression, she whirled and headed for the door. The absurdity of the situation struck him. His sharp laugh at his inept behavior stopped her. With one hand on the doorknob, she glanced over her shoulder and gave him a last questioning look.

He had one chance to make it right. "Listen,

please don't leave. I've handled this badly. I wasn't expecting a woman in the dressing room. My sister talked me into the auction, but forgot to mention I was supposed to wear this…." He gestured toward the wetsuit and the swim trunks. "I was irritated. Not at you. Mainly at myself for getting into this position. Then you came along and… well spending time with you seemed like a lot more fun than looking like a fool on stage."

He imagined playing lover's games with those still faintly swollen lips, but the time was past as her cheeks returned to their normal color.

Her eyebrow quirked up, she gave him a slow look from his head to his feet still sporting those ridiculous black socks. A smile tugged at her lips as he squirmed under her inspection.

"With all these costumes, surely we can find you something." She scanned the room.

His gaze followed hers. "No way. I'm not going in drag, either. These are women's costumes."

Ignoring him, she crossed the room and bent over a pile of clothes and dug out black spandex bicycle shorts, a neon red and black jacket, gloves, sunglasses and a helmet.

"Try this on." She tossed him the clothing and returned, wheeling one of the bikes to the center of the room.

"No shirt?"

She studied his open jacket and his chest. "No, you'll look better without one. After all, you do want women to bid on you."

The shorts were tight and almost as revealing as the skimpy bathing suit, but he was covered enough he didn't feel naked. "Whose clothes are these?"

"One of the waiters."

The door opened. A young man wearing a headset stuck his head inside, whispering. "Time to go." He gestured impatiently.

He turned intent upon thanking her, but she'd disappeared behind the clothing racks.

The darkened backstage area where he and the other bachelors waited allowed him to think about the attractive woman. Her brown eyes and raspy voice stayed with him. Her taste lingered on his lips. After this fiasco was over, he'd find her. All he knew was that her name was Lily, but it wasn't her name he was after.

"Are you finished with the staging area?" Dori asked Lily when she appeared in the darkened auditorium. The sing-song chanting of the auctioneer provided background noise.

Lily attention was on the stage. "The equipment is stacked ready to be transported to the van. Send Rodney and Shawn."

As Dori stepped away to issue instructions, Lily moved closer to the tables, eager to figure out what was happening.

"Six-hundred-six-hundred-six-hundred. I've got six-hundred, do I hear six-fifty."

"Up" A spotter standing in the crowd yelled and pointed toward a raised paddle on the far side of the room.

Standing center stage was a basketball player in a black and red Blazer uniform. Tattoos decorated his muscular arms. He dribbled the ball, pivoted to the rear and shook his butt from side to side as he tossed a grin back over his shoulder.

Several women whistled and a few catcalled from the audience.

"Seven-fifty-seven-fifty-seven-fifty. Do I hear eight?"

Transfixed Lily hadn't even realized the bidding had increased. Her partner returned to her side, but Lily couldn't pull her attention away from the fast pace of the auction. The basketball player sold for eleven hundred and twenty-five dollars. The applause rang in the high-ceiling room.

Lily's cell phone buzzed. She tugged it from her pocket and hurried through the exit. When she returned, her mystery man stood under the spotlight, leaning against his bicycle. The introduction already over and she still didn't know his name.

"Isn't that the guy from the fire? Look," Dori whispered in her ear and pointed across the room. "His wife's bidding."

Lily searched each table, trying to determine exactly which blonde she was. Resting her back against the pillar, she waited for the blonde to bid again. "Bachelor auction," she whispered. "Not his wife."

"Doesn't say much for his taste in women, does it?"

Lily wished she hadn't spoken. What her partner said was true. How could he date Beauty Queen Barbie and molest her in the dressing room? He certainly hadn't shown much loyalty. At least she hadn't been kissing a married man.

But whatever his taste in women, he had appeared insincere. For a guy with money, he looked painfully awkward as he leaned woodenly against the bike. Arms folded; his eyes stared blankly at the audience. Lily narrowed her gaze trying to make what she knew about fit into a tidy package and came up blank.

"Seven-hundred-seven-hundred-seven-hundred. Do I hear eight? Eight-hundred-eight-hundred-eight-hundred." The auctioneer tried again for eight hundred, before beginning his downward quest. "Do I hear seven-fifty? seven-fifty-seven-fifty-seven-fifty?"

The bidding lagged.

He was going at bargain rates? *No way.* Why weren't women clamoring for an evening with Bachelor Number Three?

A woman, down in front, finally bid seven-fifty. Lily let out the breath she'd been holding. The bachelor on stage shifted his feet and gazed at the floor.

The auctioneer exhorted bids one more time, then raised his gavel. His hand moved in the air. Higher. Higher. Then the pause.

This was it.

"One thousand dollars." The words left her mouth before she'd even known she was going to speak.

The spotter pointed in her direction and relayed her bid. The room came to a standstill as her enthusiastic bid shocked everyone. Heads craned to look in her direction, not just the audience but most of her staff as well.

The audience was deadly silent for all of three seconds. Then erupted with chatter. Whatever Lily's intentions had been, she'd broken the conversational ice.

What was the big deal? Had she increased the amount of the bid too quickly or was the bidding limited to members and guests only? Was the group offended because she was only the caterer, a hired contractor? She doubted the last, but she hadn't expected to create such a ruckus.

The auctioneer hit the gavel on the podium for several minutes.

The bachelor spoke. At least Lily saw his mouth form the words. The auctioneer walked to his side of the stage to confer. The topic of the conversation was easy to guess. As the room calmed, Lily and the rest of the room waited for his reaction.

Dori stood beside her in a silent show of support, bolstering Lily's confidence. The unwanted attention surprised her. She prided herself on being invisible at a party. Members of the audience craned their heads for a view.

Between Dori, the pillar and being dressed completely in black. Hell, she was invisible.

On stage, the bachelor searched the audience while the auctioneer gestured in the general direction of the bid. Lily took a deep breath and stepped away from her shadowy position.

Without vacillation, the bachelor's lips curled upward – not truly a smile, but something more intimate, more carnal than just a simple, pleasant look. Whatever the look was, it warmed her heart and curled her toes, making Lily excited to be in the spotlight for once in her life.

The audience murmur rose in titillation. The up-to-now-bored bachelor encouraged the woman with a look held a promise worth persevering, one they all desired.

"Do I hear any other bids?" The auctioneer asked, as he returned to the podium and regained control of the rowdy crowd.

"One thousand and twenty-five dollars," a miffed reply came from the opposite side of the room. An angular blonde expressed her displeasure. Lily grinned.

So that was beauty-contestant Barbie? What a shame to piss her off.

"Eleven hundred." Another woman jumped into the melee.

"Eleven hundred. I've got eleven hundred. Do I hear eleven-fifty? Eleven-fifty-eleven-fifty-eleven-fifty. Do I hear twelve hundred?"

"Fifteen hundred," Lily parried, delighted that her mystery man hadn't so much as glanced in either of the other women's direction. His posture relaxed with the change in bidding. He lounged, seemingly at ease, using his bike as a prop as he casually awaited the outcome. His face reflected his confidence, but his attention never wavered from Lily's position at the back of the large hall.

"Fifteen fifty," Another bidder added. Lily paused to determine if the new bidder was trying to block her bid or was swept away by the moment. But rather than swaying her, it strengthened her resolve. Lily already knew he could kiss.

Boy, could he kiss!

The auctioneer opened his mouth to chant when Lily responded undaunted. "Two thousand." The bachelor's smile morphed into a triumphant grin.

From across the room, the blonde rose to gauge her opponent. With the dim lighting how much could the Bachelor see on stage? But it didn't take sight to feel the waves of anger ripple across the room.

"Two thousand and ten dollars," the blonde retorted.

"Twenty-five dollar increments, please," the auctioneer reminded her. Lily realized he'd given up any control of this bidding scenario and was fighting to keep his grin from showing. The blonde nodded and waved her agreement blindly in his direction, never taking her steely stare from Lily.

Lily smiled sweetly in the direction of the angry woman. *Stupid cow.* "Twenty-five hundred dollars."

The blonde woman gasped, open-mouthed, at the audacity of the newcomer, pressed her lips together and plopped down in her seat.

"Do I hear any other bids?" As the auctioneer gave up any effort to contain his mirth, he banged his gavel. "The bid goes to…" He paused, stared at Lily. When she didn't immediately respond, he asked, "What's your number?"

Flustered for a second, Lily quickly regained her confidence.

She had won him! Oh, Lord! What now?

With confidence, her manner took a saucy turn. "My number's twenty-five hundred dollars."

Bachelor number three laughed.

"So, it is." The auctioneer chortled. The audience broke into applause. Lily blushed.

"What're you doing?" Dori asked without moving her smiling lips.

"Having my fifteen minutes of fame."

Lily hurried to the company van to find her purse. Her feeling of elation carried her back to the cashier's table to complete the transaction. "I don't have a number, but here's my check." She leaned over the table and spoke loudly to be heard over the noise of the continuing auction in the background.

As she signed her name with a flourish, the reality of the situation struck her. What had she been thinking? The bidding was exciting, winning had exhilarated her, but she hadn't thought it all the way through. How was she ever going to face him? After being incensed at his offer to pay for her time, she had 'bought' him instead.

The cashier was a pleasant woman whose

orderly and patient manner reminded Lily of a schoolteacher or perhaps a librarian. Crisp, precise and organized.

"Congratulations on your winning bid. Fill out this card, please. You'll be contacted during the upcoming week," the cashier informed her.

"Why?"

"For the date," the older woman enunciated carefully, the way one would to a very young child. "You've won an evening on the town."

"No date! I bid for fun. Don't contact me." Lily reached for the card with her personal information on it, but the woman drew her hand back out of Lily's reach. Not that it mattered, they already had all her information on the check.

"I'll put that on your card. Perhaps Marshall Caudill will be relieved, but based on what I just saw, I doubt it."

"Marshall Caudill?" Lily couldn't help but ask. She glanced toward the stage as the roar of the crowd caught her attention.

"You didn't know the name of the man you bid on?" the cashier asked, openly surprised.

"You didn't know the name of the man you bid on?" Dori echoed, equally amazed, having just joined Lily at the table.

"No. I didn't know the name of the man I bid on." Lily mimicked her.

No one spoke as the other women pondered what that revelation could mean. Lily bit her inner cheek to keep from blurting out what she knew they must be thinking. She was an idiot.

"I want you to know," Dori said, breaking the awkward silence, "that I know you don't have the first dollar you ever made. However, I'm positive you've still got at least seventy-seven cents of it. Never, have I known you to do anything like this! Where's your brain? If you were a man, I'd wonder which body part was in control."

Dori spun on her heel and stormed off.

The cashier handed her a receipt. "I'll personally tell Marshall that he doesn't need to call. All you were doing was making a donation. But I've known him for years. That won't deter him. Marshall has a reputation for going after what he wants. And he gave every indication of wanting you."

Lily's mouth dropped open in surprise at the woman's words. She was even more amazed when the woman gave her a deliberate wink and a parting word, "Enjoy".

Chapter Four

The bachelors gathered for photos and a final appearance on stage to wild applause at the end of the evening. Marshall's kissing partner's unconventional behavior had loosened the audience and bidding had taken on a frenzied quality for the remaining bachelors.

He tapped his foot. Impatient for an opportunity to find the brazen waitress who could toss twenty-five hundred dollars to charity. What an exciting little witch she turned out to be. Once he got her naked and in his bed, he was willing to bet she'd be one wild ride. It wouldn't take much, and he'd be settling between her legs and driving deeply into her. The memory of those sweet, sexy moans taunted him now and caused him to hurry. Time for part two of their game.

His dressing room was empty of people, food, and catering equipment. Another bike with some random clothes stood in the corner, but the caterers had departed.

A quiet knock hurried his dressing. Perhaps she couldn't wait and had come to find him? "Come in," He growled, anticipation pulsing in his veins.

The door cracked open. "Are you mad?" his

sister, Caroline, asked.

His lips pulled into a tight line. "You're definitely on my list."

How easily this evening could have turned into a disaster. Yeah, he was mad, and the fault lay squarely in Caroline's court. Judging by the hesitant tone of her voice, she wanted to repair any damage before it escalated into a problem.

"Is that the naughty or nice list?" she joked.

Marshall softened his stance. "I'm not going to beat you in public. C'mon in."

Caroline entered with her husband, Steven, close behind. Her worried eyes and sheepish grin had his anger dissipating.

The strapless navy dress with a flowing skirt and twisted colors of pinks, golds and purples ended on the floor in a cloud of white, his sister had inherited their mother's sense of fashion. "You look nice."

She smiled, knowing she was forgiven. "Why are you in here? This isn't one of the dressing rooms."

"I would ask you the same question. Not only is it not a dressing room, but it was being used by the caterers, unbeknownst to me."

Caroline blanched. "Is that how you met Lily Carmichael?"

"Who?" He counted out five twenty-dollar bills and tucked them into the jacket of the waiter whose clothes he'd borrowed.

His sister frowned. "The winning bid. Why are you putting money in that jacket?"

Marshall ignored her last question and focused on what he wanted to know. "Who is Lily Carmichael? You say her name like I should know it."

"She's one of the owners of the catering company. Luscious something."

"Luscious Foods," Steven added from the comfort of a chair he'd spotted in the corner.

Caroline and Marshall exchanged a surprised look when Steven volunteered that bit of information. Caroline's husband was a lawyer, seldom aware of his surroundings or the people around them. For him to have information like that at his fingertips was out of character.

Caroline raised her eyebrow in question.

Steven shrugged, tugging on his white bow tie. "Jack Raulerson, in our office, sued them a couple of years ago in a slip-and-fall case. When it went to court, the judge dismissed the case for lack of merit –a major contributor to Jack not making partner."

"So, she owns the company?"

"Limited Partnership," Steven clarified. "She and her partner, Doralene Conners, have been in business together for nine, ten, eleven years –– something like that."

"What's she like?" Caroline asked her

husband.

"No idea. I only read the depositions. Competent. Hard working. Our client's numerous Worker's Comp claims and a multitude of injury lawsuits gave her the appearance of a fraudulent gold digger–."

"Is she married, divorced or what?"

Steven cleared his voice, then continued, "Widowed. You remember the restaurant, *Just Apps*? The entire menu consisted of appetizers. It was the hot place in town when it first opened, but the chef-owner, her husband, died in an automobile accident. As far as I know, she hasn't remarried. But my information's a couple of years out of date."

The door opened behind Steven. Blanche Donnell, the cashier for tonight's event, stuck her head in the door and peered at Marshall. "Good, you're here. Here's the winning bid information, but you're not to call her." She held out the card. "She requested her money be used as a donation."

"Like that's going to happen," Marshall murmured under his breath as he crossed the room to take the card.

"Evidently, she didn't even know who you were." Blanche's eyes sparkled.

"How could she not know?" his sister scoffed. "It's not like you were a mystery man.

You were introduced." Caroline fingered the cheap fabric of a stage ball gown and grimaced.

"Maybe she missed the intro or wasn't paying attention," Blanche said. "But I don't think she knew. For one thing, her business partner gave her hell for participating. That's a gorgeous dress. The way the colors blend it reminds me of ombre hair."

Marshall smiled when his sister glowed. "Is she still here?" He asked before Blanche could slip out the door.

"Outback – loading the vans." Blanche gave him a grin. "Good hunting, Marshall."

Marshall laughed quietly. So the little caterer thought she could avoid the inevitable?

How long it had been since a woman had intrigued him? He couldn't ever remember the last time he'd wanted to give chase. This night wasn't turning out like he had envisioned at all. In order for the woman who won him to have her wicked way with him, he was apparently going to have to catch her first.

The brisk night air was a refreshing break from the overheated ballroom. Both moon and stars lit the sky. Without cloud cover, the temperature would drop. Tomorrow was a light day. Dori sucked in a deep breath. They were almost finished. She towered over the van parked in the loading dock below.

"Is this everything?" Dori asked. A server standing nearest, nodded absently. Dori was glad she had sent Allyn back to make a final tour. "Sign out. Then you can go. Remember, you've already committed to next Saturday night."

The young man jumped the four-foot drop to the ground. The impact jarred Dori's joints in sympathy. Unaffected, the kid wandered off into the night. Shaking her head, she was momentarily envious of his age. Another server, a young woman waited by the front door.

"Is the van full?" Dori asked the driver.

The girl peered in the door. "Just about."

"Move it to the lot. The rental company will want to park here for their pick up."

Racks of dishes and glassware crowded the far end of the dock along with piles of napkins and bus tubs of silverware.

"Doralene Conners?" a deep masculine voice spoke.

She turned, puzzled to see Marshall Caudill standing behind her. Automatically, she extended her hand. His handshake impressed her. His age matched her vision of an acceptable man for Lily to pursue. His appearance did not. Good-looking men raised her hackles.

Even dressed casually in slacks and a

tailored shirt, this man reeked of money and something else − confidence, maybe? But despite Dori's hesitation something about him had finally flipped her partner's switch.

"Where's Lily?" he asked, searching the faces of the various staff remaining.

"The kitchen. Washing dishes and putting away food."

Marshall grunted in disbelief. "The owner of the company washes dishes?"

"It's like mopping the floors or taking out the trash. As near as I can figure, management loosely translated means any job left undone by others." She joked, but it fell flat when Marshall's response was a curious stare.

He gestured toward the van moving away from the loading dock. "Do you still have to unload this van tonight?"

"No. Nothing's perishable. What's in here will go home with me and get unloaded tomorrow."

"Tomorrow's Sunday."

Dori studied the tall man before she continued, waging a private battle between encouraging him to pursue Lily and protecting her friend. When she'd pushed Lily to date again, she hoped her friend would start with a different type of man. This one had heartbreaker written all over him.

"Catering's twenty-four/seven. Weekends are our hot time, but we work every day."

People not in food service didn't understand the time commitments. The truth would be enough to gauge his interest.

"So Lily will also be at work tomorrow?"

A spear of annoyance at his detailed persistence made her wish he'd go away. She already regretting telling him Lily's location. "Well, no. Tomorrow's a light day." Throwing caution to the wind, she added, "but if you think that'll be a good time to see her, you'll have an uphill battle on your hands. She doesn't date." Dori crossed her fingers and hoped her partner wasn't going to make a liar of her. "Did they tell you she only intended the money as a donation?"

"Uh-huh." He nodded, and slowly a smile lit his face. "Good to meet you. I suspect I'll be seeing you again."

That smile was deadly, and those blue eyes would be impossible to resist.

She shook her head and tried to keep her answer noncommittal "Maybe." Silently, she prayed Marshall Caudill wouldn't damage Lily's tender heart.

Chapter Five

Lily had Sunday off. But since it was already half-past-one Sunday morning, it didn't feel much like a day without work.

Sandra removed the last sheet pan from the dishwasher. "That's it," she announced from the distance of the long narrow kitchen.

"Great," Lily hollered from the storage room where she finished rearranged chafers. "Go ahead and sign out."

A few minutes later, she emerged wiping her hands on a side towel. The two girls huddled together in a corner of the kitchen, whispering as they peered into the entrance foyer.

Her fatigue vanished. "What's the problem?"

Sandra pointed. "Across the street. Some man is sitting in a car watching us."

"What?" Lily stepped toward the door, but Sandra grabbed her arm.

"Mary noticed him a few minutes ago when she went out to smoke."

Mary nodded in confirmation.

Lily's mind raced to find an answer. "Let's call the police."

Both girls looked horror-struck. "It's already

late. By the time the police get here, it'll be after two o'clock. Can't we just go," Mary protested.

Their reluctance to involve the police grated. These girls were relatively new to her staff. "What if he follows you?"

Finally, seeing their continued resistance, Lily compromised. At least the two rode together which should be some protection. "Let's all leave now. I'll monitor you as far as the freeway. If he follows you, promise you'll call 9-1-1 from your cell phone."

Lily hoped for a false alarm. Her original plan to work at her desk for another hour or so until the evening's adrenaline rush wore off vanished. But if her staff were in jeopardy, she couldn't concentrate not knowing if they were safe.

Her fears were probably groundless. A man, intent on harming them, would not sit in a well-lit parking lot where he and his car were openly seen.

The three women left the building at the same time, using the side-door kitchen exit. Lily hurried through the lock-up procedures. When the girls were safely in their car, she peeked around the corner of the building and scanned the lot for any suspicious behavior. Nothing was out of place.

Lily jumped into her van sure the girls'

imaginations were on overdrive. She cranked the ignition, and the motor roared to life. The girls exited the lot ahead of her. She put her vehicle into gear and followed, lagging only a couple of car lengths behind.

Barely had she maneuvered onto the street when lights blazed in her rear view mirror as another car pulled in behind her. Studying her side mirrors she tried to identify the vehicle, but the headlights blinded her.

Lily turned the corner paying more attention to the vehicle behind her than the road. All she could see was a light colored car, not an SUV, van or truck. She swallowed hard, sweat prickled her scalp and her upper lip. Her finger punched the power lock button a dozen times, finding the clinking noise unsatisfying. Her cell phone stood ready in a cup holder.

Four blocks later, the girls hooked a right onto the northbound freeway entrance while Lily continued through the intersection under the overpass. The sinister vehicle, lurking behind her, tenaciously rode her bumper.

She exhaled for the first time in several minutes. He wasn't following her staff, but at the next intersection, he failed to turn left to catch the southbound freeway.

Oh, Lord! What if he was following her?
What to do? What to do? Whattodo?

Her mind refused to form a coherent thought.

Wait. Don't panic. This had to be a mistake.

She varied her route. Two blocks later, she swerved into a sudden right turn, then switched lanes, sharply wheeled left and finally a block later, right again. Cars lined both sides of the residential neighborhood's streets.

As though the two vehicles were joined, the car never varied from the pace she set. She lacked spittle to relieve her dry throat and was forced to wipe her damp forehead on her sleeve.

She grabbed her cell phone to call for help. It rang, shattering the tense quiet. Lily's body jerked. She pulled the steering wheel sharply to the right. Panicked, she corrected her mistake. The van fishtailed barely avoiding sideswiping a parked car.

Holy shit.

Her driving put her at more risk than the sinister car behind her. Flustered she grabbed her phone. "Luscious Foods."

"You're driving like a demented woman. Do you want to have an accident?" The amplified male voice on the speakerphone echoed in the empty van.

Lily threw the phone into the passenger's seat. She clung tenuously to the steering wheel.

"Who are you? Why are you following me?"

He swore softly easing Lily's panic.

"Let's calm down," His rich voice soothed.

"I didn't mean to frighten you. This is Marshall Caudill, your bachelor pick of the evening. I wanted to talk to you. I should have known I was scaring you to death."

She opened the window to get a cool breath of air. "It's called stalking, Mr. Caudill, and it's against the law." Her tone didn't reflect her relief at knowing his identity.

A rumbling noise came over the phone, and she wasn't sure if it was amusement or disgust.

"Trust me, stalking is different," he said. "We need a place to talk – minus the hysteria. If you had been more forthcoming with your personal information, I wouldn't have had to hunt you down at the only address you gave. I was about to come in when the building lights went off, and I realized everyone was leaving. My intentions were simply to make sure you got home safely."

His relaxed, deep voice curled around her making her chagrined for her suspicions.

"Giving out my home phone or address is pointless. I'm never there." Lily drove without paying attention, both hands glued to the steering wheel like she was in charge of an eighteen wheeler instead of a utility van.

Gradually, her fingers relaxed, and she exhaled.

Where was she?

At the next intersection, she paused.

"Turn right here," Marshall directed from

the car behind her. His voice, which had been quiet for several minutes, startled her.

She reached for the phone to disconnect the call but before she could, he asked. "If you're never home, why do you live so far away from work?"

"Ten minutes isn't that far away," she protested as the light changed, and she automatically turned right onto Fourth Street as he'd directed.

"Ha! It takes longer than ten minutes for you to get home."

"Sometimes in traffic, but this late at night it's pretty much a straight shot down the Sunset." She reached the second intersection. A left turn would connect to the Sunset Highway. She pressed the signal down. Suddenly, a thought hit her. "You don't have a clue where I live. You're fishing for answers."

"And I'll have a lot more of them if you turn here."

A silent alarm rang in her head.

Driving home meant he'd follow her. Tired from a long day and still slightly unhinged, letting him know where she lived seemed like an invasion of privacy or worse.

The big concern wasn't personal safety, but control. With this man, she suspected that wasn't even a menu option. For some reason, knowing he followed her touched on her memories of his kiss, instead of the absurdity of this late night adventure. Her body shivered with the memory of his hands on her.

Refusing to turn she drove Fourth Street through the heart of downtown. The one time that red lights might have allowed her time to strategize, everything was green. She crossed Burnside into Chinatown.

Chinatown's reputation at night worried her. Too near the homeless shelters, the dubious nightclubs and the drug buying centers where the runaways and homeless youth congregated. Inert bundles sprawled in doorways. Gloom flickered beside the dark buildings. Lily closed the window and punched the lock button a few more times.

Leaves and trash danced along the street. Lily jumped when a shadow morphed into a man dressed in dark clothes and a hoody. Adrenaline raced through her, but her nerves were shot, and her mind was numb.

Marshall's car remained behind her. Silence reigned for several minutes, the phone line still open. Now she sought the comfort of his presence.

"Turn left now," his voice directed.

She didn't object. Heading into the Pearl, a recently renovated upscale neighborhood got her out of the seamy area. This was crazy! Who was it she needed protecting from?

Marshall. Maybe. Her recurring fantasies were what had gotten her into this mess in the beginning. A red light brought her to a halt. *Where to go?* It was difficult to think with his constant presence hovering.

His voice interrupted her anxious thoughts. "In the middle of the next block, turn left into the building, where the garage door is rising."

Halfway down the street a large metal door cranked noisily grinding upwards. The cavernous opening suggested underground parking, below an expensive high-rise condo building.

"No," she declared, fighting her rising fears. He'd limited her options. How had she arrived in this situation?

What was she doing? This was insane. She was a calm, rational, mature businesswoman. Was Marshall's presence so exciting to her that she reverted to acting like a teenager? Something about him dredged up daring and naughty feelings. As frequently happened when she was stressed, inappropriate laughter bubbled out of her.

"What's so funny?" the voice on the telephone asked.

When she didn't answer immediately, Marshall asked. "Are we just going to continue driving around all night, talking on our cell phones? We're at my place." His soothing voice was reasonable. Again, the question of her sanity appeared.

His place? The light in front of her turned green and then red again. Neither vehicle moved. The garage door rattled closed.

"I'm not going inside with you," she announced, disappointed when her voice did not mirror her conviction. But pleased that she'd at least announced her first decision since she'd left work.

"Fine. We'll sit in your van and talk in the garage, but we'll be off the street and safe from traffic and people wandering the streets."

How could she fight such a sensible request? A more personal thought hit her.

"No. My van smells like food. Everyone hates it. I'm nose-blind to it, but you'll be offended."

"Sweetheart." He gentled his voice. "I don't care if we sit in my car, pace the garage floor or simply ride the elevator up and down, but we're going to talk. Pull in."

The light turned green as the garage door wobbled its second ascent skyward. Lily, unable to think of a counter plan, eased her foot off the brake and inched forward.

The dark garage, even with the metal grated wall lights all working, offered little comfort. The only true illumination came from the elevator cubby at the far end.

Only six cars parked in the cavernous space. Why was this space so much safer than the street? Lily took a deep breath and searched her mind one more time for another option.

No other solutions occurred to her. His persistence was going to require a head-on conversation. She flicked the van's vanity mirror downward and groaned. What little makeup she'd applied at eight o'clock that morning was long gone. With a sixteen-hour workday behind her, her body was encrusted with a layer of salt and sweat intermingled with the odor of food. Her feet and calves ached from too many hours standing, and her teeth felt scummy. She would kill for a shower.

When she didn't look like hell, she was pretty cute. But would he think that? He'd certainly never seen her at her best. Pieced minute-by-minute together, their entire acquaintance wasn't longer than a half hour.

He wanted to talk. Couldn't they use their cell phones? What was she doing here? She should just drive home and promise to call him when she got there, safe, sound and sane. Instead of having a face to face when it looked like she'd been a tortured prisoner of war. His interest would disappear faster than little weenies at a redneck barbecue.

But then another problem became apparent

as a desperate need for a bathroom surfaced. Involuntarily, she bemoaned her situation. Her bad habits had caught up with her. Mentally she counted back and realized she hadn't stopped working long enough to go to the bathroom for hours. And now time was of the essence.

She pried herself out of the van, her feet hit the hard concrete floor. Her tired muscles protested with the jolt. A solid night's sleep might make her feel human again, but right now she hopped on one leg and then the other attempting to regain her lost energy.

Marshall unfolded from a small silver car. The make and model were obscured from her vision, but if this was his address, it was a safe bet that the sports car had a hefty window sticker connected to it.

Impatience now drove her; she clutched her knees together to avoid the bathroom dance ritual.

"Can I park here?" she asked, longing to scream to pleeease hurry.

"Yeah."

When he rounded the car, his walk had a predatory grace that she might have admired under different circumstances.

"You're sure?" she demanded, attempting to regulate the impatience in her voice.

"I own the building." He lounged against the silver passenger door. "What's your preference, darling? Inside my car or standing out here? I doubt if we'll be disturbed, but you won't be very comfortable."

Lily rolled her eyes in self-disgust. "I'm sorry to tell you this, but I have to find a bathroom … quickly."

Marshall's face was expressionless as he pushed away from the vehicle. He gestured toward the elevator. "After you."

Inside the paneled elevator, he inserted his key and pushed the top floor button. "What would you be doing now if you were home?" he asked as the elevator slowly rose to the top.

Shifting from one foot to the other, she said, "Alone? I'd pour a glass of red wine, ease into the hot tub until the kinks of the day had unwound, then brush my teeth and go to bed."

He nodded. "The hot tub is on the deck. I'll even pour the wine."

Lily's only reply was an unladylike snort, which produced a slight smile from Marshall.

He pointed when the door opened into his spacious loft, "Bathroom's down the hall under the stairs to the left."

The rooms rushed past her in a blur, as she raced down the hall eager to reach her destination without embarrassment. The bathroom was luxurious. There was simply no other word for it. The sleek, elegance of cool gray slate floors and the coordinating marble struggling half way up the walls only to end in a staged jagged edge delighted her sense of style. The swirl of celadon in the stone was subtly expanded in the shower dominated by four shiny heads. Each silently promising to reach every aching muscle group.

What if he wanted to kiss her again? She sniffed herself. If she took a quick shower, she would feel refreshed even in clothes she already worn for hours.

Her head sank to rest on her hands. She couldn't believe she'd even think that. A shower in his house no matter how appealing was unacceptable. She ran the water until it was cold, then splashed her face, finger combed her hair and pinched her cheeks. The final glance in the mirror told her it wasn't good, but at this time of night it wasn't going to get better. She opened the door and marched toward the light.

At the end of the hallway, Marshall leaned against the wall. A snowy white terrycloth bathrobe hung from one finger. He'd read her mind? His expression plainly told her she'd be a fool not to take him up on his offer. Without too much of an internal fight, she surrendered. A hot shower was too enticing to resist. Barely mouthing a "thanks" she scurried back down the hall.

Peeling off her clammy uniform was a welcome relief. The water felt wonderful. Hot streams of clean water cascaded over her skin and beat against her tired muscles as she stood with her eyes closed, savoring a few tension-free minutes.

Her nervousness evaporated. For the first time in several hours, she could pass for human again. That feeling lasted right up until the moment she turned off the water and reached for a towel.

Her clothes left scattered over the floor, were missing. Only the plush robe hung from a hook on the back of the door with spa flip-flops for her feet. A glass of red wine, a comb, toothpaste and a new toothbrush still in a cardboard package sat on the sink.

Oh, Lord! This was not good.

She glanced at the clear glass shower door. What could he have seen? Everything. No, this wasn't good, at all.

Chapter Six

Muffy Parsons lounged on her rich Egyptian cotton sheets and shifted restlessly. She flipped the pillows and tossed the duvet aside, but then her skin chilled and she pulled the cover over her. Unhappy with the evening's end, she berated herself for not outbidding the woman who'd won Marshall. For her to spend money on something as foolish as a bachelor auction, when she was already dating the bachelor was abhorrent to her fiscal sense of responsibility. But letting that caterer outbid her made her appear cheap and uncaring.

Money wasn't the issue. Thanks to two generous ex-husbands, she had plenty of money, but twenty-five hundred dollars could have bought a new outfit or maybe that Louis Vuitton bag. As it was, it cost her one hundred and fifty dollars for a ticket to attend the Cancer League Fundraiser. Had Marshall been a gentleman he would have purchased her ticket.

She'd spent months appearing at all the right events to catch his eye. He had a reputation as an elusive confirmed bachelor.

Once he bedded a woman, his interest waned. Work was his mistress.

She'd heard it all, but she wanted to marry again. They looked good together, and his wealth was appealing, so she played her hand carefully. Determined to strike fast and hard for marriage while keeping him out of her bedroom. Anne Boleyn became the Queen of England by doing the same thing. Why not her?

Moonlight streamed through the windows. She reached for the hand controls and raised the bed's head until she sat almost upright.

Her plan wasn't working. Marshall's bizarre behavior worried her. Tonight, he outright encouraged the caterer to bid against her. At the time, she's dismissed it as an ego thing. All men loved being pursued. But instead of seeking her out afterward, to comfort her because she'd lost. He ignored her completely – never emerging from backstage at all. She'd lingered, spoken to several friends until it had become awkward for her to remain. Finally, she spied Caroline and her husband returning from backstage and headed in their direction.

But Caroline informed her, in that snooty way she'd perfected, that Marshall had left by another exit. As a result of that little superior gleam in his sister's eye, Muffy now tossed and turned. If Caroline's attitude was going to be a continual problem when she and Marshall married, she would simply have to insist he no longer see his sister.

Her thoughts drifted. While he hadn't

proposed quite yet, she'd already spent three days this week house hunting. The winner was a classic Dutch Colonial with an imposing yard and a panoramic view of the Willamette River.

It would take time to sell her home and his dreadful loft, but she could easily imagine being the envy of her friends. Older homes often required extensive repairs, but the bathrooms and kitchen had already undergone crucial design changes. Perfect for a discerning owner or a magazine layout. Maybe both.

The thought almost brought a smile to her face which she quickly squelched. Night cream sat on the side table, and she dabbed it around her eyes as she visualized the home.

When she and Marshall entertained, the caterers would have ample room to work, but the one caterer they would never hire would be Luscious Foods. That woman could eat her heart out.

Her wedding plans crystallized. She'd wear a nice tailored white suit, simple with classic lines or maybe a simple white dress like Caroline Bessette had worn when she married John F. Kennedy, Jr.

Her daughter, April would be her bridesmaid. April lived in California with her father, Muffy's first husband, but at ten, she'd want to be included in the wedding.

She could see it in her mind's eye -- the purity of white and the femininity of peach. A church filled with exotic orchids. A harpist played concertos. This time, everything would be perfect.

Lily eased the door open, listening for any sounds of movement. One end of the hallway took her back towards the front door; the other opened into a dark room. Marshall's robe dragged the floor. The sleeves had been rolled into cuffs. Why was she behaving like a coward? Go out. Face him. Go home. If he refused to relinquish her clothes, she'd steal his robe and simply leave.

Lily paused. Marshall was only part of the problem, not even the biggest part. The full wineglass in her hand was too appealing. She took a sip for courage and stepped into the hall.

Why couldn't she glide into his open arms and snuggle into his warmth? Why not let him run his rough hands over her and smother her with kisses?

Perhaps her dream could have an actual climax.

The one thing she was positive he could provide, she wanted. Worse, she wanted it shamelessly. Over and over until he tired of her and insisted she leave, which would probably be in less than an hour. He wouldn't even want her to stay the night.

So far, her impression of him was that of the kind of man who desired a companion for nothing more than a short-term fling. Which was good news because that was all she wanted. Her fantasy man in the flesh. Finish the dream.

But the thought of having sex again, after so many long years, turned her will power to gelatin. In theory, it was obtainable. Marshall was willing.

When she dreamed of a physical relationship, it flowed, even if the ending was unsatisfactory. Dream sex didn't require her to say yes or no, or think about being naked in front of a stranger, or to even leave the bathroom. She merely had to close her eyes and let the magic occur. For the first time, she had a thorough understanding of the phrase 'reality bites'.

She was afraid.

Of what? That he'd say no? Unlikely.

That she'd be embarrassed? Probably.

That he might leave her unsatisfied? She couldn't even contemplate that thought.

Taking a deep breath and clutching her wineglass like it was the Holy Grail, she forced her feet to move. Silently, she drifted down the darkened hall toward the light.

A fire roared. Music played from unseen speakers and the comfortable butter-leather couch beckoned. Everything present for a seduction but the host. No doubt he tired of waiting for her and fell asleep.

Lily stared at the stairway that floated from the first floor to the loft above, the most likely place for the master bedroom. No visual supports gave the stairs a magical feel as though constructed by smoke and mirrors.

There wasn't enough enticement in the world to make her climb those stairs. Crawling into bed with a sleeping man wasn't her fantasy. She wanted seduction, not candlelight and roses, but a man who would be patient enough to coax her body into wanting to open up and trust him. Not someone who would roll over and find her within easy grasp.

She opted for the kitchen. Copper pots hung from racks over a serious island workspace; a sub-zero refrigerator and a six-burner gas stove top with griddle and two dishwashers completed the picture. What a jewel of a kitchen. It would be a pleasure to cook here, but she refused to kid herself. It was doubtful that such an opportunity would ever present itself.

An open bottle of Opus One sat on the counter in invitation. Barely had the wine surged from the bottle toward the glass when a series of loud dings startled her. Her hand lurched. Wine splashed from her glass onto the black granite counter top.

"Washing machine," a masculine voice announced behind her.

Her spine jerked, and she riveted to face him as more wine slopped across the counter. Catching her behavior, she righted the bottle and made a dam of her hand to keep the wine from spilling over the edge on to his stone floors. A crimson blush stole up her cheeks.

Marshall stepped around the work island and took a sponge from the sink. Reaching across the counter, he mopped up the spilled wine and placed his empty glass beside hers.

"I'll let you pour if you think you can handle it."

He doubted her abilities? "No worries, I'm a professional."

His blue eyes crinkled. "Really? I couldn't tell."

"The robe's a hindrance." She shrugged.

"Uh-huh." The corner of lips crooked into a wicked smile. "Don't let me stop you. Feel free to take it off if it interferes with the performance of your duties."

By sheer willpower alone, she held the bottle steady refusing to respond to his taunting. Unable to keep quiet any longer, she asked. "What's your plan here, Marshall? You got me up here to talk, and now you're holding my clothes hostage. It's late. I need to go home, so say your piece and let me leave."

Marshall handed her his glass of wine. "Sit

in the living room. I'm going to throw your clothes in the dryer before I join you."

Somewhere this evening she'd lost control. How was it that she was following someone else's instructions? She found herself placing his glass of wine next to hers as she took a seat on the living room couch and waited for him to join her. Annoyed she downed her glass of wine and propped her feet allowing her to stretch out on the soul-sucking comfortable couch.

Marshall chuckled as he opened the door of the washing machine. So he was just to blurt out his wishes, listen to her rebuffed them, and then watch her march out the door. Younger women were so much more pliable, not as much fun, but certainly more predictable. Getting them into bed only required a specified number of steps including a courteous phone call for a cab to whisk them home and out of his hair.

He recalled her toned, silky back that ended at those perfect white globes he had seen in the shower stall. Her arms raised above her head the water sloshed over her skin leaving her glistening. He'd never found skinny women appealing. But it wasn't until he'd seen her naked that he realized it had been a long time since he wanted a woman for more than arm décor. An array of attractive women had paraded through his life. Some, he'd discovered, were so lean he could count their ribs.

Not so with Lily. Hers was a body finely laced with toned muscle that offered the comfort of cushioned hips and real breasts.

Still that wouldn't account for why she was so difficult to resist. For a moment in the bathroom, he had come close to shedding his clothes and joining her in the shower. She didn't even have to turn around; he'd just slip into her moist folds from behind and drive her hard against the wall. His body didn't need any prompting, and it had been that way since he'd met her. And whether the little witch chose to admit it or not, she was just as primed.

Dori's comments, about Lily not dating and Steven's memory of her husband's death, troubled him. He vaguely remembered the event. Every newspaper had written about the incident, and the mommy-conscience legislature introduced a series of bills to made construction illegal on bridges. That was four or five years ago.

While he waited in the car, he'd used his phone to Google her. News stories had reported his death but said nothing about her life, except that Luscious Food was one busy catering company.

She hadn't been out socially, but that didn't mean she'd been celibate. A little hot-blooded number like her wouldn't have been on hiatus that long. Would she?

The telephone in the kitchen rang. He'd installed the land line when he'd built the place years earlier. Even after the last remodel, he'd kept the phone lines complete with old-fashioned phones still attached to the wall. Not because he was sentimental, but he refused to give his cell phone number to most people. Particularly women, who felt entitled to call and chat. Sooner or later they realized that work always came first with him.

If someone called at this time of night, it was probably an emergency. Marshall grabbed the receiver. "Hello."

A soft, feminine voice purred, "Did I wake you?"

Inwardly he groaned. "Muffy?" He waited until she acknowledged her name. "I'm awake. What's the problem?"

"I couldn't sleep. I felt terrible about losing the auction tonight. I had to call to make sure you're okay."

For the first time since Marshall had known her, she voiced concern for someone other than herself.

He leaned against the kitchen wall wishing for his glass of wine. "I'm fine. Why wouldn't I be?"

"Well." Marshall heard her inhale before the words gushed out. "I was afraid you'd be so offended at being won by one of the kitchen help that you might be angry at me. Honestly, darling, I didn't bid more because I knew you didn't want to waste our money like that."

Kitchen help? Our money?

He'd hardly call Lily kitchen help and when did her money and his money become our money? Her choice to bid had been just that – her choice. He hadn't been planning to replace any funds she could claim as a tax deduction. The event had been for charity, and she hadn't been his date.

Marshall opened his mouth and then closed it again. It was late, no one was thinking straight.

"I'm not offended. Overall, it was fun," he assured her. "Listen, why don't I call you in the next couple of days and we'll talk then."

"No." Her voice snapped into a harsh bark. "Come over now. You're not asleep, I can't sleep." She lowered her tone to a seductive whisper. "Not talking will only make it worse."

Why did dealing with her always feel like goo that clung to his skin and no amount of scrubbing would release? "It's late. I've got a full day tomorrow; I've gotta get some sleep. Monday or Tuesday's soon enough. You did the right thing. Spending all that money would have been foolish. Try and get some rest. I'll call you."

He hung up before she could protest further.

The corkboard held dozens of scraps of paper with names and numbers. He grabbed Muffy's number, crumbled it into a ball and tossed it into the trashcan.

Her call cemented his thinking about his relationship, not just with Muffy, but with many of the women he knew. Of all the women who sat in the audience tonight, the one least able to afford to spend money had understood his embarrassment and worked to make him look good. Yeah, the auction was supposed to be fun, but it wasn't.

Had Lily not bid, his ego would have been dented, not seriously damaged. But the intrepid caterer assured that never happened. The card with Lily's information was in his pocket. Tonight would probably be the last time he saw her, but still he wasn't ready to pin her information next to the rest. He patted his pocket as he hurried to the living room to find her.

The second glass of wine proved to be Lily's undoing. When Marshall rounded the corner to the living room, he found her curled up on the couch, sound asleep, his robe tucked neatly around her. Her ruby toes twinkled at him in the dim light of the room.

The temptation to wake her was strong, he even considered carrying her to a bedroom, particularly his own, before he decided against it. Keeping himself in check would be difficult if she lay next to him. When he took her to bed, he wanted her full cooperation. And she would be as hot for him as he was for her.

Covering her with a throw, he left her asleep. As a precautionary measure, he pocketed her keys and locked the interior door to the elevator, preventing her escape. Reluctantly Marshall retired to the master suite alone.

Chapter Seven

The next afternoon Dori arrived unannounced at Lily's home. Her location was no mystery; she merely followed the sound of music to the backyard. Crouched on the moist earth, Lily planted her tomatoes in the rich soil. The iPod player blared as she and Patsy Cline sang about sweet dreams.

Dori pressed the off button. Patsy was immediately silent. Lily still managed to have a few more notes left in her.

Lily wiped the hair out of her eyes with the back of her gloved hand, leaving a smear of mud. "What're you doing here?"

Dori hopped from one set of pavers to the next, trying to avoid getting her shoes dirty. . "Why aren't you answering your phone? I've called you something like fifteen times today."

"It didn't ring. I've got it right here." Lily patted her pockets to discover the phone wasn't at her side.

She rose, her rubber boots covered in mud that spread to the knees of her overalls. Unlike Dori, she had no problem tromping across the garden bed. The boots were cast aside at the back door while she searched the house.

"Well, shoot," she said as she padded out to the driveway in socked feet to her van. A minutes later she returned looking slightly embarrassed, but with the missing phone in her hand. "I've missed twenty-six calls."

"They're not all from me. I'm betting most of those are from bachelor number three. He's called the kitchen several times, as well." Dori folded her arms over her chest. "What happened last night? Everyone's worried about you."

Lily shrugged, unconcerned. "Hey, I didn't purposely leave the phone where I couldn't hear it. C'mon, I'm ready for coffee, aren't you?"

Inside the back door, she shucked her muddy overalls and hung them on a hook; her bare legs protruded from a long T-shirt, which displayed wild mushroom varieties. The fact Lily didn't look worried eased her partner's concern.

"Sandra said someone followed you last night after you left the kitchen. Was it Marshall?" She emptied the last of the pot of morning coffee into the sink and ran fresh water.

"Uh-huh. How'd you know?" Lily yelled from the hallway on her way to the bedroom.

Dori opened the refrigerator and studied the dairy selection before deciding on skim milk. "Because you left your car keys at his house, and he quizzed me about how you got home." She sniffed the contents.

"Spare key in the magnetic holder," Lily answered, as she re-entered the kitchen wearing a clean shirt, jeans, and loafers. "That milk's good, I just bought it."

"So, what did happen?"

Lily shrugged, attempting to appear unaffected by the previous night's carousing. "Well, let's see," she said. They had been friends and business partner's way too long for Dori not to recognize stalling. She slapped two mugs on the kitchen table with more force than she'd intended.

Lily jumped. "He insisted we go to his loft – to talk." A smile curled her lips. "I fell asleep, waiting for him. When I woke this morning, it took a few minutes to get my bearings, but I snuck out without telling him. No easy feat since he'd locked his elevator and hidden my car keys."

Dori laughed, imagining her friend plotting her exit strategy. "You fell asleep? I want the whole, juicy story… out with it." Both moved to the kitchen table.

"The fire escape stairwell. He lives on the fifth floor. Fortunately, I was going down, not up." Lily's eyes sparkled with delight at outsmarting Marshall.

Dori asked leaning back in her chair. "What's he like?"

"Domineering. Bossy. Determined. Take-your-breath away sexy."

A knot caught in Dori's throat. She already knew the answer, but she asked anyway, "Did you do him?"

"No," Lily's lips curled upward, but it wasn't a joyous look. Dori's heart ached, but then Lily squared her shoulders and threw off her slump. She had seen her do the same thing a thousand times. Circumstances couldn't keep her down for long.

"But," Lily said in a happier voice. "I've got enough fantasy bait to sustain me for some time."

Dori laughed. It was hard not to admire a woman who saw the bright side of every situation. "I'm not sure I could've resisted."

Lily nodded. "Parts of me said yes, but it ended up being like downhill skiing. I can ski perfectly okay if I can get off the chair lift and on the slopes before the fear hits my brain. Last night, the fear hit my brain." She leaned closer, stirring the coffee in her cup. "What'd he say about me?"

Dori's eyebrows shot skyward. She'd never seen Lily displaying any insecurities. "Nothing revealing. He didn't mention any tattoos or that in the middle of passion you like to sing the Alleluia chorus. He was concerned and eager to return your car keys."

Lily reached across the table and grabbed

her arm. "You didn't give him my home address, did you?"

"Would that have been wrong?" She laughed at Lily's horrified face. She'd never seen her partner so interested in a man. Maybe a little heartbreak would do her good. "So, why *are* you hesitating?"

Lily grimaced before answering and ran a hand through her curling dark hair. "Aside from the fact that I just met him on Friday? Let's look at some facts, here, shall we? He's gorgeous. I'll bet he even wakes up looking good. I, on the other hand, clean up well about three days a week." She frowned at the garden dirt under her fingernails.

Dori resisted leaning over and beating her friend about the head and shoulders for such a stupid comment. But Lily continued before she could voice her opinion.

"He's rich and can have any woman he wants. My savings are embarrassing, I work all the time, and my vast salacious experience was with Charlie –- a man who didn't care if we ever had sex."

Dori was genuinely surprised. "You're afraid."

"Of course, I'm afraid. I'm forty-four. Gravity has not been my friend. My butt touches the back of my knees. My bras no longer require underwires but rather steel reinforcements and a hoist. I'm not sure that Marshall is the right man. Plus if anyone's singing the Alleluia chorus, I would prefer it to be someone grateful that I agreed to take my clothes off."

Dori poured herself a second cup of coffee and carefully considered her words. "Do you remember when you were thirteen and every night you prayed you'd have breasts?"

Lily sniggered. "Yeah, and now I wish I had less. You know large breasts kind of get in your way."

"Mmm. Do you remember how you dreaded turning thirty because your body would lose its shape? And now in your forties, you greatly exaggerate your flaws but still hate your body."

Lily shrugged, but she listened.

"What's that phrase you tell brides when they're choosing a menu? If you're happy, your guests will also be happy."

Lily closed her eyes. "And your point is?"

"It's been my experience that a man who finally convinces a woman to remove her clothes for pleasure isn't likely to reject her because he was expecting a twenty-year-old supermodel. Men tend to like women in various shapes and sizes. Face it. Betty Boop was a sex symbol, even if she was a cartoon."

Her eyes flew open. "I can't believe you'd bring up the Betty Boop thing, after all this time."

Dori chuckled. "Charlie was wrong about a lot of things, but he was right about the fact that you have a strong resemblance to Betty Boop."

"It's not flattering to be compared to an animated character with a baby doll voice whose brightest comment is 'boo-boop-de-doop.'" Lily imitated the cartoon voice and batted her eyes. "Do you think we've had enough coffee, now? I'm ready for a glass of wine."

Dori laughed. "I've got to go. Beating up my best friend was only the fourth thing on my agenda today. I still have a long list left to accomplish, and unless I'm mistaken, you've still got tomatoes to plant."

The light from Marshall's tablet illuminated the dark room. The words failed to make an impact. He hadn't moved for the past forty-five minutes except to twirl Lily's keys around his fingers.

When sleep had eluded him, he'd come downstairs to his home office in hopes work would help take his mind off this woman, but the words inscribed on the screen failed to make an impact.

No calls could only mean good news. Lily hadn't died in an accident. She'd made it home safely, but he wanted to hear her throaty voice assuring him she was okay and that he hadn't moved too quickly and scared her off.

How ludicrous – he never scared women off. Sometimes Caroline teased him that he needed to beat them off with a stick, but he never frightened women. Of course, Lily might disagree if she was still hot about that stalking misunderstanding.

He reread the latest report from Peter on cetaceans and their prey. Peter, one of the fifteen marine biologists who worked for Caudill Marine Institute, was currently in the Florida Keys researching echolocation, the high-frequency clicking noise dolphins used to locate their prey. The goal of CMI was to determine whether the fish forewarned by the dolphin's sounds, altered their behavior defensively.

He'd read the second paragraph twice before acknowledging his concentration was zip and dolphins were not his main concern. The provocative Lily with her tousled hair, her liquid chocolate eyes, and sultry red lips still danced before his eyes taunting him. When was the last time a woman had distracted him like this?

Inexplicably, the memory of another woman came to him. Brigit Ingemar, the blonde, beautiful, Swedish au pair, had been the object of his fantasies for the better part of his fourteenth year. At twenty-four, her perfect body enticed him as few ever would again. As summer drew to an end, so was her time in

America.

The Oregon Coast and Caudill summers were intertwined. He'd spent months at the family beach home. One scorching hot July night, his parents left the kids alone while they attended a neighbor's party. After Brigit had put two-year-old Caroline to bed, she introduced Marshall to a different nighttime game.

With the sound of the waves hitting the beach outside his open window, he tasted her salty skin as she stretched beneath him. It was the first time he'd seen a woman's eyes glazed in passion from his actions and heard quiet muffled moans she made when he plunged into her time and again.

Marshall was not so foolish as to believe her behavior was based on love, but at fourteen that hardly mattered. If she was willing to teach, he devoted every spare minute of his time to learning. Their summer romance blossomed, continuing until mid-August when the family returned to the city.

Marshall loved the rambling old house and the library with its floor-to-ceiling books and highly polished furniture. Musty leather and citrus. The scent still enticed him. He stood at the patio doors, staring at the moon, glad to be home.

Behind him, a door opened. He turned to see

his father and Bridget tiptoe into the room. Quietly his father closed and bolted the hall door, then pulled the girl into his arms for a deep kiss. Marshall froze in his position debating whether to duck behind the bookcase or open the patio door and sneak out. He refused to look away, fascinated by his girlfriend's response to his father's touch.

When Henry Caudill released her, the younger girl staggered slightly.

"Now, what's so important that you had to see me immediately? You know I have no control over the INS. If it were up to me, you could stay, but it's not. The only way you can remain in this country is to marry a citizen."

His hand stroked her face. Bridget tilted her head to encourage him. "I'm pregnant."

Henry snatched his hand back and stepped away from her. "Bullshit!" He crossed his arms over his chest. From the far side of the room Marshall quaked. His father's stance did not bode well. "If you're pregnant, it's not mine."

Wishing with all his being that he'd escaped earlier, now Marshall prayed for the floor to open beneath him and swallow him whole. Brigit had planned well. The immediate knowledge that he'd been used and thrown away like a pawn raised his ire as he watched the argument unfold in front of him.

"It could be." She tossed her head in a manner designed to entice, but Marshall thought it was more likely to cover her intentions.

"I'm never careless," Henry declared as he walked to his desk, found a cigarette and lit it. "Two children were plenty for me. I've been snipped. What did you think? That I'd leave my wife and children because you got knocked up?" His father chuckled cruelly. His cold blue eyes lacked mirth.

Brigit's eyes narrowed, and her back tensed, but before she was able to drop her well-executed bomb, Marshall stole her thunder. "You swore you were on the pill."

Both Brigit and his father looked in the direction of his voice. Marshall stepped away from the windows into the light. Standing straight and tall, he attempted to appear older than his age.

"Oh my, aren't you the sneaky one," Henry Caudill said, shifting his vision between Marshall and Brigit. Unsure which of the two of them his father meant, Marshall kept quiet. His father took another puff and regarded them intently.

"How long?" he demanded of his son.

Marshall counted in his head. "Three weeks."

A smug smile crossed Brigit's face. Never

had Marshall wanted to slap a person as much as he did her. Instead, he took his cue from his father and kept his face as expressionless as he could.

"I want ten thousand dollars," Brigit demanded. "Or I'll tell your wife."

Henry burst into laughter. "Go ahead and tell her. She probably already knows about us. But I guarantee that when she finds out you seduced her baby boy, you'll think you've opened the gates of Hell. Her anger is something to behold."

Bridget took a step backward. "There are laws against this kind of thing." Her voice rose with each word until she squeaked by the end of the sentence.

"Yeah, there are. It's called statutory rape. My son's a minor," Henry calmly ground his cigarette into the ashtray. "Tomorrow morning, I'll take you to a doctor and if you're not pregnant, you'll be on a plane for Stockholm in the afternoon. I suggest you pack tonight."

Color faded from her face. Momentarily, Marshall felt a twinge of sympathy for her, but then her eyes glinted, her mouth drew into a tight hyphen, and her look of pure hatred shocked him into rethinking his pity. The door slammed behind her echoing in the quiet of the room.

Marshall's attention returned to his father, expecting anger. To his surprise, Henry smiled conspiratorially at his son. "Was she your first?"

Marshall was stunned. His father was proud of him? He nodded.

"Did she approach you?"

"Yeah," he admitted.

"Next time, you make the moves," Henry told him, glancing down at his desk. "One more thing. I'll take care of this time, but never, ever let me hear that you had unprotected sex again. I don't care what cockamamie thing the woman tells you. The only way to protect yourself is to make sure you always use a rubber. They're in the bottom drawer of my bathroom."

His father pulled a large checkbook from a drawer in his desk and tore a check from the sheet. "Remember, son. Women will always be available, but the one you marry becomes a Caudill, and it's up to you to make sure that she and her background represent what we stand for. Love's for children and romance novels."

Marshall nodded. As he stepped toward the door, his father stopped him with one last question. "So, back to Brigit. How was it?"

Unable to resist, Marshall grinned. "Fan-fucking-tastic."

His father laughed. "She was a hot little number. You did okay for the first time."

Marshall smiled at the memory. It had been the first time for a lot of things. Certainly, it was the first time he could remember his father being proud of him. Yeah, Brigit had been a hot little number, and something about Lily reminded him of her. Once he bedded Lily and got her out of his system, he could concentrate on work again.

He consulted his tide chart. In about thirty hours the remote beach, known as Dead Man's Cove, would have the lowest negative tide during the past twenty years. He hadn't planned to leave for the coast until after lunch, but if he couldn't sleep he might as well go now.

The arduous four-hour drive involved long winding mountainous roads and then non-stop traffic on the narrow coast highway. He hadn't even packed. Marshall rubbed his eyes knowing tomorrow would be more difficult if he didn't get some sleep before attempting several hours in the car alone.

That thought stayed with him. Why should he be alone? Without hesitation, he pushed the redial button on his telephone. On the second ring, a sleepy voice mumbled. "Hello."

"Did I wake you?" Marshall asked softening his voice to a seductive level.

Lily made an exasperated noise. She didn't sound enticed; she sounded irritated. "Don't you ever sleep? Or do you stay up all night like Spiderman?"

He grinned, amused by her instinctive flare up. It was fun to rile her. "Wrong superhero, darling. It's Batman who stays up all night."

"Great. Let me write that down. Why aren't you asleep? Don't you have a real job, Marshall?"

"That's why I called you, sweetheart. Do you know what a negative tide is?"

"Of course," she said yawning. "I'm in food service. '*The ocean sets the table twice a day.*' I don't know who said it, but everyone understands that when the tide goes out, an entire edible world is laid bare."

He imagined her snuggling down in the covers the phone stuck to her ear as he whispered exotic fantasies into the receiver. Would she respond? No, this wasn't the right time. If she hung up on him, he'd never convince her to come to the coast.

"There's more to it than just food. When the tide recedes, an entire microcosmic world is exposed. Some of which is easily seen and some of which is studied microscopically. But you've walked the ocean floor during a negative tide?"

She didn't speak, making him wonder if she'd fallen asleep. Finally she answered, "In grade school we went tide pooling if that's what you mean. I've always wanted to go again. It's just difficult for me to find time for the research, so I'll know what I'm seeing."

He baited the hook. "Tuesday morning's a

minus two point seven negative tide."

"Is that good?"

That's right, come a little closer. "The lowest in twenty years. I'm going down after lunch today to see it. Would you like to come?" He tossed the lure.

"I'm not prepared."

She circled but didn't say no. He waited.

"Would I learn any more than I did years ago?"

He smiled and reeled the line toward his boat. "Darling, not only am I a Marine Biologist, but I'm one of the most knowledgeable men in the State of Oregon. I doubt that you want to get into a discussion of semi-diurnal tides, but trust me, you'd learn a lot more from me than your fifth-grade science teacher."

"You're a Marine Biologist?" Still, she hesitated. "You don't seem like a scientist to me."

Marshall chuckled. "Lily, you know nothing about me. Why did you bid on me?"

"Let's go back to the first question. Would I like to see a negative tide with 'one of the most knowledgeable men in the State of Oregon'? Yes, I'd love to. What do I need to bring?

Marshall gave her a short list that he could rattle off without too much thought. Lily may be tired but she wasn't a fool. If he gloated, she'd back out, so he kept his voice professional, but after he hung up the phone, he rubbed his hands together.

Come to Daddy, darling.

The next morning, Lily arrived late at work. Dragging herself into the office she shared with her partner, she dropped the paperwork in her arms on her already cluttered desk.

"Would you be offended if I said you were not very attractive today?" Dori asked. "Maybe you shouldn't have days off if this is how you return to work."

Lily groaned not up to Dora's verbal challenge. "I'm just tired. Thanks to my new friend, Mr. Caudill, I haven't slept well for two nights." She ground the sentence out between her teeth and plopped down in her chair.

"Oh!" Dori's interest picked up. "What *have* you two been doing?"

"He called at three AM to invite me to a negative tide at the coast." Lily rested her head on her desk and closed her eyes. "After his call I had trouble going back to sleep."

"It's the lowest in twenty years. To view it with a Marine Biologist would be amazing."

Lily opened one eye to peer at her partner. "How did you know he was a Marine Biologist?"

"I Googled him. He's reputed to be brilliant.

Are you going?"

"Why not? It's a quiet week." She refused to raise her head, not wanting to see her partner's look of disapproval.

"Great. I can handle things until the Goldstein Bar Mitzvah on Saturday morning." Dori's tone sounded absolutely perky.

Lily raised her head. Dori grinned. She wanted her to go? She couldn't possibly want Lily to get laid as much as she wanted it.

Dori rose from behind her desk and walked to toward her. "If you aren't back by then, I can manage that, too."

"I'll be back long before Saturday morning," Lily assured her, surprised when Dori took her arm and propelled her out of her seat.

"Doesn't his career choice seem out of character? He seems more like someone who'd come up with the concept for Hooter's Restaurants. I can even see him as the owner of a troubled professional sports team. But a scientist? It stretches the imagination."

Dori shuffled through the pile of paperwork on her desk and found her purse. "Looks like he may surprise you then. Take off until Saturday anyway. You're going to be at the coast. Have a fun time," Dori thrust the handbag at her and guided her toward the door.

"I'm betting by tomorrow afternoon, he'll be sending me home. Let's face it, he only invited me to fulfill his obligation as an auctioned bachelor."

For the first time, Dori stopped, bent over and almost choked on her laughter. "You know when men call me at three in the morning, my first thought is always that they're just performing a social obligation." She straightened and fixed a pointed look at her partner. "Go home. Get some rest before you go. Pack your black bra."

Lily couldn't leave without being honest with her friend. "Listen, I only agreed to go because I want to have sex with him. He makes me crazy. I've known him less than sixty hours, and I've wasted more energy thinking about him than any man is worth. Maybe the celibacy thing's gotten old. I figure with my luck, I'll go to bed with him, it'll be a total bust, but then I'll get back to what's important by Saturday."

Dori gaped. "And what is important here?"

"You know I mean work." Lily let annoyance creep into her tone.

"Well, it's a documented fact that most people's dying wish is that they'd devoted more time to their careers." Sarcasm laced her voice. A hard shove found Lily on the other side of the threshold. Without another word, Dori slammed the door in her face.

Chapter Eight

Marshall followed the directions Lily had given him and pulled into her driveway around noon. The small Cape Cod cottage was attractive, well-tended, but more homey than affluent. The yard was a riot of pinks and purples with rhododendrons, azaleas, and impatiens in bloom.

He'd barely turned his engine off when his cell phone rang. Glancing at the caller ID, he answered, "Hello, Caro." His sister, Caroline despised nicknames.

"Friday night." Her voice was tight in that formal way she used when annoyed. "Steven and I are having a few friends for dinner. Shall I invite Lilith Carmichael?" She emphasized Lily's full name.

"Stop making plans, Caroline. I'm sure by Friday we'll have gone the distance in this situation."

After Marshall had spoken to Lily in the middle of the night, he'd finally slept. Now refreshed, his attraction to her had diminished. Tomorrow, when he had his fill of her, she would no longer haunt his dreams. And he could close this chapter on an unusual woman who had drifted through his life.

"One day love will tackle you around the ankles and drive you to the ground. I want to be there when it happens." The disgust in Caroline's voice amused him.

"Oh, come on, Lily's a nice woman, but she's just a little too…" He'd been going to say Betty Crocker, but looking at her front yard upgraded his answer to "Martha Stewart for me. She does not have, as our father would have said, Caudill potential."

"She also doesn't have a prison record," A peevishness had entered Caroline's voice. "Marshall, I love you, but our parents were not role models. Consider this, have you ever met anyone who had Caudill potential? And if you answer yes -- think about it -- did you actually like that person? Plus I read some men find the thought of Martha Stewart, clad only in a tool belt and a smile, a real turn-on."

Marshall ignored Caroline's philosophical take on their parents. Their lousy marriage could be contributed to many of the beliefs they espoused. But while Marshall didn't necessarily agree with everything, he knew that marriage had a different set of requirements than just hormones or emotions. Caroline could chastise him for his ideas, but she had married Steven – a Zonnheiser – one of the richest families on the West Coast.

"If Lily seems like the clingy type I'll be sure and mention the tool belt thing to her."

Lily stepped out the front door and placed a small overnight case by the stairs. Marshall stared at her, entranced. Seeing her again was like a punch to his gut.

Her curly hair was momentarily tamed, and fresh makeup made her eyes appear larger and her lips more kissable. Even from the distance of the driveway, he could see the curve of her breast under her t-shirt, and her shorts emphasized her shapely bare legs – legs that he could easily envision wrapped around his waist.

Lily raised her hand in greeting but didn't wait for a response as she returned inside, leaving the front door open.

Marshall followed. From his observations of the outside, he expected the house to be decorated like a magazine layout rather than the eclectic hodgepodge he found. His walls were soothing beige. This woman didn't own a beige wall. He inhaled deeply, and the cinnamon apple scent of her house reminded of a childhood he'd only seen only on television.

The jeweled-toned walls effectively offset the cool whites and light colored wood in the furniture, making her artwork literally jump off the walls. In the living room, he noticed a signed Agam, which changed with every movement he made. Interesting her taste ran to such sophistication in art. A lighted alcove housed a piece of blown glass resembling wild stargazer lilies. He was confident the glass was a Chihuly original.

Well, wasn't she turning out to be just a fancy piece of work? Her husband must have done well in his career for her to be able to afford this level of luxury. He wouldn't have guessed she was the type.

"Don't let it frighten you," she called from the kitchen.

"What?" He walked in the direction of her voice.

"The house. It's the diametrical opposite of yours."

Marshall looked at the crowded tables and counters. "Different styles. You don't lack for stuff."

Lily scrubbed the mud off well-used rubber boots in her kitchen sink and laughed. "What a polite statement. In this house, a clean counter is a homing beacon. I've lived here ten years and just keep collecting more stuff."

"Everything seems to have a place. It's attractively arranged. I like it."

"Do you? I hate to tell you that I was envious of the clean, minimalist look of yours."

Once again his image of her was incorrect. "You must be one of the few women I know who owns rubber boots."

"I've got some cowboy boots and spurs, too, but I save those for special occasions." The saucy smile she gave him had his heart racing as he visualized her in cowboy boots and little else. He stepped closer, trying to get the scent of her, but other odors interfered -- the soapy residue from the boots, the cinnamon-apple smell of her kitchen and the underlying scent of pine cleanser.

"Why does your kitchen smell like apple pie?"

"I'm baking a strudel to take with us. It's just about done." She set the boots on the edge of the sink to dry, rinsed her hands and opened the oven door. "You said on the phone that others would join us. How many?"

"Ten or twelve." Her kitchen may have looked like something out of grandmother's house, but she had a serious stove. Longer than normal, six burners -- a professional stove in a home kitchen. His kitchen had been designed for a professional chef, but it was all for show, Marshall didn't use it.

She lifted a long pan with two pastries. The apple filling bubbled between the lattice golden brown dough.

"Good, we've got plenty, and the quiche is done, too." She lifted another pan with three quiche pies and carefully jiggled each one before satisfying herself that the egg dish was set.

She was bringing food? "Did you think we

wouldn't feed you?"

Lily stood upright, a stricken look in her deep brown eyes. "Not at all. It's an ingrained habit. I always take food. It's the curse of my career. If I've offended you, we don't have to bring it."

He leaned casually against the wall and tried to remember if he'd ever dated a woman who cooked. "No way. I'm just afraid if you cook for the team`, they'll never let you leave."

"Naw. The novelty wears off after a couple of meals and then everyone will start to complain that I'm making them fat."

He doubted that would be the response. "How long do those need to cool?"

"Ten minutes. Then we wrap them in towels and take them warm." She shook the boots once more over the sink to encourage them to finish drying.

"Why don't you give me a tour of your house while we wait?" he asked when she'd finished.

"Okay, then we can figure out what to do with the other nine minutes."

Marshall refused to offer suggestions on how to fill a void of time, although several ideas occurred to him.

The tour was short. A long hall covered with artwork and a quick stop to view a den with a television, a guest bedroom, and the master bedroom. Each room had a different motif; the den was western with cowhide print fabric on the furniture. NW Indian tribal masks, Karl Bodmer, and Bev Doolittle framed prints decorated the wall.

The contemporary guest bedroom had lime-green walls with smatterings of brightly colored modern art. The white wicker headboard screamed Pier I. The expensive and the inexpensive lined right up next to each other.

"It's very bright," was the only comment he could manage.

"When the lights aren't on, it glows in the dark," she said. He was sure she was joking especially when she added. "I have to provide eye masks for my guests spending the night.

As he followed her down the hall, he walked behind her so he could watch her butt sway with each step. What was it about her that drew him? She was nothing like other women he knew.

Her bedroom was his favorite. Authentic Asian furniture and the subtle color palate appealed to his style. "Very nice."

"Thanks, I just finished it last year."

The fact that her husband hadn't slept in this room pleased Marshall. Maybe it was the bedroom itself or perhaps he was unable to resist her. He stepped behind her and placed his hands on her shoulders drawing her back against his chest.

Two feet in front of her stood the tidy king-size platform bed inviting him to lay her across the raw silk comforter.

"This room would look good in my loft. I should have you decorate my bedroom."

As his hands slid down her arms, thoughts of the way Lily could decorate his bedroom crossed his mind. Her body shivered beneath his hands, her thinking ran on the same track. Slowly, he pivoted her to face him.

Lily's eyes were half closed allowing him to recall how quickly she succumbed the last time they kissed. He bet this time would be the same. She was half gone now, and all he'd done was rubbed her arms. Maybe they would put off the drive to the coast.

His pulse racing, he traced the outline of her lips and slipped his thumb into the warm cocoon of her mouth. The flickering of her tongue almost made his lose control. He eased his hand back before he dropped to his knees and ripped her clothes off.

Her pouty lips with tilted upward. His fingers stretched around her neck to hold her in place while his right arm wrapped around her waist securing her to him then he lowered his head to hers.

"That's right, sweetheart, want me back," he murmured as his lips brushed hers. Lily sighed, opening her mouth. He tightened her against his body until thighs touched, and breast met chest. Her arms encircled his neck.

The touch of their tongues was electric. She tasted of apples and chocolate. With his thumb on her neck her blood thundered, and she squirmed impatiently in his arms, but he was not into more speed. This time he wanted to savor – to touch everything that would be his. His hands stroked her gentle curves, drifting lower until he cupped her derriere.

A familiar tune jarred the scene as his phone rang. This was the main reason he refused to give his number to anyone, but, as a result, every call was important.

"Sorry. I've got to take it," he apologized, watching her so intently he never glanced at his Caller ID.

Lily nodded, her eyes still unfocused, but the spell was broken. She slid out of his reach, but by then his attention had turned to the phone.

"Hello." His tone huskier than normal would alert an astute caller to his state of arousal. He prayed the other person wouldn't recognize his voice for what it was – a man about to get laid.

"Marshall," a high pitched voice whined into the receiver. "You never called me back."

Marshall groaned.

Muffy! How had she gotten his cell number?

"Let me call you back." Marshall turned away from the woman in front of him as he attempted to extricate himself from the call.

Undaunted by his brush off, the woman on other end of the line said, "Fine. Just don't forget about Thursday night."

"Thursday night?"

"The opening of the De Goya exhibit at the Art Museum." Her clear enunciation conveyed her annoyance. "You agreed to take me."

Marshall racked his memory to recall when he'd agreed to such a thing. It wasn't that he was opposed the Art Museum, although De Goya tended to be a little too macabre for his taste. He couldn't believe he'd given two thumbs up to going with her. Continuing to escort Muffy to social affairs was not on his agenda but breaking up with one woman while standing in another's bedroom was complicated.

"I doubt I'll be back from the coast by Thursday. This week's hectic. There's a tide series--"

"That's lovely, Marshall," She interrupted before he could get his full excuse formulated. "The Coast isn't that far. Drive back Thursday afternoon for the gala, spend the night and then return on Friday." A sultry tone entered her voice as she added, "I'll make it worth your while."

Inwardly, Marshall winced. It had been a long time since he'd balanced two women, and he didn't want to be doing it now. "Not this time. Find someone else." Muffy's insistence irritated him. "I'm not free this week."

He hated confrontations. How had he gotten involved with a woman he didn't like?

"Marshall," she sniffed. "How will it look if I take someone else?"

Oh, no. They weren't going to tears. He paced the room, aware Lily had left. "Like I was busy?"

"No," Her sad tone plucked at his guilt. "Like I was dumped after the bachelor auction fiasco last Saturday. People talk, you know."

A dozen responses came to his mind, all of which would end up in an argument. He knew his temper, if he pursued this discussion, he would say things he would regret later.

"Thursday night's out." Never had he let a woman interfere with work and he wasn't starting now. If the women he dated complained about anything, it was his time spent at the coast. She knew his reputation. They had too many mutual acquaintances for her not to know. "I'll call you when I'm free and we'll talk."

She started to protest, but Marshall disconnected the call.

Lily peppered Marshall with questions on the long road trip. Two hours had passed before it dawned on him that she had not told him one personal thing about herself.

He'd rattled on about CMI and with her prodding had included a detailed character sketch of everyone she was likely to meet and their areas of research. His family, which he normally did not think of as fodder for a comedy routine, had her laughing so hard tears trickled down her cheeks. She insisted upon hearing in detail how he'd chosen Marine Biology for a career, and he'd spent twenty minutes rhapsodizing about his childhood ambitions. Every time a personal question was directed her way, she would deflect it back to him and the next thing he knew he was discussing his personal life in a way he never did.

They now drove in comfortable silence while he thought about how she was able to maintain the conversation without revealing any personal information. One, she was a great listener, but two, she asked insightful questions that demonstrated her ability to assimilate data—the skills of a good scientist.

He pulled the car into a rest stop.

"Do you want me to drive for a while?"

"No." He removed his sunglasses. "I've got

a picnic lunch in the trunk. Are you hungry?"

"Not really. What did you bring?"

"Don't get too excited. It's not foie gras or caviar. Grocery store roasted chicken, a couple of salads, some fruit, bottled tea and wine for later."

Marshall moved a wicker picnic basket to the back seat. "What would you like?"

Lily stifled a yawn. "I'm fine."

Marshal smiled. "Take a nap, if you like. We still have quite a distance to go."

By the time the car pulled out of the rest stop, he heard her deep breathing.

Her face, relaxed in sleep, gave her a younger, wilder appearance. Her hair, which had been subdued earlier returned to its riotous state, giving her a gypsy-like appearance with dark hair, dark eyes, and an elusive wild spirit. Taming that spirit would be like trying to keep water from trickling between one's fingers.

Marshall pulled his gaze back to the road with a start. He refused to think of her in those terms. By this weekend, he'd be moving on.

Her hand scratched her stomach. He found himself eyeing her legs and wishing it was his hand instead. Reaching into the box he grabbed a piece of chicken. The seasoning was off, but he continued eating -- more to keep his hands busy than anything else.

Chapter Nine

Two hours later Lily woke with a start. Falling asleep hadn't been part of her plan, but exhaustion had overtaken her. With all the grace she had displayed so far, she had probably snored or worse drooled. Surreptitiously, she felt around her lips for moisture and was relieved to find none.

"Almost there." Marshall patted her bare leg just above the knee. His touch held both affection and promise when his fingers lingered longer than was necessary. His warmth against her cool skin was comforting. When he added a circular motion with his thumb, she sat upright and clamped her knees together.

He removed his hand as the car slowed to make a right onto an unmarked gravel road at the most inauspicious entrance she had ever seen. A small sign indicated the road was a dead end. Nothing designated the location as the entrance to Caudill Marine Institute.

"How can anyone find this place?" Lily asked, wondering if this could possibility be the right turn until a clearing and buildings came into view.

"We're not open to the public like an

aquarium, although the public doesn't always understand that. Oregon has no private beaches. As a result, Dead Man's Cove is a remote beach separated from the land by a sheer terrain of rough rocks. Building stairs would help us move our equipment more easily. But as it stands now few people use the beach, other than CMI due to the lack of accessibility."

The compound resembled a rustic fishing camp, nothing like the gleaming, white, sterile environment that the Institute's name inspired. Had the area not been electronically fenced, one might never have known that this was a research facility. Six satellite cabins surrounded a larger two-story rustic lodge. Marshall drove around the circular gravel drive and parked in front of the lodge.

A younger man, no more than thirty-two or thirty-three, bounded out the door as Marshall shut off the engine.

"San Diego's on hold waiting for you," he said eyeing her with interest and a welcoming grin.

A brief frown crossed Marshall's face. "Help Lily get our things inside. Lily, this is Josh. I'll meet up with you when I get off the phone."

Josh grabbed the bags from the trunk. "You're here for the tides?" His friendly hazel eyes gleamed in the dappled sunlight. His face was freckled, but the kiss of the sun had tanned his skin making them blend.

Lily nodded. "Are you a biologist?"

While Marshall didn't fit the profile of a scientist, neither did Josh. With his disheveled appearance and wild sandy blond hair, he was the antithesis of Marshall's dark well-groomed look. Based upon the two she'd seen so far, they promised to be a diverse group.

The aroma of the salt, the algae, and the damp ocean air hit her. Inhaling deeply, she filled her lungs with the scent of the coast.

Josh handed her the towel-wrapped quiche. "Yeah. I've been here for about two years. No place else smells like Oregon, does it? What's your discipline?"

"Discipline?" she asked.

He placed the luggage on the porch and returned to the trunk to gather the remainder. "You know, sea stars? Algae? Eelgrass? Marine mammals? What's your specialty?"

"Lemon bars."

His constant movement ceased. He raised his head and stared at her over the trunk lid, a frown across his boyish features. "Lemon bars?"

"I'm not a biologist, I'm a caterer," she clarified. "I won Marshall at an auction. He's required to show me a good time." Lily blushed as she realized the words that had come out of her mouth had a different meaning than what she'd intended.

Josh coughed to hide his laughter. "Okay, then. Let's put your luggage inside the front door," he directed. "While we're waiting for Marshall to show you a *good time*, you and I can take a quick trip to see the water."

"That didn't come out the way I meant." She attempted to amplify her words, but Josh cut her off.

"This promises to be an interesting week."

"Oh, I'm not here for a week, I'm probably going home tomorrow."

Josh's quizzical expression puzzled her, but instead of questioning him, she took the containers of food to the kitchen.

Eager to see the ocean Lily followed as they tromped through the trees and the mossy undergrowth on a narrow path where ferns and salmonberries grew abundantly.

"Don't you think it's interesting the way the forested areas butt up to the beaches? I've heard it is the same way in Maine, although I've never seen it," Lily said.

"Oregon's a unique pairing of earth and water. Do the mountains and cliffs march down into the water or climb out of it? Which force is more dominant?" Josh asked.

"I thought water was more dominant."

"Well, it's more persistent. Nothing but water could wear away stone, yet nothing in nature can contain water the way stone can."

"What about the power of a flood or a tidal

wave?" Lily wanted a definitive answer.

Instead, Josh countered with, "What about the power of an earthquake or a volcano?"

The trees abruptly ended, opening to a small clearing and a high ledge just above a sheer hazardous drop-off. The beach lay forty feet below. Large black basalt boulders, rocks and gravel comprised the cliff face.

"Oh, my. Marshall told me it was rugged terrain, but I wasn't expecting this. How do you get to the beach?"

He gestured to what might have been a trail if she'd been a ground squirrel. "We climb down."

"Carrying equipment?"

"Some. We can go down now if you want." He glanced at her open-toed, heeled sandals. "Maybe we should wait, Marshall may have another plan."

"What time's the tide tomorrow?"

"Not too early. Six-thirty. We'll need to be on the beach an hour earlier. The sun won't be up, but at least there'll be some light when you're going over the rocks for the first time."

Lily nodded, dreading the early morning and the rough terrain.

"Come on. I'll show you the lab." Josh took her arm and steered her through the trees yet again. The dense forest with massive trees and thick undergrowth that stood well above her head hid the laboratory building until they were almost on top of its rough-hewn façade.

One large octagonal-shaped room with two smaller rooms anchored it like opposing wings on a fat bug. Inside, desks, computers, file cabinets and bookcases surrounded the outer walls. A business office could have just as easily claimed residence.

In one of the adjacent rooms, she was relieved when she discovered a few lab tables with microscopes and other instruments she didn't recognize. Various small aquariums dotted the chilly room; some filled with rocks and encrusting anemones, others were filled with sand and had unusual tunneling. Above, a drip system not unlike her home garden, continually dribbled water into some of the glass tanks. Baby eels swam in one tank. In another, she recognized sponges and crabs, but many of the fish were unidentifiable.

"It's not what you expected, is it?" Josh asked as they moved toward the equipment. "This is a particle counter used to count microorganisms in water and this measures the fluorescence of chlorophyll." He pointed out a few of the pieces of equipment.

"When I picture a Marine Biologist, I think of someone who works with dolphins and whales, not a computer geek."

"Most people think the way you do, but it's

a divergent field. At CMI, research is the foundation of our work. Unless you're affiliated with the government or a major University, funding is very competitive, so we have to be ahead of the field constantly. We've flourished because Marshall's very good at doing the things that most scientists hate to do, including drumming up public support and continually soliciting those in control of major funding. You'll see what I mean when you meet the others. Most of us just want to do our research and be left alone."

Josh and Lily walked single file on their way back to the lodge. They entered through a side door. Several small offices lined the long hallway. In the largest of them, Marshall bent over a map, the phone glued to his ear. Glancing up he gave her a small wave and then returned to the phone conversation.

"If you don't mind, I still have some work to do," Josh said. "Will you be okay on your own?"

"Of course." Lily didn't mention she looked forward to exploring the lodge without supervision. Although her perusal only took a few minutes, the utilitarian structure was designed for work. Luxuries, she associated with Marshall, were non-existent. Other than standard kitchen appliances there was a coffee maker and a microwave. The generic, functional furniture in tans and browns looked savaged.

Lily delivered their luggage to Marshall's apartment on the second floor. Small and efficient it was more a sitting room and bedroom than an apartment. She smiled pleased to see only one large bed. At least she and Marshall were on the same wavelength in that regard.

Aside from a desk, computer and phone, his apartment was lined with bookcases crammed with untidy scientific journals and thick hardbound books that contained titles with words she couldn't even pronounce.

Finding nothing else to do, she plopped on the bed and stretched out. Would Marshall be thrilled to find her waiting? She imagined him coming through the door. A smile would flicker across his face as he closed the door behind him. He moved closer and she clamped her legs together in excitement. A giggle bubbled up out of her causing her to roll her eyes. Even in her fantasy, she lacked sophistication.

The front door opened on the floor below, and other voices drifted up the stairs. Perhaps now would not be the best time to be caught looking like a horny trollop. She pursed her lips together and exhaled. Another fantasy thwarted by real life. She rose to rejoin the others.

She scanned the waiting men on the floor below for a glimpse of Marshall. Josh met her at the newel post and gestured for her to join them.

"This is Lily," he announced to the group of

eight men seated around the coffee table. "She's a caterer."

Several men representing a variety of nationalities nodded politely. From under the stairwell, a woman with luminous skin the color of burnished copper, stuck her head out and peered up the stairs. "I know you. You did the food for my sister's wedding. I'm Sara."

Lily eyed Sara's apron and the bunch of broccoli in her hand. "Are you the cook?"

The entire group laughed.

"No, I lost a bet. Dinner's almost ready."

On that clue, everybody stood up and moved to the large plank table off the kitchen. Two other women entered the back door. Sandwiched between Sara and Josh, Lily ate with relish the dinner of cracked crab, melted butter, wild and brown rice pilaf and broccoli.

"I love crab," Lily said appreciating the freshness and easy availability the coast offered.

"Yeah," the dark skinned man across the table agreed, "after we finish studying them, we plunk them in a pot of hot water and serve them for dinner." With his accent, dark hair and eyes, Lily guessed him to be Indian.

She looked at her food with new eyes. It had been studied first? "Ewww." Lily grimaced, causing all the scientists to laugh.

Sara laughed with the rest but nudged her,

"Ignore them. That's Oceanology humor for you."

The table sat a crowded ten. Tonight there were eleven people already wedged around the table when Marshall joined them halfway through dinner. He pulled up a chair between Lily and Josh and squeezed in. Heat radiated from his body. Troubled by the effect his presence had on her, Lily found she couldn't face him. Platters of crab were passed in his direction, but he waved them off.

"Marshall, you don't look good," one of the men on the other side of the table commented. "Are you feeling okay?" Everyone looked, included Lily. A sheen of sweat matted his forehead, and his skin had taken on a greenish pallor.

Lily's stomach lurched. "You *really* don't look good."

"I'm okay," he growled. "Something's made me a little queasy, that's all."

Ten minutes later the room was eerily quiet as Marshall bolted from the table and hot-footed it out of the kitchen. A door slammed, and the sound of retching had all of them pushing their plates toward the center of the table. Dinner was over.

"What'd you eat on the way down here?" Josh whispered to Lily.

"I didn't eat anything. I slept, but Marshall ate some food from a lunch he'd packed. I put the leftovers in the refrigerator, but maybe I should throw them out." Several others, listening intently, nodded in agreement.

"That didn't include the strudel, did it?" a hefty red-haired man at the end of the table asked. A couple of others snickered in response.

"No, and the quiche should be okay, too. He ate chicken and salads. I didn't see a cooler in the car, so I don't know how long it wasn't refrigerated."

Marshall reappeared a few minutes later. "Excuse me, I need to lie down."

As he climbed the stairs, Lily's gaze followed him, knowing that despite the fact that sex had been the star attraction on her menu, fate had eighty-sixed any possibility for this trip. Her luck was running true to form – the great dry spell continued.

Chapter Ten

Marshall alternated between the bed and the bathroom. At some point he dozed. Hot tea and toast appeared on the nightstand. Lily. He closed his eyes as his stomach rolled. Thank goodness she hadn't stayed to play nursemaid. It was embarrassing enough to be incapacitated without an audience.

The last time he remembered checking the clock, it had been three am.

Now bright sunlight streamed into the room. Marshall rolled onto his back and flung an arm over his eyes. Without even looking at the clock, he knew the tide was long past. Mentally he checked his body. Whatever he'd had, seemed to have passed. Tomorrow he could show Lily a low tide the way it should be seen.

The hot shower kicked his body into gear. Noon. He couldn't believe it. He hadn't slept till noon since college. A little coffee and he'd be able to think.

The deserted kitchen was tidy except for three empty quiche pie tins stacked on the counter and a paper plate containing a small portion of the strudel. Voices could be heard coming down the long hall, followed by laughter and loud hooting. The next statement was clear enough to establish the direction of the conversation.

"No, the girlfriend I hated the most was one who spent the entire evening touting her athletic abilities. Took one look at the scramble to the beach and simply came back to his apartment to wait for us to return."

"You thought she was worse than the one who climbed to the beach, but refused to wear the 'ugly' rubber boots and slipped and fell all over the rocks?"

"Or how about the redhead who worked so hard appearing interested in Marshall's career that her eyes would cross when she forced herself to pay attention."

Laughter followed. Marshall shook his head as he remembered Hillary Larson, the woman who fit that description. The voices were more distinct as they moved closer.

"I don't know," Julie said, "if that beats last year's Christmas party. That girl couldn't have been over twenty-five and was so full of herself. I thought if she flipped that blonde hair one more time, I was going to snatch her bald."

Last Christmas? A blonde at the company party? Who had he been seeing then? He couldn't believe he was unable to remember.

The group lead by Julie and Connor rounded the corner. Both stopped immediately, but those behind them kept on coming. Bumped and jostled, Julie scrambled out the path and let others tumble into the room. Each wore a shared look of guilt.

Lily was not among them. Inwardly, Marshall winced. What had she done to set them all talking like this? When no one spoke, he was forced to ask. "Where's Lily?"

"Sara went back to Portland this morning, and she caught a ride with her," Josh said.

She left? Why?

Marshall cleared his throat. "Sorry, you got caught babysitting one of my dates. I shouldn't have brought her."

Everyone spoke at once in an attempt to reassure him.

"Lily wasn't a problem at all."

"No, in fact, she was great."

"She held equipment, took samples and followed instructions."

"Instructions?" Marshall asked, backing toward the stairs to avoid even the couple of hands that manage to reach and pat his back. Why the sudden patronizing? Marshall gulped a sip of coffee that churned all the way to his stomach.

"You know, the usual ones. If you turn a rock over, return it the way you found it."

"Don't turn your back on the ocean."

"Watch out for the slippery algae."

The group wound to a halt, leaving Marshall uncertain. Nobody had ever even mentioned any of the other women he'd entertained. Occasionally, he saw a set of rolled eyes or an admiring glance at a pair of legs, but for the most part he'd always assumed no one gave a damn.

"We shouldn't have been joking about some of the other women you know," Julie said. "Lily's not your usual type. She was interested in what we did."

"Plus, she got up extra early and cooked us all a hot breakfast before we went out."

A sea of faces watched his. What reaction were they looking for? He didn't need them to like his dates, but they liked Lily. And wanted him to know it? Just what he needed another group to sing her praises.

The phone rang, and Josh grabbed it before anyone else could get there. After listening for a brief moment, he held out the phone to Marshall. "Port Renfrew."

Marshall took the call upstairs largely to escape his colleagues. After he had hung up the phone, he debated placing a quick call to Lily. He glanced at his watch. Between here and Portland, cell service was spotty at best.

And she'd left without telling him. If she wanted to speak to him, she could call. He didn't need to chase her. He had work that needed his attention.

After several moments he opened the door, leaned over the balcony and spoke to those still in the living area below him. "A chopper's picking me up in a couple of hours. The tides have washed up something on Vancouver Island's coast. It's probably a giant jellyfish or maybe part of a squid, but they're requesting a positive ID."

Lily glanced at the clock. Two fifty-seven. For the third night in a row, she lay awake. The faceless dark-haired stranger no longer visited her. In his place, Marshall's commanding eyes haunted her dreams. Now her dream man not only dominated her physical desires, she imagined his arrogance as well, knowing he could snap his fingers whenever he damn well wanted, and she would roll over and play fetch for him. Anger flared. She was not his lap dog.

But when she was awake, the dreams worried her more than she would admit. Who, after all, was she trying to convince? Marshall's silence, since she had returned from the coast a week ago, said more about the situation than her fantasies. Perhaps her anger was misdirected. Marshall had no intention of snapping his fingers at all, much less expecting her to her roll over, sit up, beg or take off her clothes. As usual, the only person she was fighting was her imagination and secret longings.

When Lily had left the coast, good manners dictated that she should have at least left a note if nothing else thanking him for inviting her. But the trip hadn't been what she'd expected at all. Leaving quietly had been easier and much safer.

All that night she'd tossed and turned on the downstairs couch even though Sara had offered to share her cabin. Lily insisted on being close by if Marshall needed her.

She slept in spurts. Finally, she got up and prepared breakfast. Cooking always helped her think.

The Institute scientists fended for themselves. Seldom were more than two or three in residence. Prescribed times for meals were non-existent. When a large group gathered, a simple meal could be thrown together if several helped. No one catered to anyone else in the group unless it was in a professional capacity.

Lily discovered this out by cooking breakfast for them. As they gathered in the lodge, the group was stunned at the sight of a hot breakfast. While Lily expected some appreciation, the scientists gushed to the point of annoyance, making her regret her decision to cook for them. They overwhelmed her with thanks for too simple a task.

That would have been bad enough. But a

subtle change took place in the group dynamics. The previous evening, everyone had been open and casual, joking with her. Now each one had a mission. Unfortunately they all had the same mission.

On the beach, the scientists encouraged her to help, and under the guise of discussing the starfish varieties or the defensive mechanisms of the varied species, their conversation focused on Marshall.

Detailed information on his life, such as he'd never married, was offered to her without any solicitation on her part. And it wasn't that she wasn't interested. Each nugget of information was stored away for evaluation when she was able to analyze the data further.

"Feel the tough texture of the bullwhip kelp. Early coastal Indians harvested and dried the kelp to make fishing lines, nets, and ropes. Did you know that Marshall received the Humanitarian Service Award for his research on medicinal uses of the kelp in treating thyroid? He's brilliant, you know."

Twenty minutes later, Sara demonstrated how to draw water from the pools. "Hold the test tube like this." Lily followed her example.

"Marshall told me a funny joke the other day." A man spoke over her shoulder. As he proceeded to tell the joke, Lily listened with interest grateful that her job kept her face turned. Several people around her laughed, and she did, too. But she hadn't the faintest idea why everyone thought it was funny or even what it meant.

"Of course, you know he founded the Caudill Cancer Ward in memory of his parents."

But when the group wasn't trying to sell her Marshall wrapped with a gold ribbon, they took their precious time away from their jobs to give her an impressive lesson in the tides. They showed her how to sit beside a pool and study the details. Things she'd assumed were pebbles began to move. Tiny animals crawled out of shells. And microscopic creatures that she had missed at first glance became apparent to her.

Almost three hours later, the group was ready to head for home.

"It's time," Josh said to Lily.

"So soon?"

"Look behind you."

The tidewaters surged toward shore. Pools, not ten feet from where she stood were covered with a foot of heaving ocean. Kelp and seaweed sprang to life. Like fields of wheat waving a protective cover over the delicate ocean life. And then it too was obscured by the opaque blanket of the white foam capped ocean waves that rushed toward the small strip of sandy beach.

Lily was one of the last to climb to the top. Sara and Josh waited for her, offering support as she picked her way among the rocks.

"You're going back today?" Josh quizzed Sara as they negotiated the dense woods to return to the lodge.

"I wanted to be here all week, but I'm scheduled to go to the Aleutian Islands on Thursday, and I need to pack."

"Look the trillium's in bloom." Lily pointed to the tri-petal flower. "This is early for it, isn't it?"

Josh and Sara smiled. "We've had a warm spring,"

"Are you sure you can't stay another day?" He asked.

Sara shook her head. "It's important I drive back this morning."

"I'd be happy to ride with you," Lily said.

"You can't leave," Josh protested. "Marshall's expecting you to stay."

"No, he's not. He only invited me because of the auction. Really, he's done his part."

They emerged from the woods into the open grassy area surrounding the lodge. Neither Josh nor Sara commented, but Lily caught the look they exchanged.

"Really, I doubt if he'll even notice I'm gone," Lily said. "I never planned to stay longer than today, anyway," she added, attempting to reassure them.

"You're more than welcome to ride with me if that's what you want," Sara said.

Lily, exhausted from the sales job the scientists had already given her, eyed the younger woman. "Really it is. Just promise me we won't talk about Marshall all the way back,"

"Not a problem."

"Great I'll get my things and join you in a few minutes."

Lily was almost inside the main lodge when she heard Sara laugh. "Do you *really* think, she *really* meant what she *really* said?"

Josh sniggered. "Are you saying she protests a little too much?"

Sara balanced on one leg and pulled the other to her chest. "She could be the one,"

Josh blew air between his lips in disagreement. "No way, she's not like any of the women he usually sees."

Now that she was home, Lily was heartsick. After Marshall's co-workers had spent hours trying to persuade her that Marshall was Mr. Perfect, the one indisputable fact was that Mr. Perfect wasn't Mr. Right. She'd wanted an affair with a dark-haired stranger who wouldn't be important enough to interfere with her day-to-day life. This thing with Marshall was turning out all wrong.

Her imagination played havoc with reality. Expecting to hear from him, she had constructed an elaborate defense, a detailed scenario whose entire purpose was to hold Marshall at bay.

Instead, he hadn't called.

Looking at it one way, she got her wish but if this was what she wanted, why wasn't she happy? The knowledge that Mr. Perfect didn't want her was hard to take.

Maybe it was the combination of sunspots and negative tides or perhaps global warming added to the week, but from Canada to Mexico the unusual nature of the tides had Marshall zipping from one location to another. The entire West Coast had been affected.

Marine mammals washed ashore in several locations; the microhabitat of the sea spiders had been disturbed which produced a ripple effect on the entire ecosystem. Newport Beach reported an unidentified bacteria near the site of the previous outbreak of killer algae alarming the scientific community. Had the chlorine used to kill the invader been more harmful than the algae itself? Or was this a deep-ocean microbe that exhaled toxic gasses? How had it gotten so close to shore?

Marshall trudged from one location to another. It was a good time to be a Marine Biologist.

After a long week on the road, he finally headed home to Portland. With concentrated effort, he would finish his latest research paper within the next two weeks. His mind had already determined how to structure the material for the possibility of another grant. But each time he sat long enough to focus on a paper of this nature, Lily Carmichael's face danced before him. Like a luminous trail, Lily's presence lingered long after she was gone.

Why had she left? He'd talked to Sara twice, and but the scientist been closed-lipped.

A parade of women had marched through his life. Some stayed longer than others, but eventually each moved on. Together they had provided a sensual backdrop of physical enticement. One woman had pretty much been the same as another. None had ever met his father's version of acceptable, according to the Caudill standards. Lily wouldn't either, but he couldn't seem to shake the hook she had buried in his mind.

In Portland, he'd deal with her and then get on with writing the new paper. Time was too precious for him to be fixated on a woman.

Dori opened the door to Lily's office. "Flour delivery." She lugged a huge basket wrapped in hot pink cellophane and tied with an elaborate bow.

Lily updated next month's calendar events on the whiteboard. "Those aren't flowers."

Her partner set the basket on Lily's desk. "Not flowers. Flours."

Intrigued, Lily came to see. She slipped the fussy pink and white bow off the top and allowed the colored plastic wrap to fall away

"Oh, Lord. It is flour – quinoa flour, buckwheat flour, rye flour, bread flour, AP flour, cake flour, even gravy flour." She picked up the individual packages and read the name before returning each to the basket.

Dori fingered the delicate flowers woven into the edge of the basket. "Also stargazer lilies,"

The lilies decorated the edge of the charming basket. Each flower sustained by a separate tube of water. Pink and green confetti lent a festive air. This was more fun than Valentine's Day where men dutifully sent flowers because it was required.

"So I see. Where did this come from?"

"Oh, did I not mention there was a card?" Dori widened her eyes to look innocence.

Lily gave her an exasperated look and held out her hand as Dori handed over a sealed envelope. The card read, "Who, but someone who appreciates your unusual talents, would send you flours? Have dinner with me? Marshall."

"Where did this come from?"

"Oh, did I not mention there was a card?" Dori attempted innocence. Lily gave her an exasperated look and held out her hand as the other woman handed over a sealed envelope.

The card read, "Who, but someone who appreciates your unusual talents, would send you flours? Have dinner with me? Marshall."

"Marshall," Lily said, doubting she needed to clarify the obvious to her perceptive partner.

"He's back in town?"

The casualness of Dori's tone had Lily searching her face. "How did you know he was out of town?"

Dori laughed. "There's a new invention called television. You might want to check it out sometime. With the weird tides, he's been in the news almost every night."

He'd been on the news. He was working not ignoring her. "Really?"

"Lily, I love you, but there is life beyond catering and gardening. What does the card say?"

Her stomach fluttered. "He wants me to have dinner with him."

She should go. Maybe she had time to shop for a new dress and do something with her hair.

"You're free tonight."

She was, but how would that look. They were back to the snapping of his fingers, and she'd come running and then, what? Even if he was Mr. Perfect, he wasn't Mr. Right. She needed to remember that. "I don't think so."

"It's a clever gift. You're turning down cleverness?"

Lily sighed. "I'm turning down a lot of things."

Dori shook her head but said nothing. Before she shut the door behind her, Lily heard the distinct clucking of a chicken.

"I'm not afraid," Lily spoke to the closed door. "I'm just protecting myself." Unable to believe how utterly lame that excuse sounded, Lily laid her head on the desk and tried to ignore the clucking of her inner voice.

A week later, Marshall opened the door of his Portland loft to Sara and Josh, both of whom he had expected for an afternoon of work. A UPS delivery driver stood behind them.

After ushering everyone inside, Marshall stepped back as the UPS driver rolled a hand truck with a large cardboard box into the entrance area and set it down in the middle of the floor.

"What's this?" Marshall signed the delivery pad.

"Some furniture store in California, Ecotec For Homes," Sara read. "I've never heard of it."

"Strange. I didn't order anything."

"Let's open it." Before Marshall could respond, Sara pulled out a pocketknife and slit the tape, then opened the flaps to reveal a large salt-water aquarium in tightly packed molded Styrofoam.

"Perfect –- just what I don't need –- another aquarium," Marshall groused. "Who's it from?"

"Lily?" Josh knelt beside Sara.

Why would Lily send him something? "I doubt it. Last week, I sent her some baking flours because I thought she'd see the humor in it. Instead, I got a brief 'thanks, but don't call me' email."

"You sent her baking flour? What a romantic you are!" Sara scoffed barely glancing up from her hunt through the box

Sara thought he was an idiot?

"Anybody could send her flowers and jewelry. I wanted to send her something different." Marshall couldn't believe he was defending his actions. He'd shopped for the flours in the basket himself. Didn't that count for something?

"Do you know why men send flowers and jewelry?" Sara pulled a flyer from the container. When Marshall didn't respond, Sara said, "Because it works. Since Lily refused dinner, I'd say you might rethink the baking flour idea."

Josh flipped open the flyer, Sara had pulled out of the box. "Why would someone send you a home-style salt water aquarium, anyway?" Josh asked. "Do they think that because you're a Marine Biologist, you enjoy sitting around admiring pretty fish on your days off?" He chuckled.

Sara joined with a snicker of her own, but Marshall failed to see the humor.

She continued searching until she unearthed a note wedged between the Styrofoam and the cardboard. "Who's Muffin Parsons? And why is she signing notes to you with little Xs and Os?"

"Damn." Marshall held out his hand.

Sara ignored him and opened the envelope to find a hand-written note. Holding the paper away from her face, she grimaced and fanned it in the air. From the distance of five feet, Marshall could smell the sweet perfume.

"You'll be glad to know," Sara said as she scanned the missive. "That she's forgiven you for not taking her to the Art Museum since you were on the news." She continued reading, lapsing into silence as she turned the note over. "Well, that explains the aquarium."

"What?" Marshall asked afraid to hear the answer. Muffy's determination was awe-inspiring, as well as frightening. Most women understood when you didn't call for weeks on end that the relationship was over.

"The aquarium's the perfect size for the

workspace at your new home."

"What new home?" Marshall gritted his teeth to keep from directing his anger at Sara and Josh.

"Apparently the one the two of you are buying together." Sara frowned and reread the words again. "She's eager for you to see the place now that you're back in town."

Marshall snatched the note from Sara's hands. "What *is* her problem?" His voice raised in volume. "I'm trying to break up with her and she decided we're buying a house together? Next thing, she'll be proposing." He read the note then threw it to the floor. "Is it still traditional for the man to ask a woman first? Or has that changed in the twenty-first century?"

Sara jumped to her feet. "What do you mean you're *trying* to break up with her? Why haven't you broken up with her?" She glared at Marshall.

Marshall snarled. "I was attempting," he said, barely hiding his irritation, "to let her down easily, to avoid hurt feelings. We don't have time for this, let's get to work." He scowled, hoping to discourage any additional questions.

Josh picked up the note off the floor and read it. "Since you're seeing someone else, would you mind if I called Lily?"

"Yeah, I would," Marshall added indignation to his outrage. "Aside from the fact that I'm still seeing her, Lily's too old for you."

He expected the easy-going man to laugh and shrug it off. Instead his eyes narrowed and his jaw twitched. He'd never seen the younger man angry.

"Bull." Josh didn't raise his voice, but it chilled Marshall with the ring of resolution he heard. "She's older than I am, but if she turns me down it wouldn't be for that reason."

When had he become Captain Bly of the Bounty while his crew mutinied? "Well, unless your resume is up-to-date, don't call her." Was Josh the reason Lily left the coast early and wouldn't return his phone calls?

"You're not seeing her and Lily deserves a man who's looking for more than a quick fling."

Marshall growled, astonished. Josh liked her. "Fine. Call her if you want."

"I don't poach. But you're one lucky son-of-a-bitch. And you don't even appreciate it."

Marshall wanted to bang his head against the wall. All his life he'd avoided entanglements with women that required more commitment than he wanted to give. Now he had two women. One, he wanted to get rid of, but wouldn't leave and one he couldn't convince to stay. And his colleague had become his competition. When had he gotten old?

No longer could he sit idly by, this had to be

resolved. His life had to return to normal.

Chapter Eleven

The phone rang at Luscious Foods after lunch on Tuesday. With no one else in the office, Lily grabbed the receiver on her way to the kitchen.

"I know it's the last minute, but my husband and I decided to throw an impromptu summer party. Would it be possible for you to cater a small evening patio party? A week from Saturday?" the woman on the telephone asked.

Lily scanned the calendar. "Number of guests?"

"Oh, I don't know. A hundred. Maybe a hundred and fifty. It's summer and lots of our friends are gone. We have a large backyard, and I'm thinking of a garden party. You did such a wonderful job at the bachelor auction, we hoped you'd be available."

Lily smiled pleased by the compliment.

Usually, last minute parties had such a tiny guest list that the hassle to get it done wasn't worth the miniscule profit. Plus, this woman had a gift for understatement. A "small impromptu party" in one's home usually did not have a guest list of one hundred and fifty people.

Lily tested her client. "So, the menu could include something like seared Ahi tuna, an array of fresh salads, maybe a cold beef tenderloin with a whole grain mustard sauce?"

"Exactly. That's precisely the kind of menu we'd like. Could we add a cold shrimp dish and maybe some passed hors d'oeuvres – like crab cakes?"

"Of course. I can send you some menus to get things started."

The woman hesitated. "Our timeline's so close, perhaps we should meet and set it up. That way you can see my house."

"If you'd prefer. When can you meet?"

"Today's good for me."

Lily raised her eyebrow. No wonder this woman was comfortable putting on a sizeable party in only a few days as goal-oriented as she was. Lily ran her afternoon appointments through her mind.

"If it works for you, I can come now."

"Let me give you my address."

Caroline Zonnheiser hung up the phone and looked at her brother. "Okay, she'll be here in about twenty minutes. I can't believe you're making me put on a party this fast."

Marshall grinned, unrepentant. "Paybacks are hell."

⚙

The address Lily sought was in the West

Hills, a mere twenty minutes and several million dollars from her home. The cobbled walkway wandered gracefully up to a stately English Tudor with a stone façade and leaded windows. Understated, yet tasteful, in a manner that screamed *'real money lives here.'*

An hour later, Caroline and Lily worked out a strong vision of the party, complete with menus and several pages of notes. The yard was perfect; shaded enough a tent wouldn't be required, yet spacious, easily able to accommodate a wealth of guests.

At the doorway, she and Caroline made their farewells when a familiar silver car pulled into the driveway. Marshall Caudill. Lily faced the brunette woman. Marshall's words came back to her. *"My sister's making me do this…"* Caroline had mentioned the bachelor auction as her connection with the catering company.

And why hadn't she noticed the similarity in appearance? Caroline may have been younger and more petite, but Marshall's dark hair, golden complexion, and intense blue eyes screamed a family connection.

"My brother," Caroline added, smiling sheepishly.

Lily nodded, hesitant to say anything. Could the party be a hoax? A sneaky way for Marshall to see her? Or if the party was real what could she say that wouldn't have the hostess calling another caterer. Several thousand dollars hung in the balance. Lily fingered the deposit check in her pocket.

"Well, well, if it isn't the runaway girlfriend," Marshall greeted her as he strolled up the cobbled walkway. He leaned over to kiss each woman's cheek. Lily didn't move. She tried to smile, but she feared her look had more snarl than grin to it.

"Party set?"

. The family genes were exceptional. She was a gorgeous as he. The covered porch shielded the bright sunlight from their eyes. Marshall stood cool and refreshed in his light gray shirt and dark gray slacks. Standing next to the golden couple, Lily felt crumpled in the sundress she'd worn since early morning

"Everything's coming together." Caroline smiled. The Caudill trademark smile. On her brother's face that smile made Lily's toes curl.

The party was a go. People with money were oblivious to how much it meant to people who didn't. Was this Marshall's party or Caroline's? Maybe she was reading too much into this. Maybe Marshall had simply recommended her as a caterer, but he called her the girlfriend in front of his sister. She was hardly a girlfriend.

"Are you coming in?" Caroline asked her brother.

"Not just yet. Lily and I have some business to discuss."

Lily's pulse danced as Caroline closed the door.

"I didn't know I qualified for the status of a girlfriend," Lily joked, stepping away from him.

"It's been three weeks since the coast. You've avoided me for the past two weeks. I don't know that you're worthy of that nomenclature either," Marshall agreed.

"I haven't been avoiding you," Lily lied. "I've been busy. In fact, another client's expecting me in just a few minutes." Lily glanced at her watch to underscore the bad timing.

A dubious look crossed his face, but he acquiesced. "I'll walk you to the van."

Lily started to protest but instead clamped her lips together. Why was it she was never herself around him? Just once, she needed to feel like she was the one in control.

"Are you free for dinner?"

Without hesitation, Lily said, "No."

Marshall's lips quirked upward slightly at the corners and wondered if her words had issued a challenge to his ego. "Do you always say 'no' before you say 'yes'?" His voice was laced with amusement.

"My staff claims I answer the phone 'yes, we can'," she said. "I rarely say 'no' to anyone. For you, I'm making an exception." She wanted to smile. Finally, the scoreboard was weighed in her favor. After all, it was bright daylight in the middle of the afternoon in front of his sister's home, what options could he possibly have?

He reached out and caught the scoop neck of her dress. His warm fingers slid down between her breasts and hooked inside her bra, giving him enough leverage to pull her closer.

Lily swatted at his arm to make him move his hand, but he stayed one step ahead. His free arm captured her waist and pulled her next to him, as he slowly removed his fingers from her cleavage. The nearness of him, his masculinity, not to mention his determination made her nervous. And excited.

"You don't like me?" he whispered leaning into her. His lips were so close that their breath was one.

The words *what does like have to do with it?* caught in her throat.

Thigh to thigh, chest to breast, he pressed closer. The day hadn't been nearly so warm a few moments earlier. Her eyelashes brushed his cheek. His scent surrounded her. Her senses were so overwhelmed she was unable to identify his scent, but she recognized it for what it was – the dangerous scent of a male predator. Worse, her body responded with a pulse-jumping, nipple tightening *hooray*.

"I don't have time for this," she choked out.

"For what?" His lips moved closer to her ears for a quick nibble.

Lily clamped her knees together in a feeble attempt to keep the flow of fire from spreading through her. If he released her now, she'd be too weak-kneed to stand and crumple like a rag doll would bring her mortification to new heights.

Why did he always affect her this way? When he wasn't close it was easy to make firm decisions not to see him again, but when he was near – touching her – it was never enough. She not only wanted to see more of him, she wanted to touch him and taste him, too.

This was bad. Very, very bad.

His lips brushed her ears and inched down her jaw line. Her breath came in ragged spurts. Her chest heaved, and her blood surged, driving her. Making her want.

He moved with such confidence that he appeared to have all the time in the world while she had none, but she willed herself not to move – not to surrender. His lips trailed down her neck allowing her traitorous head to tilt, allowing him more access.

The burning infused her, filling her with anticipation and fear. Afraid of him, afraid of herself, but mainly afraid that this might be the only true feeling she would ever have for any man, except in her dreams.

Marshall struggled for self-control. Close to dragging her into the back of the van and ending this game they played. How easy it would be to push her skirt up and take what he wanted. But what did he want? A quick tumble? Josh's words reverberated in his mind. "*Lily deserves a man who's looking for more than just a quick fling.*"

He found he no longer needed her for just a night or possibly two. When had his feelings changed? He couldn't remember the last woman who had given him this much trouble. Not just playing hard-to-get, but the damn chemistry between them wouldn't let him go.

His lips touched hers. Tasting. Testing. She'd lost her will to resist, but acquiescing wasn't the correct answer either. This was a woman who needed to be wooed. If she said yes tonight, would she be angry tomorrow? One night to explore her depths wouldn't suit his purpose at all. Some things took time and a devoted interest. Some things took a scientist to investigate.

He stepped back but continued to hold her. "Tell me why you won't have dinner with me."

Lily took a long deep breath to steady herself. "Time," she ratcheted out. Inhaling she started again. Her breasts rose and fell. His eyes devoured her movement. "I have no time. At first I thought, slipping between the sheets with you wouldn't be emotional, just physical – sort of like having a great massage."

Marshall winced. Talk about a left-handed compliment.

Lily rubbed her forehead. "Okay, that probably wasn't a good example, but you know what I mean. I was prepared. Then I found out that the people who know you best -- the ones you work with -- really admire you. While you were sick, I heard hour upon hour of what a great guy you were. If they like you that much, I'd like you, too. I don't want to like you because then I'd want to keep you, but you're not a keeper. You'd die in captivity."

She was protecting him? Who was this woman? He didn't need her as a safeguard. Every woman he'd ever dated assured him he was the black heart – one emotionally bankrupt son-of-a-bitch was how one very angry woman had put it. While others hadn't used those exact words, they had thought it.

Did she think this because she'd saved him from embarrassment at the auction?

Before he could think of an appropriate response, she continued. "When you got sick, I thought I was safe. The fates had intervened. Sex wasn't destined. But did you catch on? No, you pursued, sending a clever gift to wear me down. So, even if you succeed, what then? I can't have a relationship because I have no time. Frankly, I'd be better off with a dog in my life at this point, and any animal I owned would die of loneliness." As Lily's conviction reared so did her emotions. A brittle quality entered her voice and a shadow of pain she was no longer able to hide reflected in her eyes.

Marshall took a step backward. Was she being honest with him? With herself? The rigidity of her stance was a problem he couldn't solve right now when her solution was to run. Not this time.

"We're not done." He released his hold on her. Unsteadily, she walked the few feet to the van door.

"Suit yourself," she attempted a cavalier voice but missed. "Don't be surprised at the results. I can't afford to get involved with you."

Grabbing the sissy bar she pulled herself into the van, cranked the engine and backed slowly down the driveway. He waited. Sure enough at the bottom of the drive, she looked back. He raised his eyebrows only to have her purse her lips in annoyance as she sped off.

His grin was difficult to hide as he strolled the path to his sister's door.

◎

"Thank goodness it's a quiet week," Dori

said the next morning. She and Lily sat at the work table in their office trying to hammer out the weekend. "You're a million miles away."

Lily's shoulders jerked. "What did you say?"

"What's up with you, today?" The only thing that could have her this distracted was a man. And not just any man, but Marshall Caudill. When had they talked? "You're not yourself."

Lily twirled a curl of hair and studied the duty roster like it held the secrets to the Universe.

Years ago, Dori counted her blessings that she been lucky to find a partner who was married but put her career first. When Charlie died, change was inevitable. Sooner or later the man would come along, and work wouldn't dominate her life. But after five years she worried that if Lily blew off every chance at love that the natural exuberance so much a part of her partner would fade and work would become drudgery.

Lily cheeks flushed. Her eyes closed. "I kissed him."

Whoa! "Him. Who?" This meeting was taking an interesting turn for the better.

"Marshall."

She knit her brow. Where was Lily with this? "You'd already kissed him. Why was this time different?" And when the hell did you see Marshall long enough to kiss him?

Lily shook her head. "Nothing. Never mind."

Never mind? Was she crazy?

She approached with care. "What kind of kiss was it?"

Something in her words sparked Lily because she sighed, and a small smile crept across her lips. "Intense. And in broad daylight!"

"Oh." Before Dori could quiz her further, their assistant, Ginger, put her head in the door. "Your appointment's here."

Dori didn't have an appointment, and Lily's flustered appearance told her partner she'd forgotten.

"What appointment?"

Dori gathered her papers and stood, needing to post the duty roster and check on the kitchen. She grabbed the upcoming menus and clipboard with a product list and headed toward the door.

Marshall crossed the threshold, looking as unflappable as usual. Dori hid her grin. Mr. Caudill was determined to bring the situation to a head. *Good for him.*

Nestled in his arms was a dainty puppy with black and white curly hair. A sweet face and alert brown eyes peered out from the ball of fur highlighted by a little pink tongue darting out in greeting. Ooh! And he was fighting dirty. One had to admire a man who put it all on the line. Lily was in for a skirmish if she thought she could avoid this man.

"How adorable! What kind of dog is this?" She tried not to laugh.

"Havanese." Marshall's intense look lingered a little too long, making Dori wonder if knew exactly what she thought. No wonder her partner was ensnared.

"How are you doing?" He focused on her like her answer was important.

"Great." She petted the dog's head. "Cute dog."

"Are we having a tea party?" Lily's voice didn't hide her irritation.

Dori wrenched her head toward her partner surprised by the tone of voice, but Marshall grinned. She restrained her laughter until she'd closed the door to the office. What was it they said in New Orleans?

Laissez les bons temps rouler.

Let the good time roll.

Lily hissed. She hated that damned knowing smile of his. Obviously he was pleased, he'd gotten to her -- again. She hated he'd appeared before she'd come up with a plan of action to keep him away. And mostly she hated that her body was glad to see him. Her breath caught, and her nipples tightened and he hadn't even crossed the room. Hell, if her breasts hadn't been tucked in her bra, they'd be winking and waving in welcome.

And his eyes reflected the fact he knew exactly what she thought.

"So, are Timmy and Lassie just out for a walk?" Lily tried attitude to establish her disapproval of his surprise visit, but the fact he laughed aloud made her want to throw up her hands in surrender. She was seldom out-gunned in a fight, but this battle was over before it began, and her body rejoiced with the happy dance. "I've known you for less than a month. What's that in dog years?"

"It seems longer, doesn't it?" he crossed the room to the round table and sat uninvited in the chair, Dori had vacated. "I've brought you a present." He held out the puppy. "She needs a good home."

"No." Lily shook her head but reached out to stroke the adorable pet who wagged her tail with such fervor, her entire fuzzy little body shook. Unable to resist Lily gathered the animal to her chest. The dog's tongue immediately sought her lips. Just like his master. "No kisses."

Marshall's knee touched hers under the table, and Lily shifted. He appeared not to notice.

"I'm picking you up for dinner tonight. Is six

good?"

"No." The dog snuggled against her breast like he belonged there.

"Well, if you'd rather cook me dinner, okay, but I think it would be easier and you'd probably be more comfortable if we went out." His casual attitude was reflected in his slouch and his wardrobe. Khaki slacks, a brown leather jacket and dress shirt open at the collar. He stretched his legs under the table. Lily tucked hers under her chair to avoid any accidental contact.

His face was solemn, but his eyes twinkled. He knew exactly what she was doing. As he taunted her, she found her determination.

"And yet, no again." No one would protect her heart, which meant keeping him at a distinct distance. She'd given him fair warning in his sister's driveway.

And the dog, cute as she was, was as risky as the owner. Both would tug on her heartstrings. "How big will this dog get when she's fully grown?" Lily examined the dog's petite paws.

"She's a year old, housebroken and fully grown. Her papers are in the car."

"Were you listening when I said I didn't have time for a pet?" Lily nuzzled the dog. "Lord, you're precious." The dog thumped her tail in agreement. "What's your name?"

"Princess." Laugh lines softened his face making him appear more approachable. That night at the auction, his face had been sterner. A definite commanding presence, not that she'd paid any attention. Half-dressed the way he'd been he could have been a scowling Quasimodo.

"I can't own a dog named Princess." Lily pushed the dog back into Marshall's lap. Politely, Princess rested her head on his leg, and his large hands played idly with the dog's head. Long and lean, he had the fingers of a composer, but the tiny white scars and calloused pads said more about the kind of person he was than his rich-boy clothes.

"Where did you get that dog? She's devoted to you." Lily wanted desperately to give the impression she wasn't staring at his hands, but rather at the dog.

"I met her last night, and she told me she wanted a good home with a lady who gardens."

Marshall stroked the dog's head and was rewarded when Lily's crossed her legs. Twice.

Never had he met such an excitable woman. Her desire lay so close to the surface, he was surprised she was able to keep it suppressed. The atmosphere between them, as always, was highly charged. One thing could only cause her nervous tapping on the table with her pen, and the constant shifting in her chair. He was prepared to let her squirm.

"This dog has already bonded with you. Maybe you appeal to dogs and children."

He grinned. "I appeal to some women, too."

"I'm so glad." She stood and adjusted her already neat stack of papers. "You need to go and take little Rin Tin Tin here with you. I've got to work."

He didn't move. Instead, he stroked the dog's head and continued to look at her. "You're afraid."

"No," she said. "You bring out an aspect of my personality that I'm having trouble accepting." Her librarian tone combined with her look of annoyance was designed to get Marshall on his feet and to move toward the door that he had no intention of letting work. He wasn't leaving until they had overcome this hurdle.

She reshuffled her papers and walked a wide circle around the table to avoid any possible contact as she headed toward her desk. Instead of her free-swinging gait she adopted a prissy walk. Head held high, she refused to look in his direction.

"You know what I think?" Without waiting for her to answer, he continued. "I think what's pissing you off the most is that you aren't in control. And you're a woman who likes control."

"Thank you, Dr. Freud." But his statement had made her look.

"You're uncomfortable. Maybe I've rushed you. Or maybe you won't admit what's really happening – there's something between us. Or maybe I've disturbed your nice, tidy life by bringing out an *'aspect of your personality you're having trouble accepting'*. Who knows what the issue is? You may want to discuss this with Oprah before you make a decision.

"But here's where I am. You turn me on, too. And I want to explore this effect you have on me, but we need to slow down until you get on comfortable ground."

Lily shook her head, but before she could argue, he said, "Let's start by having a quiet dinner tonight and get to know each other better. In essence, we could become friends and then see where it goes from there. How do you feel about that?"

She tilted her head as she considered his words and played with an amethyst drop on her necklace. He focused on her eyes, but his peripheral vision kept him posted on what the hand was doing. The fact that she wasn't trying to be sexy made it worse, but he certainly found her to be the most desirable woman he had met in a long time.

"Not tonight, I have to work."

"Till when?"

"About seven, maybe seven thirty."

Marshall nodded. "That's great. I'll order Thai. That way, if you're uncomfortable, you can leave whenever you want."

She consulted her schedule. "Tomorrow would work better for me."

"I fly to DC."

"Next week, then."

"Tonight."

She paused for several minutes before saying, "I couldn't be there until around eight, and I'd have to leave early because I'm doing a breakfast in the morning."

"Good." He purposely gave her a wicked look. "Then I won't have to put up with your incessant pleading to spend the night and keeping me awake with your insatiable desires."

She'd turned her head, but even from her profile the color crept up her neck into her cheeks. "I think you're safe."

He'd won the first round. Now it was up to her.

Marshall stood to leave. He wasn't sure if she walked him to the door out of politeness or fear he wouldn't leave. Her lips called to him, but he resisted fully kissing her. If spooked, she might not show. Instead, he settled for a hug.

"Stay," he sat the dog on the ground. Princess sat, her sad brown eyes conveyed her disappointment.

"Toto goes with you, Dorothy," Lily swooped the dog off the ground and urged her into Marshall's hands. She didn't move from the doorway as he crossed the lobby to the front door. Just before he stepped out onto the street, he winked.

Let her think about that for a while.

Chapter Twelve

Marshall loved living in the Pearl. Restaurants, coffee shops, a grocery store, and retailers selling clothes, household goods, books, and jewelry were within walking distance.

Princess marched beside him on the leash for four blocks. When she reached her limit, she sat, refusing to walk another step.

He tugged on the leash. "Let's go." Princess spread all four paws out and lay belly down on the ground. "We're walking." He drug her about a foot before he capitulated and bent over to lift her into his arms. She wagged her tail and gave his chin a lick of reward.

The jewelry shop display caught his eye, tucking the dog into his jacket he headed inside.

He wandered past wedding rings, watches, and even earrings. The stylized lapel pins slowed his steps as he studied the intricately jeweled daffodils, roses, and tulips.

A salesman rushed to help him. Marshall leaned over the gleaming glass counter when Princess thumped her tail. He looked up surprised to see Caroline at his side. He smiled. "Why are you here?"

"Steven was free for lunch. On the way to my car, I saw you and this dog a block away."

Knowing he was being discussed the dog's tail went into overdrive, and he squirmed to get away.

Marshall tightened his grip. "Good, I need some advice."

The shop owner, a dapper man in his sixties, stepped up to the counter and nodded at Caroline in greeting. "Is this what you wanted, Mr. Caudill?" In his hand was a delicate piece of jewelry. Clusters of diamonds and rubies designed as a stargazer lily pin. Stamens of garnets and delicate pink tourmalines gave the pin realistic color and depth.

Next to him, Caroline inhaled sharply and reached out to stroke the stones with a rose tipped finger.

"What do you think?" he asked.

She searched his face. "For Lily?"

"Of course."

Caroline was quiet for several moments before she said. "What are you doing? The pin is lovely, of course, but you're spending thousands on a party and buying her jewelry, too?"

Caroline would search for a motive. He didn't want to be questioned except to find out if Lily would react the way that Caroline had. "Will she like it?"

"What woman doesn't like expensive jewelry? She'll love it," Caroline's finger drummed the glass countertop. She wasn't going to let this drop. Silently Marshall counted down. Five. Four. Three. Two…

"Is something going on, I don't know about? Why are you buying her this? And where did you get that dog?"

Marshall smiled. Caroline would have made a good detective. He should suggest it as a career choice if she needed a job in the future. "The dog was a miscalculation and someone told me jewelry was a sure thing. You think it's too much?" He laughed at his joke. Caroline's confused look didn't bother him. He handed the jeweler a credit card.

"When have you ever needed a 'sure thing'?" Caroline asked as soon as the man had stepped out of earshot.

Marshall shrugged. "Lily is a different breed from most of the women I've known. I'm still figuring her out."

Caroline's delicate eyebrow rose. "By making money the basis of the relationship? I don't understand what you're hoping to gain by this."

Marshall signed the credit card receipt. "Nothing. Lily needs a little spoiling in her life. She doesn't appear to have had much of that. Do you think I'm wrong?"

She tentatively petted the dogs head. "No. I'm just surprised. Forty-five hundred dollars seems like a lot of money to pay for a gift for a woman you've just met."

Marshall smiled. "Funny I didn't hear you complaining about how much she bid on me the other night. Proportionally, I'll bet the money she bid was worth a lot more to her than this is to me."

Caroline drew her lips into a tight line that reminded him of their mother. "What is it you disapprove of?"

"Nothing."

Marshall leaned his arm on the counter and waited. Caroline shifted and glanced toward the store. Finally, she said. "You just seem so different with her. I wondered if you were serious."

"As in marriage serious?"

"Yes."

He picked up the bag and stuffed it in his pocket as he led the way to the door. "No. She's just another pretty woman."

At five-thirty Lily sat on her bed, chewing her fingernails. She replayed their conversation in her mind, knowing she'd lied to Marshall about what time her work would be done. Was there a way she could call him and weasel out? Did she want to?

What did one wear to seduction disguised as

a getting-to-be-friends dinner? What had she worn when she dated before? Blue jeans and high heels. Two things she never wore now. And she had had sexy underwear back then, too. Now all she wore was practical white cotton underwear. When had that happened?

Why was she worrying about underwear?

But she knew. Part of her wanted to wear sexy underwear and have an affair with this man who was a virtual stranger, and another part was angry to be considering it. This was a relationship that couldn't possibly work out. They ran in different social circles. They worked different hours and in different locations. Marshall saw her as a fling.

Lily wanted desperately to have a fling, but she'd waited too long. Now, she liked him. She *really* liked him. He would have a brief fling and move on. She would have a broken heart.

His behavior today was a complete surprise. Not at all what she had thought he'd be like. Certainly this morning had been interesting, bringing her that dopey dog. She found herself smiling just thinking about it. When was the last time, anything like that had happened to her?

She was still smiling when she got off the bed. Digging in a bottom drawer she found a long forgotten, pink lacey camisole and matching panties from a different time in her life, and she dressed with care.

With the right underwear, she could

overcome her nervousness.

Marshall straightened the already neat kitchen for the third time. The refrigerator contained chilled white wine and a six-pack of microbrews. Except for dressing, he was ready.

Princess slept on the rug, appearing to sleep, but she was vigilant even in her slumber. Every time Marshall left the room, she sprang to her feet and followed dutifully on his heels. Even as a child he'd never had a dog quite as devoted to his every move. They'd taken two long walks up and down the park blocks that ran in front of his loft. He hoped that would hold her for the night.

At six o'clock he headed for his bedroom to shower and shave. Three-quarters of the way up the steps he heard whimpering. The little dog sat at the base of the stairs, one paw on the first step.

"C'mon up."

She rose upward, but it was obvious, the steps with the open back worried her. Marshall encouraged, but the dog only whined.

"So much for tough love." Marshall came back down the stairs and carried the dog upstairs. "You're going to have to learn to climb these stairs because I'm not going to carry you all the time."

The dog wagged her tail. Marshall wasn't sure if the dog agreed to try harder or was pleased that he was so easy to train.

Ordering food was a challenge. Lily was a caterer. What would she eat? Should he wait until she got here to order? He studied the menu and made selections. What if she changed her mind?

Jeez, this wasn't a date. He was as nervous as if he'd been condemned to death and prepared to go before a firing squad. What he needed was Don Corleone to slap him around and tell him to act like a man.

The front door buzzer rang, and his relief was palatable. She'd arrived early. Things were working out better than he hoped. He punched the intercom button. "Hello." His reflection in the glass showed him grinning like a kid on Christmas morning.

"Marshall, I'm glad you're here." The cool female voice came over the intercom.

Oh, no. This couldn't be happening. "Muffy?"

"I was in the neighborhood and took a chance you were at home. Ring me in please."

No way. "I'll come down."

He opened his door, and Princess sprang up to accompany him. "Wait."

The dog barked.

"Just what I need. Another female to argue with me." Marshall grumbled. "Sit," he commanded. The dog sat.

But as soon as Marshall had closed the door behind him, the little dog yipped.

"Enough," he said loudly through the closed door and amazingly Princess quieted down. If only Muffy would cease and desist as easily. He stepped into the elevator.

The previous week he had returned the aquarium to the store and left a message on Muffy's recorder thanking her for the gift. But − and he'd stated this clearly − she'd misunderstood his feelings. He had no intentions of getting married or buying a house with her. His message had stopped just short of telling her it was over, but any woman with a lick of sense would have been able to read between the lines. A quiet week passed with no word in response. He believed all was settled until she arrived on his doorstep.

Muffy's svelte form was visible behind the glass entrance. Every blonde hair in place, her distant expression focused on the park across the street.

As irritating as he found her, he was once again struck by the perfection of her appearance. All his life, elegant blonde goddesses attracted him, and she was certainly one of the most beautiful, so, why was he, now waylaid by a short, feisty, tousled brunette?

Marshall walked toward the entrance,

watching one woman and thinking of another. Getting Muffy out of here before Lily showed up would be a trick. He opened the door and stepped outside.

"Let's walk, shall we?" he suggested, gesturing toward the park across the street.

"Walk?" An appalled look crossed her face, which might have been funny if her eyes hadn't welled up with tears. "What have I done to make you hate me?"

She buried her face in her hands, and a wretched sob overwhelmed her. Marshall put out his arm to touch her shoulder, but she stepped into the opening and clung to his shirt. He had no choice but to put his arm around her and offer her comfort.

"Muffy," He searched for the right words.

Her sobbing escalated. He stood, uncertain what to do or say. Her hand traveled across his chest as she shifted, pressing her breasts against him. Grabbing her hand to stop its movement, Marshall placed a finger under her chin and raised her head. Her pale eyes were bright, but her tears remained unshed. .

He hadn't seen fake crying this bad since Caroline had begged for a car for her sixteenth birthday. Politeness had not worked. Subtle hints had not worked. Now he had to be the bad guy. He hated this.

Muffy's BMW was parked half a block down. Catching her upper arm, he propelled her down the sidewalk, as he struggled to master his emotions. She must have known the jig was up because loud caterwauling replaced her sobbing. Someone would probably call the cops any minute thinking he was manhandling her. He needed her out of here without any outside interference.

He walked to her car as fast as possible narrowly resisting his urge to throw her over his shoulder and carry her. All the while, he surveyed the street for any vehicle that might belong to Lily.

Pushing her into the passenger's seat, he grabbed her purse and emptied the contents into her lap. From the jumble of makeup, checkbook and loose papers, he snatched her keys and climbed behind the wheel. Marshall's mind raced. Leaving her on the street in plain view of his front door would only invite additional problems when it was already clear that this woman's perception of their relationship was askew. In the car, her sobs reduced to sniffles, giving him time to consider where to drop her that allowed him to return in time. And yet left no misunderstanding about his intentions. They were never going to reenact this scene again.

As he shifted the car into drive, an idea came to him. He'd met her while dating Liv Shelton, another woman who'd wanted Marshall to dance to her tune. His relationship with Liv hit the skids once she demanded he compromise his work hours.

Now that Liv was dating a successful dentist, her anger had faded. At least he thought so because she'd been polite the last time they'd run into each other. Fortunately, she lived reasonably close.

Liv's black Lexus was parked on the street in front of her home. He pulled Muffy's Beamer in behind leaving the keys in the ignition. "Liv's home. Go visit her. She'll have no problems commiserating with you. I'm sure the two of you can dissect what a bastard I am, but we're done. No more. This is over."

Without waiting for her response, he jogged two blocks back to Burnside and searched for a bus stop less than a block away. In only a few minutes he hopped off the bus four blocks from his home, amazed once again by the incredible convenience of the Portland transit system. As he sprinted along the edge of the park, a white utility van pulled alongside him.

"You know when a man asks me to dinner, he's usually home when I get there," Lily yelled to be heard over the engine. "Would you like a ride?"

"Perfect timing." He dredged up a smile. Lily's eyes met his as he climbed into the van.

"What's the problem?"

Her astuteness surprised him. "Tell me," he

said. "Do you think all women have the characteristics of the psycho in the movie *Fatal Attraction*?"

Her eyes squinted as she imitated a suspicious person. When he laughed, she grinned. "Probably to one degree or another. Are we having bunny for dinner?"

"No," he admired her spunkiness, "but it would be best if you parked under the building rather than on the street."

Lily nodded and mumbled to herself. "No wonder Dori wants me to date more. I've been missing this kind of adventure."

Marshall couldn't help but compare the personalities of the two women currently in his life. He didn't comment but instead handed her a plastic card to wave across the infrared beam that operated the garage doors.

"You're right," he said as she handed back his card.

"About what?"

He sniffed the air. "Your van smells funny."

She snarled. "Either learn to suffer in silence or walk."

"Too late, we're here now."

While Marshall dashed upstairs to change clothes, Lily took a self-guided tour. His loft was delightful in the daylight. The place was vast. The light from the skylights gave the contemporary furniture an eerie glow. It was easy to understand why he liked his loft, but she couldn't imagine living without her garden.

She admired the fact he'd gone green with the bamboo flooring and the ceiling to floor waterfall took her breath away.

He rejoined her in a matter of minutes. "So what do you think?" The blue knit shirt intensified the blue in his eyes. Lily forced herself to admire the downtown skyline through his windows instead of ogling his body. His turf. His possessions. His kingdom. How was she supposed to resist him when she was going under for the third time?

He poured them each a glass of red wine, and they moved to the cream-colored leather couch and sat companionably together with a reasonable distance between them. Princess reared up on her short back legs and pawed the empty air until Marshall picked her up and laid her across his lap.

"What happened this evening?" Lily asked.

Marshall shrugged. "A misunderstanding. Have you ever ended a relationship with someone where you tried to be kind and instead were forced to be mean? Other than with me, of course."

"Not really." She grinned relieved to hear he'd broken up with Beauty Contestant Barbie. "I told you, for you I'm making exceptions."

The subject changed to work. Lily told

Marshall about the upcoming Library Gala in two weeks, and Marshall updated Lily about the Washington DC trip.

Lily listened, but it was obvious from her questions, she'd never been to the nation's capital.

"You've never been to DC?" He stretched back against the couch and propped his legs on the coffee table.

"My work doesn't allow much time off. And would you be going to DC if it weren't for work?"

"Not this trip, but I love to travel. There's a great trip to Antarctica in January I'm considering."

"Antarctica?" She asked hardly able to contain her disbelief. "What's in Antarctica besides penguins and ice?"

"Wildlife. True penguins are predominant, but it's a seal sanctuary and home to numerous species of fish, whales, cormorants and microscopic animals. Look at the geography. Did you know that there are no accurate maps of the region because ice covers the land mass that continually breaks off, shifts, moves, and buckles?"

"Would you fly?"

"No. Cruise. The smaller Russian ships get you close enough in that you can get off the boat, but I hear the water can be rough. That in itself would be an adventure."

Lily laughed and held up her hands in surrender. "Okay, Mr. Scientist. You've convinced me. Antarctica would be an interesting location to visit," she said. "And a cruise would probably be fun."

"You've never taken a cruise, either?" he asked. Sheepishly, Lily shook her head, and he said, "You've lived a sheltered life."

The doorbell rang. Marshall left Lily on the couch while he dealt with dinner. He surprised her by suggesting they eat out of the cartons on the couch. At home, Lily might have done so, but with company, never. His home. His rules.

With a haphazard flair, Marshall opened container after container of various Asian delights. Almost every one of Lily's favorites had been included, which was a very good sign. If he couldn't order an interesting meal, even friendship between them was doomed.

When he finished, Lily studied the quantity of food he'd ordered. "Did you think we'd be snowed in or were you just stocking up for the winter? Because I hesitate to mention that winter is still several months away."

"I like a woman with a healthy appetite."

"That attitude will get you fat thighs. So watch it," she warned. "Wow! These green beans are fabulous!" She offered him a bean suspended on her chopsticks. He leaned over to put them in his mouth. His eyes met hers and her self-protective instinct almost had her jerking her chopsticks back.

Clamping her knees together, she cast about for a safer topic. "Do you have any children?"

"Nope. Never married. Close once."

"That's amazing. I thought everyone was divorced."

"You're not." When she studied the Pad See Ew longer than necessary, he asked. "Do you want to talk about it?"

One shoulder shrugged upward. "There's not much to say. After fifteen years of marriage, one icy night in January, he and our Irish setter, Jackson, ran an errand. It was late. There was construction on the Marquam Bridge. In a freak accident the truck became airborne, cleared the guardrail and landed in the Willamette River. Investigators thought he might have fallen asleep at the wheel since the construction was well marked."

She never spoke of that time. Nobody ever asked anymore, but now information flowed out of her mouth. "Death is a terrible thing under any circumstance, but unexpected death is the worst. You're never prepared." She stared out of the window, refusing to look at Marshall.

"No one knows what to say, so they say the wrong thing. The widow doesn't want to hear that God has a plan. Or at least he died quickly and didn't suffer. Or how fortunate it was that he left you with some insurance money. Or the cruelest one of all was how lucky I was, because I didn't have small children. No one said what should have been said."

"Which was?" Marshall scooted closer to her. Not in a sexual way, but in a hovering protective way. As though somehow his presence could shield her from any future tragedy. Lily told him the truth.

"'Damn, girl, this sucks' would have worked better than most of the comments I heard." Her voice broke.

Marshall stroked her arm.

Lily finished her story quickly. She had to get away from him. "Eventually, because it was awkward for everyone, we stopped talking about it. I went back to work, and everyone pretended everything was okay. After a while it became, if not okay, at least tolerable."

"Were you counting?"

She squirmed out of his embrace and stood to put some distance between them. "It's a silly little trick I learned to keep from crying. You count backward from one hundred by thirteen's. Unfortunately, I've done it so often that it has lost its power." She couldn't talk about Charlie and let another man touch her.

Marshall didn't move. With his arm thrown across the back of the couch, he casually asked.

"Did you want children?"

"Yes. No. I don't know." She shook her head. "We agreed to wait until we were better established, but when he died, I regretted that decision. It would have been nice to have an anchor in another person."

She stared out the window. "Charlie was driven to make his restaurant work. It's unlikely we would have ever reached a comfort level for the commitment of a child. Fifteen years is a long time to wait to start a family."

Marshall nodded. "It could have been worse."

Lily snorted. "Yeah, just imagine if I'd had small children and no insurance money. I'd certainly be living a different life today."

"But he loved you enough to leave you well insured."

Lily laughed. "Don't be ridiculous. I insured us. When we bought our house, we needed both incomes to make the payments and pay the bills. I insured us so that if anything happened to one, the other would be protected. At the time, Charlie argued that it was a stupid waste of money."

"Protecting those you love is never wasted money," Marshall shrugged. "You should be pleased you had that kind of foresight."

She'd returned to the couch and picked up

one of the cartons, but he noticed she was counting again. "Are your parents still alive?"

"My dad died when I was nine. My mother has remarried and is living in Florida."

"Are you close?"

"Not very," she admitted.

"You're spilling rice."

"It's hard to eat rice with chopsticks." She picked up the grains from the floor. "Are you finished? I'll put the food away." Anything to get away from him and shake the melancholy that had swept over her.

As Lily finished in the kitchen, the clatter of floor-to-ceiling drapes in motion caught her attention. Marshall pushed buttons on an elaborate remote control. Lights were going off, and others were coming on. A roaring fire blazed in the fireplace. Contemporary soft rock replaced Mozart in the CD player. Lily swallowed hard. Despite Marshall's assurances that they would be friends first, he was setting a seductive mood.

Wasn't it Oscar Wilde who said the only way to rid oneself of temptation was to give into it? If she agreed, knowing the seduction was just a game to him, would she care when she never saw him again? What difference did the answer make? Trapped between her body's needs and her heart's desire, she had to make a decision.

The room had grown darker, more intimate. The light came from the waterfall on the far side of the room and the glow of the fireplace. Marshall continued to play with the buttons, adjusting and re-adjusting the setting.

"That's the ultimate masculine toy," she commented. "Sit down if it's too much of a testosterone rush."

"I have one for upstairs, too." Delighted with his toy, he reluctantly set the control down.

"Life is good." She strove to keep her tone flippant, as she rejoined him on the couch. It was finally going to happen and tonight she'd go with it. But even with that knowledge, she sat as far from him as the couch would allow. He hadn't even touched her and yet her skin tightened, and her nipples hardened in expectation.

Marshall lounged casually. He patted the couch next to him. "Give me your feet."

"I've been running around without shoes all evening." She wished she had never taken her shoes off.

He leaned over and clasped her ankles with one hand and brushed off the bottoms of her feet. "Do you feel better now?" he asked as he placed them on his lap and rubbed her toes. "Lie back."

Reluctantly she did as he requested. His foot massage was pure heaven, and she let out a noise that wasn't exactly a sexual moan, but reflected her pleasure.

"Close your eyes," he coached.

It was very difficult to relax when he touched her feet. What an aphrodisiac!

"Breathe," he commanded as he reached over and put his hand on her lower abdomen. "Here. Make my hand go up and down. Breathe down here."

Lily's body tingled in all sorts of ways. Her thoughts volleyed between wanting to be far away from him and why couldn't he'd go faster.

Marshall removed his hand from her stomach and returned to massaging her feet. The soft gray jumpsuit, Lily wore, had wide flowing pant legs. A gray and pink lightweight jacket covered the bib and straps. The width of the pants material gave Marshall easy access to her calves.

The song changed, but the mood didn't. Opening her eyes, she watched the flames leaping in the fireplace. Marshall had moved up her leg from her foot to her calf and back down again. Oh, Lord, his touch had reduced her will power to nothingness. How was she ever supposed to resist him?

Chapter Thirteen

She struggled with her emotions. When he'd touched her stomach, she'd jumped six inches. His plan to take things slowly had been working, but he was having trouble sticking to it. Particularly, when she made involuntary noises of pleasure and was so excitable about being touched. Such a sensual woman was a new experience he planned to enjoy.

"One dance. Then you need to go home." His voice had deepened.

She gazed at him. "You may regret this. It's been a long time since I've danced."

Her husky voice was already making him regret it.

"Believe me, we're not going to do any complicated steps," he muttered and pulled her to her feet. Putting both of his arms around her, he drew her in close. He hadn't realized she was short, but the top of her head fit neatly under his chin. They stood swaying to the music locked in an embrace. His body's warmth radiated to the point of being hot. Lily shifted enough to drop her jacket to the floor. One of his hands rested on the top of her jumper and her cool velvet skin while the other stroked the small of her back.

The song changed. She relaxed against him in a way that took all his control not to drop to the floor and take with him. Unable to resist further, he sought her lips.

When he pivoted slightly more than she expected, her nails dug into his shoulder blade pushing him over an invisible edge. His breathing turned ragged, and he forced himself to hold back. He held her at arm's length until she had sure footing.

"Where are your shoes?" he asked hoarsely.

"By the sliding patio doors." Her throat was so dry the words came out in a whisper.

"I'll get them for you."

As she bent to pick up her jacket, she understood that the sands in the hourglass had run out. Lily yearned for more. Her body wanted to stay, but to keep her heart intact, she needed to leave. Going home was the smart thing to do, except wild horses, couldn't have dragged her out the door at this point. When had being smart ever made her feel like this?

This was not a stranger, nor her mystery man. This was Marshall, a man she liked, more than she wanted to admit. No matter how much she wanted to avoid it, she had to make a decision. He was not going to make it for her.

✿

Marshall's restraint was frayed to the breaking point; he berated himself for letting it get this out of hand. Sending her home was the only way his plans would survive his desires. His prized control wavered in the face of her lack of resistance.

If she acquiesced, would her lust turn to embarrassment in the light of the morning after? Then refuse more than a solitary night? Would pushing her be his swan song?

Even understanding the odds were not in his favor, he still wanted to corral her –- right into his bed. His need to mark her as his and dive deeply into her ruled him. Hell, he'd even give up slogging through tide pools if it meant he could claim her now.

Marshall stopped. Where had that come from? This couldn't be anything more than casual. Caroline had been right. Giving her the pin would smack of commitment. Where was his mind? Women like Lily didn't separate the sensual from the emotional.

Balancing her shoes in one hand, he dug in his pocket for door keys. Lily stood in the corridor only about ten feet away. With only the fireplace for light, it took him a moment to realize her eyes searched his. Purposefully, he slowed his movements. With arms crossed over her breasts, she resembled an Egyptian sarcophagus lacking only the tools of power.

She lowered her arms. Caught in a slow motion dream, the shoulder straps of her pants outfit released and the billowy material floated to the floor. Sensual music played, and she swayed her hips, wearing only a lacy camisole and panties. He'd misread this situation.

He held his breath as he inspected her face, but the dim light made a true read impossible. Her unexpected response had him frozen in place.

Neither spoke.

Neither moved.

Finally Lily said, with a clearer purpose than he felt. "I'd like to see the waterfall from the second floor."

Not trusting himself to speak, Marshall covered the several steps between them dropping both shoes and keys along the way. One hand slid around her neck and the other her waist. He bent her back and lowered his lips to hers in a feverish kiss – devouring her. Kissing her the way, he'd wanted all night. Gradually he pulled her upright and guided her movements he propelled her backward toward the stairs. At the steps, he surfaced for air and eased his lips from hers.

"If we don't stop, we'll never make it to the

top," he whispered not wanting his words to break the mood. For the first time, her face was clearly visible. She wore that same unfocused look she'd had the first time he'd kissed her.

Did she have enough presence of mind to climb the stairs?

Did he have enough strength to resist her all the way to the second floor?

But Lily found fortitude he didn't have. Her shy smile caused his blood to race. His wonder changed to worry. What if he couldn't make it up the ten required steps?

He was unprepared when she leaned forward and lightly touched her lips to his. But even less ready when she took his hand giving him time to rally as together they climbed the stairs.

His massive bedroom was the only room with carpeting. The bamboo floor below had always been his preference, but now, her murmur of delight when she stepped onto the tightly woven floor covering, pleased him with his choice. The room, cast in gray shadows from the waterfall below and the skylight above, created a sensual mood.

He kicked off his shoes and pulled his shirt out of his pants. Lily watched transfixed. An awkward moment surged between them as she fidgeted. Her gaze darted around the room, and her hands twisted a corner of the camisole top.

Marshall's eyes never left hers. In one smooth move, he yanked the shirt over his head and dropped it to the floor. His lust ruled him, but in her eyes he could see the underlining of hesitation and doubt. Would she stop him now?

One of his arms circled her waist enclosing and stroking the silky material she wore. He drew her close enough that the material brushed his bare chest and caressed his skin.

Her full breasts surged over the inadequate covering of the camisole top. His arm rested in the indention of her waist as his hand slid underneath allowing him to feel the warm velvet skin. While her clothes were reduced to mere wisps of silk, he wanted her naked.

His mind cautioned him to take it slow, give her time to change her mind. Her lips, already swollen from his attention offered more, making him unable to resist. When his tongue delved inside, she trembled in his arms. Masculine pride soared. He was invincible. But her touch was tentative making him pause.

He felt certain it had taken a lot for her to remove her clothes downstairs. It was an unfamiliar boldness then. Now she held back. Her body language confused him. While her arms dangled at her sides and didn't come up to circle around him, her torso arched toward him. She allowed him to take but held herself back from giving. While her response to his touch was languid and accepting, she didn't ignite in his arms as she previously had.

Had she finally been the one to find control, just when he'd lost his?

Lightening his kiss, he nipped at her lower lip with his teeth before slipping his tongue between her lips to explore her mouth. Her smell, her taste, and the feel of her in his arms overwhelmed him, he wanted more than simple caresses. He wanted all of her.

His hand slipped beneath the elastic waistband to the luscious curve of her derriere, kneading and squeezing her buttocks. She offered no resistance. Lifting her to her toes, he aligned their positions, center to center. The hard ridge of his penis pressed against her, nestling in the welcoming adjunct of her legs. A harsh intake of breath let him know that she was not unaffected by his movements.

The dance of surge and retreat first, with his tongue and then his hips. Breaking off the kiss, he nibbled down her neck, stopping to suck her pounding pulse before skimming across the rise of her breasts. His hand cupped her breast lifting it above the material. An exposed nipple beckoned him, and his lips offered solace surrounding and sucking.

A low-throated moan escaped from her, sounding like a wild animal struggling to get free. She opened her lips to let it escape. Marshall was surprised by a strong, wave of passion that tore through her. Her entire body rippled with movement. Had she just had an orgasm? Was that possible?

Hesitantly, he pulled back to watch. A flush covered the upper part of her chest and neck. Had he ever known a woman capable of climaxing from just kissing and a little petting? He hadn't even explored below her waist. If this was true, then all his experience might well be next to nothing. Lily was different from any woman he'd ever known. Her arousal excited him more than he'd been for years.

His lips found her neck and the thin straps holding the satin to her body. He eased the fabric off and reached beneath to cup her full breast glistening with his recent attention and rubbed his rough thumb against a puckered nipple.

His lips and teeth followed as he lowered her to the bed. Her hesitancy was a thing of the past. Now she clung to his shoulders, and her hips urged him to hurry by thrusting upward in an undeniable invitation. Soft mewing sounds like a kitten emanated from her.

Unable to release his hold on the woman in his arms, in his need to see her naked, he tugged at the camisole until both her breasts were bared to him. His clothes didn't matter, despite his body's demands. Her head tossed and turned with frenzy as he attempted to soothe her with meaningless words.

With her nature so excitable, he exercised more care. Marshall had always been a considerate lover, but seeing to another's happiness was more. A lot more.

But if he was aroused, Lily was ablaze.

An electric current ran through her. Her arms rose to his waist and slowly inched up his shoulders. Clinging to his back while arching against his front, she found the match for her flame. Her head dropped back in surrender, and her voice urged him to hurry.

Little things overwhelmed her. It had been a long time since a man had held her close enough for her to appreciate his clean, masculine scent, the warmth of his body pressed against hers and the safety she felt wrapped in his arms. She also missed something she hadn't even known existed; she missed the way he moaned and whispered heated words driving them both upwards in passion. As his hands stroked and explored, her body came fully alive, perhaps for the first time in her life.

Marshall's caresses became more urgent.

His hands sought her heated center. Dipping his fingers under the satiny underwear, he touched her gently, but when her body rippled with explosions, his fingers intensified their exploration. He spread her legs wider to gain better access to her body. She was wet. Ready. Tonight would be the night.

How long had it been for her?

A mature woman, married for fifteen years, should not feel like a young virgin, even if sex had been missing for a while. Exhaling, he drew upon all his resources and stamina for control.

His fingers slipped through the soft folds of her body. One finger, followed by a second while his thumb lightly flicked over the hooded nub. Her ferocious response triggered his primitive nature.

Anxious hands clawed at his arms and back urging him closer. He eased his grip on her as he unzipped his pants. His fierce erection jutted proudly, free at last from its confines and eager for her touch. He guided her hand downward until she grasped him firmly and stroked. With more certainty, she caressed the width and length of him, taking his measure.

She froze. He rolled off her to give her better access. In a swift movement that left Marshall unprepared, Lily disengaged herself, lunged off the bed and backed against the bedroom wall.

Naked from the waist up and panting, she was exquisite. Full heaving breasts, a narrow waist, and nicely rounded hips gave her a sexual quality he hadn't expected to be so enticing.

The appeal of Marilyn Monroe had been lost on him. Now, jiggling curves beckoned him and offered him erotic comfort and the chance to bury himself in the sweet, dark oblivion of a woman.

Primal hormones surged until her wild eyes caught him – arousal mingled with something else. Fear.

"Lily." He spoke her name. Almost a whisper. He held out his hand urging her back to bed. She refused to meet his eyes, looking everywhere in the room, but at him. Measuring the distance to the stairs on the far side of the room and escape.

Did she suddenly think this was a mistake? With great caution, he rose to the edge of the bed, attempting not to alarm her. "What's the problem, sweetheart?"

As Lily struggled to regain control of her breathing, big tears rolled down her cheeks. She closed her eyes, but it didn't stem the tide of tears. Marshall came to her side gathering her in his arms and maneuvered her back to the bed. At the edge, he pulled her down to sit on his lap.

"Shhh," he crooned. "Hush now, tell me why you're crying." He buried his face in her neck inhaling her aroused scent.

She gulped for air. Surreptitiously, she wiped her eyes with the back of her hand. "I'm so sorry, I didn't intend to lead you on, but I couldn't stand it if you're disappointed." She hiccupped.

Marshall struggled not to laugh. "Disappointed? How could you disappoint me? This has been one of the most fascinating nights I can ever remember. Meeting you was the best thing that has happened to me in years." As he said the words aloud, he knew them to be true.

He stroked her back and murmured soothingly. "What's wrong, sweetheart?"

"I'm not built for pleasure," Lily admitted between hiccups. "I've got some weird physical abnormality. It never occurred to me that you were so much bigger than Charlie."

Pride warred with confusion. His size had been an asset when he was younger. Now, it was fact. It had been a long time since anyone had commented.

But, her statement that she wasn't built for pleasure baffled him. Women with better bodies and more experience had passed through his life, but never one more responsiveness to his touch – one who could climax with a mere kiss! How could she think she wasn't built for pleasure?

"What weird abnormality?" he asked using caution as his guide.

Lily hesitated. "I'm too small for your size. I

know women are supposed to stretch, but I can't. Sex was always painful for me."

"Did I hurt you?" he inquired, stricken by the thought.

Embarrassed she hung her head and shook it. He laced his fingers through her thick curly hair as he considered her answer. How much stretching had been required? Granted she was tight, but she'd managed to accommodate two of his fingers without pain.

Marshall tried hard to convince his brain to return to his head. There was more to this story than she was telling him. "I think," he said as he drew her back on the bed, "that you need to tell me about your previous sex life. Did you and your husband have sex during your marriage?" He had heard of married couples not having sex.

"Of course, we had sex." She attempted to sit up. Marshall's weight kept her pinned, but his fingers were gentle and caressing. Finally, her meager struggles quieted, and she relaxed against him.

Marshall reverted to using her words to determine her meaning. "Did you think you weren't built for pleasure when you were married?"

Lily closed her eyes and even in the darkened room he could see a blush coloring her breasts and cheeks. "Yes."

"How's that possible?"

"I'm too tight," she mumbled. He leaned close to catch every word. "Charlie was never able to get completely inside me before it was all over."

Marshall suppressed a groan. "Every time?"

"No, but most."

"Why did you think it was your body rather than his problem?" Hell, why hadn't she gone to a doctor if she had a problem?

"Because he had never had that problem with other women before me."

"And you were how old?"

Lily stopped to think back. "Twenty-two or three."

"A virgin?"

Lily blushed. She hesitated before she finally blurted out the truth. "Yes, but sex was never what it was touted to be. Some women can't enjoy it. I didn't mean to mislead you. I thought maybe it would be different with you, but then when I touched you, I knew you'd be miserable, too. I just can't go through that again."

Pieces fell into place. Her husband had been a premature ejaculator who blamed his wife's body rather than his performance. Lily had been young and inexperienced enough to buy it. What a waste!

But the impact of the precious prize dawned upon him. Without a doubt, this was the best gift he had ever been given. A sensual woman waiting for her passion to be awakened. By him. Vowing to ignore the primitive side he'd focus on her pleasure until she was able to accept her own nature.

"Listen to me. You, of all women, were built for pleasure."

Lily opened her liquid brown eyes and gazed into his blue ones.

"Let's say, for the sake of argument, that you're right. Your body's unable to accept mine. Do you believe there's only one way?" He doubted the problem was physical, but if necessary, he would personally take her to a doctor. This woman was not getting away from him. Not now.

As he spoke his hand moved to cup her breast and tweaked the nipple, which immediately responded to his touch. She inhaled a sharp breath, her chest thrust upward as his lips lowered to capture his prize. Not meant for pleasure? This was the most sensual woman he'd ever met.

"Marshall," she moaned.

His heart soared, but he hesitated prepared to stop if she said 'no.'

Her hands speared through his hair, she tugged him closer.

His lips sought hers. Their tongues met and

dueled while his hand caressed her stomach. Within minutes, the passion they had kindled earlier returned, but with a subtle difference. Lily responded in earnest.

Now the peaks he drove her to were more intense. Her vocal qualities took on a new dimension exciting Marshall even more. Smiling to himself, he was grateful not to have close neighbors. Lily, when excited, was a screamer and, as it was becoming apparent, somewhat of a little wildcat in bed.

Better and better.

His lips and fingers did an intricate little dance that left her peaking time and again, as her body movements jerked with frenzy reflecting her urgent need.

"Soon," he murmured as he dipped his face between her legs and tasted all of her, grateful that as she reached acappella range her thighs blocked his hearing.

Pausing for breath, she moaned his name with a renewed sense of desperation, clasping his shoulders with her hands.

Marshall rose above her and entered her with a single stroke, sheathing himself to the root. The look of shock on her face said it all.

Slowly, he drew back and thrust forward again. Instinctively, her hips surged to meet him before she tensed and stopped all movement.

Withdrawing, he eased inside her again. There was no hesitation, and he saw no pain reflected in her face, but still her body remained as rigid as a two-by-four. His movements altered between gentle and vigorous while she refused to budge from a catatonic state.

Frustrated, he asked, "Am I hurting you?"

"No." Her voice was strained.

His motion stopped, and he waited until she opened her eyes. "Why have you stopped moving?"

"You want me to move? Charlie always told me to stop moving now," she whispered.

"It's not only okay to move, but more fun." He grinned, slowly he slid in and back out again. Her eyes widened and then fluttered as he repeated the move.

It was the invitation she needed. Her body rose to meet his strokes, uncertain at first but soon with an instinctive confidence. He encouraged her to wrap her legs around his back and let herself go. She did so with an abandon that drove him crazy.

His careful behavior vanished.

Growling and cursing, he pumped into her like a piston engine.

Pounding. Pushing for more than release. Searching for something deeper he couldn't define. He'd been raised in a life of privilege. He wanted for nothing, but he needed her.

His release came with a howl and a blissful

darkness.

Chapter Fourteen

The room cooled as his breathing returned to normal. He eased his body from hers and rolled to the side as he pulled up a sheet to cover them both.

Her eyes stayed closed. Marshall lay stunned. Not only had it been the most intense orgasm he'd had in years, he'd failed to use a condom.

Since his occurrence with Brigit, thirty-two years prior, Marshall had never had sex without protection – until now. And he was not the only one demanding body armor. His sperm had always been treated like terrorists – to be protected against at any cost.

Tonight he felt free. If this was wrong, why did it feel so right?

He took a deep breath and pushed the thoughts away.

"Shower?" he asked, not adding before we go again.

Opening her eyes, her mortified look made him realize he pushed too fast. If the experience had moved him, a woman with a sketchy sexual history would be overwhelmed.

He smiled and stroked her cheek. He sighed.

Okay, individual showers. Not as much fun, but perhaps a little privacy was what she needed. For now that was acceptable. Later, he would persuade her there was no need for such modesty.

"I'll be right back." Kissing her forehead, he climbed out of bed, heading to the bathroom.

Hot water righted his world, sending any stray thoughts down the drain. One more round, then he'd send her home. Or maybe he'd let her spend the night. She had to leave early anyway.

Several minutes later, he opened the door. His bed was empty. And after an in-depth search so was his loft.

The runaway girlfriend was gone again. Dammit.

He sat on the edge of the bed, debated dressing and going after her. What was wrong with him? He'd had her, now he needed to let her go.

Except his mind kept replaying their evening scene by scene.

He stared at the jeweled pin and knew he had to be on a flight to DC in only a few hours. They weren't done yet.

The plague of erotic dreams was no longer Lily's nemesis. Now the turmoil of her life kept her awake. She rose to a sitting position in bed, tired of tossing and turning. Marshall had already kept her awake half the night, why would she want to sleep the other half? Although, it wasn't Marshall who was keeping her awake now. It was Charlie.

Her husband had lied to her.

And deep inside she'd known it.

Lily may have been a problem solver at work, but in her home life, she had developed equally good skills at avoidance. She'd hated sex with Charlie. It had been easier to drift apart than to work on a solution that might involve more sex. And Charlie hadn't cared either. Or had his avoidance been even greater than hers?

They were so young when they met. Love hadn't cemented the arrangement. Comfort had. The fifteen years had drifted by.

The first year after he died, Lily, whose life had never been dependent upon his, couldn't imagine living without him. All of his bad qualities were forgiven and forgotten.

Now, she remembered all the years of fumbling in the dark. Of pain and guilt. Of believing sex was misery and best to be avoided. That there was something wrong with her body.

And then Marshall arrived. With a few practiced moves, he slid home like he'd lived there all his life. And her non-orgasmic body cranked out climaxes like a Pachinko machine on the fritz. Every ball – a winner.

She hated Marshall. She hated that he wasn't the arrogant over-sexed fantasy man she wanted desperately to believe he was. She hated that he was warm, tender and caring.

But even the sincere Marshall was not a keeper. The facts bore this out. Late forties, a bachelor –- not divorced –- never married. She and the western half of America would be able to hear the loud crack when her heart snapped in half.

But little things like a broken heart, the humiliation of her tears, her embarrassing inexperience and her wanton behavior didn't matter. Those things were in the past.

Because now, she knew the truth. She was not a failure as a woman. She could have real sex with a man. Marshall had taught her that. But in teaching her, he understood how stupid she'd been and for how long. He wouldn't respect her; he'd laugh, not to her face, of course. To her face, he'd be compassionate until he tired of her, which had probably already happened.

The office door was closed which was unusual, particularly with Lily's van in the parking lot. Dori knocked and heard a muffled reply. She pushed the door open. Lily lay on the couch with a damp washcloth covering her eyes and her feet propped up.

Panic swept up her throat. "What's wrong? Was there a problem with the breakfast this morning?"

Lily groaned. "Breakfast went fine. They were off on their count and only had about thirty-five people, so there are leftovers. Ginger's calling the homeless shelter to see if we can drop them off," she said from under the washcloth.

Dori warred with her brain. Yes, she was glad Lily had found someone. But it was more roller coaster than she'd expected. "Rough night?"

"The Japanese fall on their swords when they've humiliated themselves. Don't you think that's a sensible solution?"

Wasn't there a rule about the hour of the day that was acceptable for drama? "Depends on the problem. How did you humiliate yourself?"

"Sex with Marshall."

She swallowed. *Oh boy, here it comes.* "And?"

"And I foolishly trusted him."

Dori stood still. But she prepared for fight mode knowing if she had to kill Marshall, she would.

"I behaved shamelessly," Lily moaned.

Dori relaxed glad that her friend couldn't see her grin. "Kinky stuff?"

"Only if you count screaming and moaning

and being totally out of control."

"Lily, you worry me, girl. If he can't drive you completely out of control, why'd you bother to take off your clothes? I hadn't realized you were so repressed."

"I'm not repressed," Lily's indignation rose with the tone of her voice.

"Good, then what's really bothering you?"

Lily shifted raising an arm to cover the washcloth. "Shit. I think I'm in love with him. What's the first word that comes to mind?"

Dori groped for a seat. *Love? So quickly? What was the first word that came to mind?* "Congratulations?"

"Not hardly." Her partner huffed. "It's fool. As in: *there's no fool like an old fool, and fools rush in where wise men fear to tread.* I'd do the one about a fool and his money, but I don't think it applies here."

Dori raised an eyebrow. "I don't know, the money you spent on the bachelor auction might dispute that."

Lily ripped the washcloth off her eyes and glared. "Thank you, I'm starting to feel better already."

If Lily could resort to sarcasm, she felt better. Even if Marshall dumped her, for the first time in years, Lily was back in the game.

"You didn't get a read on his feelings?" Dori attempted sympathy.

Lily's response was to shake her head.

When that didn't work, she went for the probe. "How was the sex?"

Lily flopped back on the couch.

Time to drop the bomb. "A large envelope arrived for you by special courier."

Lily sprang to a seating position. Dori left her chair, moved to the couch handed her the large brown envelope. The shape indicated more than a letter inside.

"It's probably a kiss-off present." Lily unfastened the brad and ripped the envelope open.

Right. "Boy, you haven't dated for a while. Men don't send kiss-off presents. They promise to call and never do."

Inside Lily found a note and a small square box.

The note read:

"Who do you think you're fooling by hiding? Last night was only the beginning."

Lily read the unsigned note several times before she released it to Dori's eager hands. "Hiding?"

She shrugged. "I slipped out while he was in the shower."

Was she kidding? Dori stared at her friend in disbelief. "Hoo, boy. I've always wondered where the phrase lily-livered came from. Now I know."

"I couldn't face him. Just before he showered, he let out this disappointed sigh. And I knew I had to go."

"You left because he sighed?"

"No, I left because I told him things about me that make it impossible for me to see him again." Lily re-read the note several times more before Dori thrust the box at her, demanding she open it.

Neither spoke when they saw the elegant ruby and diamond lily pin lying pristinely in the box.

Dori broke the silence: "I'm betting he doesn't know it was a one night stand."

"I can't keep it."

"Are you crazy? Expensive gifts of jewelry for a man are like buying an insurance policy. When he behaves like an idiot, the chances are you'll think about this pin and forgive him. What was the name of that professional athlete who had sex with another woman? When his wife found out, what was the first thing he did? He purchased a four million dollar ring. I'm not condoning sex outside marriage, but a four million dollar ring can forgive a lot of sins."

"Well, I'm sure this pin didn't cost four million dollars, but it wouldn't matter if it did. I'm returning it, and I'm never going to see Marshall again."

Dori leaped to her feet. "You're insane! Do you know how many guys out there would send a gift like this? Nada. Zilch. Zero. Nyet. No way, Jose. None. Plus you're doing his sister's party on Saturday."

"You do it without me."

"Where's your backbone?" Dori snapped. "Grow up, Lily. We're running a business here. You *will be* there, and you *will be* a smiling, professional caterer. If you encounter Marshall, you can damn well deal with it on your own time. This is not a group of people we can afford to piss off because you were caught kissing Johnny behind the barn."

Dori whirled and marched out of the office, slamming the door behind her.

Lily sat on the couch and stared at the pin for several minutes. Dori didn't agree, but to Lily, it felt like payment for services rendered. She glanced at her watch.

He had to have purchased it earlier before last night. No jewelry store was open this early. Her fingers stroked the beautiful stones. Except for a band of gold, no man had ever given her jewelry.

And she was an idiot. Not about the pin, she was going to return it. But letting her past dominate had thrown her off her game. No more. Marshall wasn't Charlie, and she was no longer a naive twenty-three-year-old.

If Marshall wanted to play, she would meet on the field, but maturity had added to Lily's arsenal and she had a few tricks up her sleeve. She rose from the couch and opened the blinds, letting sunlight pour into the room. Then sat at her desk. Up to now, he'd been in charge. It was time to chart her next move.

Send me in Coach, I'm ready to play.

Suzanna Gerland laid her tennis racquet on the bench and glanced at her watch for the third time. Court time was four o'clock, and it was four minutes after. Muffy was a serious player. She was never late.

A distinctive giggle reached Suzanna's ears.

She spotted her friend two courts away. Shielded by Muffy's stance, a man knelt, hunched over her shoes while she bent over and ran her hand through his hair, flirting. Apparently, she wasn't too torn up about Marshall Caudill, no matter what the gossip circle reported. Suzanna walked toward them.

The man uncurled and rose to stand beside her, his back still to Suzanna. In a manner that conveyed more intimacy than friendship, his arm was wrapped around the woman's shoulder as he whispered in her ear. Another giggle. Suzanna saw her blonde ponytail flip as she nodded her head.

Muffy turned. Their gazes connected. She murmured something to her companion, who straightened and raised a hand in greeting.

Jim Alden. Muffin Parsons flirted with Jim Alden? Suzanna's Jim Alden.

Pasting a smile on her face, Suzanna waved back.

"Sorry, I'm late," she said, sounding anything but sincere. "My shoe had a problem. Fortunately, Jim rescued me." The women exchanged air kisses.

"Yes," Suzanna injected a sultry quality into her voice. "Jim's specialty's knots and ties."

His lips curled in an arrogant smirk as he leaned in to kiss Suzanna. She stepped closer, but the bastard didn't offer anything more than an obligatory kiss. *Is that how he thought this game was going to be played?*

Keeping her face passive, she watched Jim's knowing gaze survey the two women as he tried to disguise a masculine smile of satisfaction. "I'm off to the showers. Have a good game, ladies. Suzanna, call me when you're done."

Don't wait by your phone.

He sauntered off as the women walked to their reserved court. Muffy dropped her bag and removed her racket. Suzanna tugged her hair into a knot and jerked a sun-visor over the top. Usually, the two women were well matched, but today Suzanna was determined to wipe the court with her opponent. After three games, the other woman called uncle.

"My game is off, today," she panted, pleasing Suzanna, who had run her all over the backcourt. "I haven't been feeling well." Muffy collapsed on the bench and dug for her water bottle.

"You poor dear. We were all so sorry to hear about the breakup with Marshall. I know you were mortified to have him turn around and immediately start seeing that caterer. It taught us all a lesson about the bachelor auction."

"He's dating the caterer?" Muffy sputtered, leaping to her feet. "What's her name? Lily Something?"

Suzanna turned her head so Muffy couldn't see her delight. "You hadn't heard? I was sure you knew. Well, you'd have run into them sooner or later anyway. Caroline must be beside herself with anguish. You know how the Caudill's feel about propriety."

With two bright spots of color emblazoned on her cheeks and a frown that Suzanne hoped would create wrinkles, she couldn't resist a last dig. "Imagine dating a caterer. That's about one step above one of those high school cafeteria ladies."

Muffy gritted her teeth. "Well, at least she owns the company."

Suzanna laughed to herself, knowing that

defending the other woman rankled the other woman's pride, but if Marshall's judgment of women were questioned how would that reflect on the fact he'd dumped Muffy for such a low life?

"You're such a dear," Suzanna said, hiding her smile. "I wonder what Marshall sees in her?

The memorial service ran long. Lily and Dori's plan to make Marshall crazy backfired. After the tenth or so inquiry about Lily's absence, Dori, who was in charge of the Zonnheiser party, called.

"We're almost done," Lily whispered into the phone.

After another forty-five minutes had passed and Lily hadn't shown up, she made a second call to no answer. The third call caught Lily as she bustled the staff out the door.

Dori stepped into the deserted kitchen to ask, "Where *are* you?"

Lily leaped into the driver's seat and slammed the van door. "We're leaving now. Big family who apparently they didn't know they were supposed to mourn on our schedule."

"Drop the others off at the kitchen, then get here. I need the help." Dori pleaded.

"I'm not even going to the kitchen. I'm coming directly there and bringing Sharon and Lydia with me. The others can join us after they've unloaded the first van. So, what's the problem? Were you not set up on time?"

"No, we were ready long before the guests got here. But you've been asked for about fifteen hundred times, and when Marshall isn't inquiring, he's giving me a look that would do a preacher proud. I've nearly confessed every sin I've ever contemplated. But the real surprise of the evening turns out to be Caroline's husband. Guess who Steven Zonnheiser is?"

Lily shrugged. "Other than one of *The Zonnheisers*?"

"He's a lawyer and, you'll love this, a partner in Rassman, Temple, and Zonnheiser."

Lily paused. *Why did she know that name?*

Dori answered because she put two and two together.

"The law firm that sued us two years ago."

"You're kidding."

"No, and I'm betting every one of those vultures is here tonight." Dori lowered her voice even further.

Lily drove at breakneck speed; the cell phone propped against her ear with the radio cranking out country and western music. The red light in front of her surprised her, had she not heard Lydia gasp, she might not have slowed down. "I can't believe you even recognized them after all this time."

"You know I never forget a face." Dori continued unaware of the near death experience her partner was undergoing. "Jack Raulerson, the lawyer who led the charge against us, came up and demanded to know why I was here. That's when I put a name to the face. Then he started spying on me in kind of a creepy, lurking way."

"Ewww."

"You're not kidding. Finally, Mrs. Z realized what was happening and intercepted Raulerson. I don't know where he is now, but she diverted him."

"Marshall's there?"

"Oh, yeah. He's outside at the bar. By the way, Maker's Mark is his liquor of choice. And from what I can tell, he likes a lot of it. But get this – he's not leading the pack. We're dealing with a hard-drinking crowd. Our bartenders have been hopping all evening long."

"It's not even nine o'clock. How's the food holding out?"

Dori sighed. "Fine. No one's eating it."

"Oh no," Lily moaned. "You know what that means. About eleven thirty when we want to go home, they'll all get the munchies. I hate parties like this. I'm pulling up to the driveway now. Do you have a clean uniform for me?"

"The laundry room in the basement. Go there first."

The basement's laundry room was little more than a large closet, but her black jacket hung over the cabinet doorknob above the dryer. Lily removed her old jacket and reached for the new one. A shiver had her spine trembling. She wasn't alone.

Marshall's liquor-scented breath curled around her neck. "You're late."

She inhaled sharply, her body on red alert. Before she could turn his warmth covered her from toes to shoulders. His arms wrapped around her and caught her hands in mid-reach to grab the hanger. He wrapped her fingers around the shiny gold knobs that lengthened her arms above her head and growled in her ear, "Don't move."

Don't move? How could she? His legs bracketed hers. The length of his body forced hers against the still warm dryer. But as his hands left hers, his meaning became clear.

She clung to the doorknobs as effectively as if he'd tied them with cord. He stroked his way down her arms.

Marshall lowered his head to her shoulders. His throat rumbled, a low animal sound, as he nibbled the pulse beating in her neck, marking her tender skin. Lily moaned as hunger hammered at her.

One hand unfastened her lacy bra and

clasped her taunt breasts stretched by her arms above her head. Her nipples responded, greeting him like a long lost friend. Her breasts behaved like separate entities from her body the way they competed for his attention. Pouting, hardening and puckering for his pleasure.

A large hand slid down her abdomen and wormed its way between her body and the dryer. Lily tensed, a groan escaped her lips.

"Shh."

Lily's head dropped between her arms unable to release the door handles. Marshall's fingers caressed between her legs through her slacks, while his firm erection found a home between her buttock's cheeks. Lily's body surged against his hand demanding more, as a torrent of moisture soaked her panties. She pushed to widen her stance to give him better access, but her legs were wedged solidly between his. She hissed at her entrapment.

"Shh. Be vewy, vewy quiet," he whispered, giving his best Elmer Fudd impersonation. Lily could hear the amusement in his voice, frustrating her further.

"Stop tormenting me," she ground out, finding her voice.

"Are you ready to leave?" he asked.

"No. I just got here, and I'm working." His fingers never stopped teasing her body, making it difficult for her to think.

"Then we'll have to take care of things now. I can't wait."

"Are you crazy?" she gasped, as his fingers inched further between her legs. "We're in a laundry room at a party, dammit. I can't stop and have sex here, just because you're ready."

Marshall said nothing, but she felt her slacks being unzipped. "Really, Marshall, we can't do this."

"This is what I should have done to you the first night I met you, sugar." He pushed her slacks and underwear to her knees, and they puddled onto the floor. "Step out," he instructed. She would have argued more, but her movement had given Marshall an access that enabled his questing fingers more freedom, leaving her speechless.

He gave a harsh bark of a laugh. "Well, aren't you the naughty one?" His voice was husky with arousal. "You're as ready as I am. And what's this I feel? Silky smooth? I can hardly wait to taste you. Next time…"

The low growl combined with questing fingers amped her response. She was as revved as he was.

"On your toes," he instructed as he bent his knees and rose behind her, impaling her on his way up. Oh, Lord. He was larger than she remembered. Her body stretched to accommodate his width like an overfilled sausage whose casing could give way at any moment. Marshall's breath was heavy on her neck. The potent fumes from the strong smell of bourbon intoxicated her.

"You're so tight," he grunted, resting his head on her neck when he was sheathed to the hilt. "Just being inside you makes me want to come."

Lily froze. What if the last time had been a fluke and she really was too small, but the thick ridge of his penis head moved inside her. One arm wrapped around her waist cushioned her hips against the dryer. He pulled her feet off the ground, supporting her weight on his muscular thighs. His free hand eased between her legs and rubbed against her clitoris.

Lights exploded in her head, and she let go of the doorknobs. She grabbed the back of the dryer to hang on while reaching for a folded bath towel to jam in her mouth in a futile attempt to muffle her vocal accompaniment.

Marshall pumped hard increasing his speed. Cursing low in her ear. He thrust heavily into her, pounding toward orgasm. Her body had been flung into the fire, her hips rose repeatedly to meet his, demanding he satisfy the coiled tension of her loins.

Her body erupted. Shivering and pushing hard against him, she buried her face in the towel to control her screams. A harsh, guttural cry rumbled up from his chest as his head fell back, and he pushed forward shooting into her like a machine gun firing live ammo.

Her cell phone, in the pocket of her pants, waddled up somewhere on the floor, rang. They groaned in unison.

"That's Dori's ring," Lily moaned, her hoarse voice scarcely above a whisper.

Marshall bent down, groping in her pants pockets until he retrieved the phone. Instead of handing it to Lily, he pushed the button and growled into the receiver. "What!"

"I see you found her." Dori's voice came distinctly through the speakerphone.

"Tell her I'll be there in a minute," Lily grunted.

Dori responded before Marshall could relay the message. "Take your time."

He took the towel from Lily and ran warm water in the sink. He handed her the wet towel first, and she quickly wiped between her legs before returning it to him. He re-wet the towel and cleaned himself.

"Don't even think about leaving without me. If you run away again, the next time I'll tie you to my bed."

Fastening his trousers, he stepped out of the laundry room. Lily bent her body forward and rested her head against the top of the washing machine as she worked to regain her composure.

The cool night air was a welcome relief. Just a few more minutes and her flushed cheeks would return to normal. She placed her used jacket in the van and then pressed her forehead against the cool glass of the driver's side windowpane. Behind her another van pulled up and three more servers spilled out.

"The Calvary's here," the driver announced. Lily peered into the darkness. Her staff from the funeral had arrived.

Earlier in the week, Lily had objected to Dori's arranging to have so much staff arriving late, but now she was glad to see them. She didn't have enough energy left to pick up a heavy tray or to even think about sorting glassware.

Lily found Dori rinsing glasses in the kitchen sink.

"Sorry, I'm late."

Dori snorted. "No, you're not. You're regretting that you have to stay, but I don't believe you're sorry you're late."

Lily grinned at her friend in gratitude. "We've been partners too long."

"Was he appreciative of any changes you might have made?"

Lily rolled her eyes. Foolishly she was hoping Dori hadn't been aware of the two-hour break she had taken yesterday morning for her spa appointment. "Waaay too long," she emphasized.

"Marshall's more relaxed since you've arrived." Her eyes twinkled with mischief. "We've got enough help here now, you could leave any time the mood strikes you and take any interested parties with you."

"I'm prepared to stay," Lily responded without looking at Dori. She was conflicted. Marshall had only served the tantalizing appetizer course in the laundry room. Lily was pretty sure the entrée was yet to follow. She wanted to go, but leaving would be disloyal.

Dori frowned. "I know you're prepared to stay, but if you leave now, I won't feel so guilty when it's my turn to behave badly." Dori smiled like a naughty child with a secret.

Lily studied her friend. "Will that be soon?"

"Maybe," Dori said.

"Do tell." Lily rested her back against the counter and admired Caroline's state-of-the-art kitchen.

Chapter Fifteen

Dori turned off the water. "Jack Raulerson asked me out."

Lily had her complete attention. "What? When? You'd date the sleaze ball who sued us?"

"I said no." But Dori smiled that Cheshire cat grin. "Go make a round outside and make sure everything's going well."

Luscious Foods had enough staff present that there was nothing for Lily to do, except nod to guests and make her cameo appearance. As she neared the buffet table, Marshall gripped her upper arm. "C'mon. They're playing our song." He led her unresisting onto the patio by the gazebo where a few other couples swayed together. Folding her into his arms, he danced her around the patio away from the band.

"How did this get to be our song?" Lily murmured against his chest.

He bent his head to whisper in her ear. "Every time I hear it, I see you standing by the fireplace with your clothes floating to the ground. That makes it our song."

Lily blushed but snuggled closer. She listened in hopes she could later identify it, but his nearness distracted her. Normally dancing with a guest would have been considered taboo, but as Dori had predicted it was a hard-drinking crowd, already three sheets to the wind. She doubted that anyone even noticed. Relaxing in Marshall's arms, Lily enjoyed herself. When was the last time she had been a guest at a party?

Marshall maneuvered her into a dark corner under the trees. Their dancing slowed. Their bodies were pressed so close they moved as one swaying to the music. "How long do you have to stay?" he asked. His hands caressed her back, and his voice coated her like warm molasses.

Moving required more effort than it was worth. If she could just stay like this forever, she'd be happy. Instead, she murmured. "I can leave anytime." Even if Dori hadn't given her permission, Lily was ready to have her fill of Marshall.

She could feel his head nod in acknowledgment of her statement, but he didn't loosen his hold. The song changed to something else with the same mellow rhythm. Neither spoke. It would have broken the bubble of isolated perfection they'd created. Marshall's hips played a game of touch, grind and retreat with hers. By the end of the song, her breathing had quickened.

The next song's melody changed, and Marshall pulled back and studied the woman in his arms.

"Let's go now," he said, a wicked grin

appeared when he added. "We still have show-and-tell ahead of us." He stepped back prepared to lead her to the parking area.

Lily hesitated and turned to face him. Gently he smiled, looking down at her, and stroked her cheek with his thumb, surprising her with the tenderness in his eyes.

Her plan to be daring hadn't anticipated his caring, "Your house or mine?"

His blue eyes burned with an internal fire. "Definitely yours. That way, you'll have no place to escape to. I'm not waking up alone tomorrow. Get used to the idea," Marshall's expression dared her to defy him.

He planned on spending the night? Butterflies took flight in her stomach. Her body trembled and he hadn't even touched her yet.

A dropped plate has a certain distinctive sound even if it doesn't break. When Lily heard the sound Friday night, she didn't give it a second thought since she heard almost every week of her life. Someone, somewhere was always dropping dishware. Especially during an event.

Out of habit, she did a slow perusal of the room while she continued to speak to the

Romers. Laura Romer wanted a fiftieth-anniversary dinner for her parents, and Lily listened intently enough to be able to send them menu ideas and costs the next day.

"Are you thinking of a plated dinner or a…" Lily's eyes fell on her partner. The look of sheer panic on Dori's face made Lily take in the full scene.

Lily glanced at the Romers, who were spellbound by the unfolding situation. "Please excuse me."

Immediately, Lily crossed the Library floor to the food tables.

The children's library was a large crowded room, dotted with low bookshelves. Lily moved quickly, keeping a reassuring expression while she tried to discern what was happening. With six hundred guests in attendance, only a hundred or so currently milled in the children's library. Music played on the upper floors, so the crowd had thinned out.

An elegant woman with white-blonde hair slicked back from her face in a tight bun stood in front of their table. The satiny beige gown flowed around her svelte body enhancing her golden skin. Exquisite jewelry sparkled at her neck and ears.

As the regal woman reached for a glass plate, Lily's eyes widened when Dori slapped her hand on the stack of plates and said something Lily guessed to be belligerent, based upon her partner's defiant expression. The blonde then stepped back, spat out angry words and hurled her almost empty martini glass toward the bookcase behind Dori. Unlike the earlier crash, the martini glass had the distinct sound of shattering. Lily watched the uneaten olive jump to safety like a pilot ejecting from the cockpit.

"You ruined my life." The blonde raised her voice above the din of the crowd, her features distorted in her anger making her less attractive.

Dori's body was coiled, ready to attack. "I don't know who you are, but you need to leave."

"We were going to be married before you stole him from me." The unknown woman wailed as she reached for an hors d'oeuvres tray filled with hard cooked pesto eggs garnished with prosciutto.

Lily managed to wrestle the tray from her. The eggs skidded precariously, and several slid over the edge to land on the buffet counter. She set the tray down a safe distance from the woman who enjoyed throwing things. "Can I help you?"

"Who are you?" the blonde demanded, her word slurred slightly. She smelled of alcohol with an underlying scent of expensive perfume. Her stiletto heels tapped out a nervous tattoo on the marble floor.

"I'm Lily Carmichmael, one of the owners of Luscious Foods."

"You told me you were Lily Carmichmael," the woman accused Dori pointing a long rose-colored fingernail. Her body swayed.

Great. A drunk.

"No. You asked me if I was the owner of Luscious Foods. I said 'yes.' I'm one of the owners. Lily and I are partners. Who the hell are you?"

The blonde woman lunged unsteadily toward Lily, completely ignoring Dori. "You made me look cheap at the auction. How could you afford that much money? You're a caterer for God's sake."

So this was Muffy. Up close.

Lily exchanged a quick look with Dori. Lily studied the younger woman's face. Her glassy eyes were unfocused. Her perfectly sculptured lips sneered. Her wrinkle-free completion lacked character. Even angry, there was no inner fire. No animation. Dori's assessment of a Barbie doll was deeply accurate on so many levels. How could the passionate Marshall ever have found satisfaction with her?

Alcohol played a part in the woman's actions, but a devious mind lurked behind the picture-postcard appearance. Muffy scanned the room, making Lily suspect that the mannequin enjoyed being the center of attention. Causing a dramatic scene over a lost lover would suit her well. Only Luscious Foods would suffer from adverse publicity. Lily changed tactics.

Leaning toward the vain woman, Lily whispered, "You've got spinach between your teeth."

Muffy's next words were forgotten in her mortification as she closed her mouth and ran her tongue over her teeth searching for the mythical spinach.

Had her cold eyes not dominated her face, Lily might have felt sorry for her. Her confusion gave her an unbalanced appearance. This was the woman who worried Marshall on the night of their first dinner.

Finally, Muffy gave Lily a condescending look and whirled unsteadily on her heels, but before disappearing into the crowd, she turned toward the caterers, adding in a shrill voice, "He's incapable of love, you know. The only thing he cares about is his work with smelly fish. He doesn't even like sex."

In seconds, she was swallowed by the crowd and swept into the foyer. With the drama over the children's library crowd drifted.

"Are you okay?" Lily murmured to her partner.

Dori bobbled her head. "Yeah. She just startled me."

Both women worked to redo the buffet. Dori

picked up the thrown glassware while Lily tossed damaged hors d'oeuvres and added new tarts to fill out the Queen of Hearts' tray. Fresh garnish was added. Green eggs and ham were replenished.

The Romers had disappeared. No doubt searching for a less controversial caterer.

Lily laughed, and Dori looked up from gathering glass shards. "What?"

"Marshall doesn't like sex? He's part mink. I've never known anyone who likes sex more." She grinned to herself. *And he's fused with parts of pony. If ever a man was large and in charge, it was Marshall.*

"Did she offend you?"

"Are you kidding? Look at her. She's every woman I envied in high school. Cheerleader, Homecoming queen and if she wasn't a beauty contestant for her home state, I'd bet she considered it. She's thirty-something, in great shape, perfectly groomed and the man she wants, wants me and it's not some cruel high school joke."

Dori kept her thoughts to herself, but her lips were drawn into a straight line. "How's it going with Marshall?"

Mentioning his name, made her body want to boogaloo to a beat only she heard. "He's been good for my ego. You remember a couple of weeks ago when I told you I wanted a man who wanted to sing when I took off my clothes. Well,

Marshall doesn't sing, but he's so appreciative, it wouldn't surprise me if he'd named each of my breasts."

Even though Dori laughed, she held up a hand in protest. "TMI. What I want to know is how do you feel about him?"

Lily froze. *How did she feel?* "The jury's still out."

The following Monday Marshall pulled into Caroline's driveway, having just returned from a week at the coast. Caroline's car was parked in the garage along with Steven's collection of antique roadsters. They hadn't talked since the party, and he was eager to hear her reaction.

Searching her house, he found her in her bedroom unpacking suitcases.

"Were you gone?" he asked after he greeted her and studied the clutter on the bed.

"We went to Pebble Beach this weekend and got in several rounds of golf. It was great." Caroline eyed his dog. "That dog had better not pee on my carpet."

"She won't." He sensed underlying tension but wasn't sure of the reason. "Did you enjoy the party?"

She looked away. "It was nice."

He sat on the chaise lounge and picked Princess off the floor. The dog immediately took possession of his lap. "Whoa. Damned with faint praise. Why're you unhappy? Did Lily do something to tick you off?"

"Lily isn't the problem. You're the problem," Caroline said looking Marshall in the eye.

"What'd I do?" he asked bewildered.

"I don't understand you at all anymore. First, you buy her an expensive little sissy dog. Steven told me that breed cost over a thousand dollars. Is that true?"

Marshall nodded unsure where she was going with this. "So?"

"Yet, you end up with the sissy dog. Of all the people I've never imagined with a little ankle biter like that, you'd be number one. A man's dog reveals a lot about his character."

"That's right. The more effeminate dog, the more secure the man. In fact, if I could get fur to grow on a marshmallow…"

Caroline's look stopped him from teasing her further.

She began again. "And you arranged for us to have a party that she catered to the tune of ten thousand dollars." She held up her hand before he could say anything. "The party was fun. Her company did a great job. I'd use her again even if she weren't seeing you. Plus you buy her an expensive piece of jewelry." She closed the suitcase and moved it to the floor. A second smaller bag remained on the bed. Caroline opened that and sorted clothes.

"Which she refused and returned to the jeweler," Marshall added.

Caroline stopped folding clothes to stare at her brother. "She returned it?"

Her incredulous expression almost made Marshall laugh. "Why?"

Marshall's jaw twitched. "Because she felt it was an inappropriate gift for our relationship."

"I agree, but I can't believe she returned it."

"You didn't say that at the time."

"Marshall, where are you going with this relationship? Muffy attacked Lily Friday night at the Library Gala. Are you still seeing Muffy? You've always been so careful to avoid the limelight, and suddenly your name is on everyone's lips. I've had four phone calls today about the library thing."

Princess went to the floor as he jerked to his feet. "What do you mean Muffy attacked her?"

"I'm not sure. I've heard the story a couple of different ways. Everyone agrees Muffy was drunk and started throwing dishes at the caterers and screaming about how Lily had ruined her life. Apparently, she thought you were about to marry her. Why would she think that?"

He gritted his teeth. "She's insane. I did

nothing to encourage her to believe we had that kind of relationship. I ended whatever was between us before Lily, even though we were pretty casual."

Caroline shook her head. "Well, she must have misunderstood. Anyway, I'm not sure what happened next. I've heard Lily became physical -- slapping and punching Muffy, who was too drunk to defend herself. But I've also heard that Lily whispered something to her, and she simply left. So I don't know what to believe."

Marshall paced the floor, running his hands through his hair. Women had always understood he wasn't the marrying kind. Where had he gone wrong?

His sister's sympathetic look annoyed him. He had to get out of here. "I guess I need to see Lily."

Caroline fisted her hands on her hips as if determined to get answers from her brother. "What is it you want? Your behavior is completely out of character."

He stuffed his hand in his pockets, then tugged them out to gesture as he spoke. "She affects me differently. I keep thinking we'll be through with each other, but then something else happens. I'm not ready to end it yet."

She narrowed her eyes and gave him a penetrating look he hadn't seen from a woman since his childhood. "Are you prepared to marry her?"

Marshall stared dumbfounded at his sister. "Hell, no."

"Why? Because she doesn't have 'Caudill potential'?" Her look of anger surprised him.

He slowly nodded. "That and we have nothing in common."

She harrumphed. "I think you've got more in common than you realize."

"Think of all the women I've dated, Caroline. Name one of them, who would say no, if I offered a spur-of-the-moment week-long trip to Paris. Even CEOs of large corporations have rearranged their schedules. Not Lily. Her constant refrain is that she has to work. And I haven't even gotten around to a Paris trip, yet."

Caroline smiled for the first time since his arrival. "It's bad when someone else likes her career as well as you like yours."

"Maybe, but I suspect she comes from agrarian stock. Her backyard is one huge vegetable garden. Do you know what she calls it? An edible landscape." Marshall's outrage amused his sister.

"Very trendy," Caroline said.

He crossed his arms over his chest. "Yeah, but I'm not Farmer Brown."

"Is she asking you to be?" Caroline sat on the edge of her bed.

He tossed his hands into the air. "No. And

her house is packed with stuff."

"Marshall, you have empty rooms at your place. Don't tell me that minimalist look is by design. You and I both know that the reason you don't have more things is because it would involve shopping or hiring a decorator, and you'd hate both of those."

Marshall threw down the final bit of incriminating evidence. "She cooks, you know."

"Everyone cooks."

"No, they don't. You don't. You have a housekeeper who cooks. I don't. Most of the women I know understand making reservations, not making dinner."

"The fact that she cooks offends you?"

"It's her house. It always smells like someone's grandmother's house. Not our grandmother, of course, but the grandmothers of fiction. The ones who always have fresh baked chocolate chip cookies and homey advice."

Caroline shook her head. "I had no idea she was that bad. You need to dump her immediately."

Marshall disengaged himself from the bantering and stared at his sister for a long minute before he left the room. The sharp little rat-a-tat-tat of Princess's nails hitting the floor followed him down the stairs and out the door.

Marshall didn't go to see Lily. He discovered he couldn't. Instead, he headed to the airport. Flying helped clear his brain. He needed to step back from this situation to gain perspective on it.

Chapter Sixteen

The heavy rain was typical Portland weather. Finding Lily's house on a street with no roadway lights was difficult. Finally, Marshall located the company van in the driveway next to her dark house.

After considering heading to his loft, he found it had no appeal. Too big. Too empty. Too lonely. Without Lily. This realization offered no happiness. Of all the women he'd known, he remained baffled why he couldn't walk away from this one.

The approaching storm had grounded his plane after only a few hours. He'd spent the rest of the evening driving on country roads, allowing the skills needed to maintain his speed and driving precision to dominate his thinking. Time got away from him, and it was later than he intended.

Setting his bag on the porch he impatiently rang the bell. Princess stamped her paws next to him, less than pleased with the rain.

A hesitant female voice called through the door asking him to identify himself.

"Land Shark," he intoned sounding like a Saturday Night Live character skit. "Candy gram."

"Marshall?" Lily asked.

"Open up, darling, it's wet out here."

Rumpled from a couple of hours sleep, her hair askew, her liquid brown eyes drowsy and inviting, She was the sexiest woman, he had ever seen. And that thought terrified him to the very bottom of his soul because he knew it wasn't his physical reaction that held him in place.

"Marshall," she cried, delighted to see him.

Her unexpected joy warmed him. Without a word of warning, she leaped into his arms causing him to stagger backward a step or two. Hugging her to his chest he gave rein to the passion that had ruled him for the past week. The wall was closer than the floor. He pressed her back against it as her legs slipped into place around his waist. Her long nightgown had climbed above her knees and exposed most of her bare thighs allowing him to slip his hands underneath. Nothing barred his path. What little restraint he might have exercised vanished. For the first time since their initial mating, her needs did not concern him, only his own and what it required to satisfy them.

Neither gentle, kind nor considerate, he moved with necessity. Lily didn't appear to miss his gentleness, for she had none herself. She pulled at his clothes making it clear, she wanted him – now.

A week without her deprived him. Without leaving the foyer with its cool white tile floor Marshall ploughed into her, rough and demanding, his need to possess her brought him only pain until he could be sated.

But his Lily did not back off. She met him with increased demands of her own. Their lovemaking took a savage turn. No longer was it the dance of two experienced partners trying out their learned steps on each other, but rather a battle of passion that ran so deep in both that neither could tell who was the aggressor and who could claim victory at the finish line.

Neither could say exactly how they made it to the floor, but in the end both lay panting for their breath. The remainder of their hastily discarded garments lay in disarray while both gasped for air and sanity in the cool room.

Princess hovered in the living room, crouching behind the chair waiting for her summons. Poor little Princess. They had terrified her. When Marshall struggled to a sitting position, the dog wormed her way between the lovers by crawling belly down wagging her tail forcing the lovers to move apart to protect their faces and exposed body parts from a cold nose, a tiny quick tongue, or the whack of a tail.

Lily rose, collecting clothing. Marshall's suitcases sat on the porch more or less protected from the rain.

"I guess I should apologize," Marshall

groped for the words to explain his insensitive actions.

Lily smile reassured him. "For what? If I recall, I was the one who jumped into your arms. How long can you stay?"

"Thursday morning." Marshall grinned glad she wasn't upset. "God! I've missed you. How busy are you? Do you have any time at all?" He stroked her back, and she arched like a contented cat against him.

"It's a pretty light week. I may be able to spare a little time for a friend," she teased. "If you keep doing that, we'll never get you completely inside."

Princess led the way to the bedroom with Lily and Marshall lagging behind, burdened with loose clothes and luggage.

"I see you still have the dog," Lily pulled a clean nightgown from the drawer.

"You're not going to need that." He tossed the gown on the chair as he encircled her body with his arms. "Princess has been staying at Dead Man's Cove while I traveled, but she's not a beach dog. It turns out, she hates water." He nuzzled her neck.

She trembled, making him want to beat his chest.

"What dog hates water?" Her voice broke on a moan. She pushed his hands away and turned to face him.

"A dog who believes she shouldn't get anything above her knees wet. And you might notice that her knees are close to the ground."

Lily laughed. "I hate to say it, but Princess is a perfect name for that animal." She searched Marshall's face carefully. "You look weary."

"I've had a lot on my mind. But I still think I can find enough energy to make you scream again."

"And they say romance is dead," she murmured as she kissed him a light, friendly kiss. The exhaustion reflected in his face. She coaxed him into bed and snuggled up next to him. Barely had he laid his head on the pillow before he was asleep. Lily lay awake and attempted for the hundredth time to sort out her feelings for him.

Her misgivings about their relationship were numerous. On one hand, she found him to be the epitome of her teenage fantasies about what a boyfriend should be. Tall, handsome, rich, generous, kind, interesting, and sexy, but she wasn't the cookie cutter match. A picture of the two of them had one asking, "What's wrong with this picture" with the obvious answer being her.

The fact that every time they were together, she completely lost control made her wonder if her body knew something her mind didn't. In some ways she knew she loved him as she had never loved anyone before, but it was a relationship that would never work and had no basis in fact other than passion. Passion created a hot fire, but how fast would it burn out?

Three thirty-six. Lily sat straight up in bed staring at the lighted red numbers on the clock as the telephone rang a second time. Lily's apprehension was a tangible thing. Nothing good ever came from a middle-of-the-night phone call. Disaster struck in the darkest hours. Sometimes it was a phone call, but sometimes it was a policeman ringing your doorbell to tell you your husband was dead. She hated the panic created by night bells almost as much as she hated the news it brought.

As though sensing her fright, Marshall rolled over and touched her lightly. "My phone, not yours," he mumbled as he leaned over to grab his cell phone off the nightstand.

Lily looked at Marshall aghast. Did he believe only she got bad news in the middle of the night, that somehow he was exempt? Had his money insulated him from problems? Or had his isolated existence meant that he had no one he'd cared enough about to receive a tragic call in the dark hours of the morning?

Marshall sat upright, propped his body against the smooth wood of the Asian headboard, managing to both answer the phone and offer Lily an arm of comfort at the same time. Lily leaned her head against his shoulder hoping she was over reacting.

His end of the conversation consisted mainly of a series of questions. When? Where? How? Now? Even without the benefit of both sides, she knew her first instinct had been correct. He ended the call by saying, "I'll be there in twenty minutes."

"Muffy's been in a serious car accident," he told her as he hung up the phone. "Either she's on drugs or not thinking clearly because she's insisting I come for her." He slid his arm from behind Lily's head and climbed out of bed. "I gotta go. Caroline gave me a second-hand account of her confrontation with you at the Library. While I'm dressing, why don't you tell me what happened."

Lily hesitated. She hadn't planned to discuss the situation with Marshall. To her, it was over and done, but since he asked, she gave him an abbreviated update.

Marshall buttoned his shirt, a frown furrowed his brow. "So you didn't slap her or touch her in any way?"

"Of course not. Think how that would have affected my business. Believe it or not, I'm a professional," She replied, indignant he could even imagine anything else.

Marshall's face relaxed. "I believe it, sweetheart. I just wanted to make sure I had the facts straight." He leaned down to kiss her. "Okay, if I leave the dog?"

"Uh-huh." Lily stretched out enticingly on the bed. "How do you feel about Muffy?" she asked in a sleepy voice. "Were you engaged to her?"

Marshall's jeans lay open on his hips while he bent over to tie a shoe. He straightened, leaving his shoe undone. "What the hell am I doing? If I hadn't told the doctor that I would come, I'd be crawling back in bed with you. She and I had a few dates, no sex. I don't love her. I never told her I did, and I never proposed. The marriage idea was an invention of her own making."

❖

Ed slouched against the hospital corridor wall, watching his former stepmother, Muffy. Like a queen, she sat on a gurney in the emergency room, her back propped against the wall, issuing orders as a harried doctor wrapped an ace bandage tightly around her sprained ankle. Even at seventeen, Ed had watched his father behavior mimic the doctor. The frustration the doctor barely concealed came directly from a woman who wasn't terribly injured but loved being the center of attention.

The doctor and a nurse helped lower a complaining Muffy into a waiting wheelchair and gestured for Ed. Both medical professionals hurried to their next patient as Ed wheeled her toward the admittance desk. At the end of a long corridor, a tall man glowered at them. Another expression he'd seen on his father's face. But this man was a stranger. Ed swerved the chair to avoid him, Muffy waved a greeting. The fact he scowled didn't bother her at all.

Marshall took in the scene before him and wasn't sure what to make of it. Except for a wrapped ankle, Muffy seemed to have no other notable injuries. In fact, she looked as she always did – perfect – not a blonde hair out of place, fresh lipstick, pristine ivory slacks and matching silk blouse. Her appearance neither reflected the time of night nor the necessity of a hospital visit.

Her face grimaced in pain, but Marshall suspected Muffy enjoyed drama more than most women. How much pain could she be in? Her bandaged foot was elevated, and she was being pushed in a wheelchair. The lanky boy behind her looked genuinely scared, but not hurt.

"How are you?" he asked striving for an even voice as his temper rose.

"Thank goodness, you're here," Muffy gushed. "Eddie's been a rock, but now I can relax." She absently patted Eddie's hand in a casual manner. Her touch made the boy jerk his hand back.

"Uh-hmm. Eddie?" He looked at the teenager. *How the hell had this kid gotten involved?*

"Ed," the boy corrected.

"Ed," Marshall acknowledged with a nod. "Push Muffy over to the admissions desk. They need additional information from her and let's find a pop machine. I'm sure it has been a long night, and everyone could use something cold to drink."

The boy did as requested and then accompanied Marshall down the hall to the vending machines.

"You're the one who called me?" Marshall waited for Ed's reluctant agreement before he continued. "Why'd you tell me you were a doctor?"

He wiped his hands on his jeans avoiding looking at Marshall. "She insisted."

Marshall dug change out of his pocket for the machine. "Tell me what happened."

"Wet streets." The boy shrugged. "She went around a corner, lost control of her car and slammed into a telephone pole." Ed gave his speech by rote like he'd recited it a dozen times and probably had.

"Are you injured?" Marshall wondered if the boy's nervousness was due to fear or the situation.

"No." Ed hung his head refusing to meet Marshall's eyes.

"You're sure? Sometimes we think everything's okay and then later, various parts of our body hurt." Marshall gentled his voice.

Ed visibly relaxed. "Yeah, my arm's been sore for the last hour. I think it hit the door."

"Did you have the doctor look at it?"

"One of the nurses did. She said it was just bruised.

"Choose something." Marshall gestured toward the machine. "Why were you with her?"

Ed's eyes darted back to the admission's desk before he looked back at the man in front of him. He shrugged.

"There's no right or wrong answer here. Only the truth. I'd like to know what really happened."

Ed studied Marshall's face before he spoke. "She used to be my stepmother. My dad's away on a fishing trip, and I was the only one home. My dad's always telling me I gotta be nice to her 'cause she's sick. Anyway, she called and begged me to meet her. I go 'no,' but she threatened to kill herself. What could I do?" He ran a distressed hand through his already rumpled hair.

Ed studied the pop machine for several seconds, as though the selection was so all-encompassing, choosing overwhelmed him. Finally, he pushed a button, and the sound of metal against metal was heard as the drink clunked to the bottom. Marshall inserted more money and chose a diet drink for Muffy while he listened to the boy's explanation.

"We drove around with her talking mainly to herself, sort of ranting, 'til she found some dark street. No streetlights or nothin'. Then she drove real slow down this street until she came to a house with a silver Mercedes parked behind a van in the driveway. Apparently the owner of the Mercedes is supposed to marry her except she thinks he's seeing another woman. She's real angry then and goes 'knock on the door' but it was three in the morning."

Marshall steeled his face to be expressionless while inwardly he reeled. Muffy spied on him. In failing to deal with her, he had put Lily in harm's way. This had to stop tonight. Ed appeared relieved at telling the entire story. Marshall bet his stepmother had controlled every sentence this boy had uttered.

"All I could see was that someone was going to get hurt. So I go 'no' making her real mad. Finally, she popped the car into gear and floored it. When we took the corner, she lost control and crashed into the pole. On the way to the hospital, she demanded I call you. She goes 'he won't come unless you tell him you're a doctor.'"

Muffy's assessment was probably correct.

Her manipulative behavior astounded him. Lily thought Marshall had stalked her. This was stalking -- complete with sinister motives.

He worked hard to keep emotion out of his voice. Ed was just a kid, an innocent victim. Marshall didn't want to upset him anymore than he already was. "Ambulance or did she drive?"

"Ambulance. Her car's a mess."

"I'm going to take you home. Here's my card," he said digging one out of his wallet. "Have your dad call me when he gets home. I know he'd tell you the same thing – don't ever get in a car with her driving again. I don't care what she tells you."

Ed's look assured Marshall that wouldn't be happening anytime soon.

The car ride was a nightmare. Ed didn't comment when they got into Marshall's silver Mercedes.

Muffy chattered gaily, her tittering giggle punctuating her sentences. Apparently, she was convinced that whatever problems they'd had were all in the past.

Marshall was silent, painfully reminded of why he had decided not to see this woman again, even before Lily became a motivating factor. Her obliviousness to all the havoc she wrecked in other people's lives astounded him.

Marshall waited until Ed was inside. As he eased the car into gear and pulled away from the curb, he asked, "All right, what's this all about?"

Muffy turned in the seat faced him. "What do you mean? Who else would I call when I was in a car accident?"

Marshall kept his eyes on the wet roadway, not wanting to look in her direction.

"Not me. Muffy, we're not dating anymore. What were you doing driving around in the middle of the night anyway?"

The rising sun gave a pink haze to the morning air. Most mornings he loved the dawn. Particularly at the coast. He wished he were there now.

"I couldn't sleep," she said.

Marshall didn't have to look to hear the pout in her voice.

"I knew you still cared about me. Why else would you have come?"

Marshall gritted his teeth and didn't spout the obvious answer. Instead, he asked, "Why was the boy with you?"

"Are you jealous over Eddie? He's been going through some tough times at school. I was married to his father, and he still misses me."

"Jealous? No, I'm just amazed that you would have him lie to me by telling me he was a doctor and that you were more seriously hurt than you are."

Marshall glanced at Muffy before he refocused on the road. How could he have ever thought this loon was attractive?

"Oh, Marshall, he's just a kid. There's no need for you to worry. As for the phone call, he made that up on his own."

At her house, he carefully backed into her driveway getting as close as he could to her back steps.

As he walked around the car, he took several deep breaths hoping to calm himself into having a rational discussion with her. Muffy raised her arms to put around his neck so he could lift her into his arms.

"I'm not carrying you. You're going to have to hobble."

"Marshall," she said plaintively.

"Here, stand up." He ignored her.

Muffy, seeing no other alternative, did as he ordered.

He helped her hop up the three steps despite her pitiful grousing every step of the way. Tall women had always drawn his attention, now he found her height irritating. He could feel her ribcage through her thin blouse and found himself thinking about Lily's appealing soft curves.

In her kitchen, Marshall gestured for her to sit at the table. From the freezer, he pulled out a bag of frozen peas and placed them on her elevated ankle.

"This will reduce the swelling."

"The doctor told me I couldn't play tennis

for at least three weeks. I'll be so out of shape by then I'll never win again."

Marshall doubted it. Her competitiveness was legendary. What Marshall had failed to realize until this moment was that she had no compunction about going after anything she wanted, not just on the sport's field, but in life as well.

"With a little practice you'll be victorious again in no time," he assured her. "Keep those peas on your ankle."

"There're cold," Muffy whined. "I'm having such a terrible week. Did your girlfriend tell you, she beat me up at the Library Gala?"

"What happened?" Marshall kept his anger tamped. It was only fair he heard both sides. Even before she opened her mouth, he expected spin. Did she lie all the time? Or was she life so convoluted she couldn't tell the different. He still had to figure out how to get her permanently over this marriage idea.

"I wandered into the Children's Library," Muffy sighed and laid the back of her hand across her forehead. "I had no idea who the food service people were. Suddenly from out of nowhere she screams at me like a banshee, telling me to get out. I was so stunned I couldn't move until she hit me. She got in a couple of good punches. I was too shocked to defend myself. So I left. Several of my friends saw me right afterward. They'll verify my story. But Marshall, you need to be careful. Not only is she crazy, she's mean. And her food looked awful. Can you imagine, she served these weird looking green deviled eggs like the hundred-and-fifty-dollar entrance ticket was for a wienie roast," Muffy smoothed her hair and glanced at her appearance in the reflective toaster. Her lips curled in a pleasant look.

Marshall couldn't take his gaze off this woman who operated in a different dimension. The more she talked, the more likely it was that his head would explode. How had he missed her craziness?

Neither subtle nor blunt had worked with her. Now he needed to be as manipulative as she was.

"We need to talk about us." He knelt beside her. She laid her head on his shoulder and clasped his hand with her own.

He stared at their intertwined fingers. "We can't get married. I've been single so long that I've gotten too old and set in my ways."

Muffy tucked her head, but Marshall slid his finger under her chin and raised it until her gaze met his.

"You need someone who's in town. I'm gone all the time. Who would you call then? Find a man worthy of you, someone, who will be here for you and treat you the way you deserve to be treated. You'd end up hating me, and I'd couldn't stand that."

Shock was written all over her face. She dropped her leg and pivoted to face him, the bag of peas and her ankle long forgotten. "Don't be ridiculous. We're meant for each other. I've even found a house for us. You're going to love it. It's located in the West Hills and has a charming view of the Willamette River and the Portland skyline. A pretty Dutch Colonial with…."

Marshall gently placed his fingers across her lips. "Shhh. Shhh. Muffy, I can't marry you." He spoke to her like a young child who simply didn't understand.

Her face was a study in panic. He could almost see her mind whirling as to how make this work. "Marshall, don't leave. Spend the night. You'll see how compatible we are."

He pulled out all the stops. "No. You've got to find someone new. It's not you, Muffy, it's me. I'm not worthy of you."

He winced as he spoke the trite words, but she accepted them. She sagged against his body unable to move for several minutes. Finally, he disengaged himself.

Wearily, she studied him. "With a little work on your part, you could be the right man."

"Never. I've long accepted that I'll never be the right man for any woman long term. It's not in me. You're still young, and, God knows, you're beautiful. There are plenty of men out there who would worship the ground you walk on for the opportunity to be your husband."

Muffy nodded her easy agreement at that assessment allowing him to make his getaway. He didn't return to Lily's. Too exhausted and disgusted after dealing with Muffy. Why was she unable to hear the truth?

Chapter Seventeen

After he'd slept a few hours, he phoned Lily mid-morning to get a read on her schedule. "How do you feel about dinner tonight? I haven't had Caroline and Steven to dinner for a while."

"At your place?" Her voice sounded distracted.

"We could do that. Should we order delivery from a restaurant?"

"Marshall, I cook." The indignation in her voice told him he'd misjudged the situation and was appalled he would consider ordering from a to-go menu.

He wanted her to enjoy herself not have a busman's holiday "That'll be like you're the caterer."

"Even caterers have dinner parties." Lily's voice changed, and Marshall suspected she was already in menu-planning mode. "Can you grill steaks or chicken?"

"Yeah." He hoped that was true. He could grill, but was it good enough for a professional? Lily may have been easy-going about some things – food he sensed was not one of them.

"Good. You can grill the meat, and I'll work

on the rest of the meal. It'll be simple, but a meal we can do together. It's always better to experiment on family anyway."

He grinned. "It doesn't sound like we'll be doing a lot of experimenting."

"Oh yeah! Two people in a kitchen who haven't worked together we're talking lots of experimenting."

She delighted him. The idea of intimate dinner parties in his home opened up a whole new concept for him.

Caroline called Steven at work to discuss the invitation. "So they're still an item?" Steven commented. His attention wandered to the file folder on his desk.

"More than an item. Marshall's infatuated with her, he just hasn't figured it out yet." Caroline laughed.

Steven stopped flipping through his paperwork to listen to his wife. "Really?"

"Apparently, Lily's led Marshall on a merry chase. She's even convinced him, he could grill, so they're cooking. I think Marshall's soon going to be desperate enough to ask Lily to marry him."

He scratched his jaw. "They haven't seen each other long enough. He's never rushed to the altar before." Steven pondered the news.

"You sound surprised."

Steven listened to his wife's voice and wondered what was bothering her. She was laughing, but she wasn't happy. "Do you think it's a good match?" he asked.

"I don't know. Lily's pretty independent. Her lifestyle's very different from his. We've heard that she works all the time. That could be a problem." Caroline seemed to be sorting through her thinking as she talked. "The thing that really bothers me the most is that... well, she's old."

Nothing she could have said would have surprised her husband more. "Why do you think that? Would you prefer he dated twenty-year-olds?"

"No, but there are a lot of ages in-between twenty and however old she is, but I would guess at least forty-three or forty-four, that might provide him with a wife capable of more domestic--" she paused "--enterprises."

Steven didn't say anything. He waited patiently. And after a minute or two she blurted out, "It worries me that she's too old to have children."

Steven nodded slowly, knowing she couldn't see it over the phone. "So you think she's too much of a career woman and too old to start a family to make him happy?"

"He doesn't realize his need to have children, yet," she said. "But eventually he will and then who will carry on the Caudill name?"

Steven grimaced. He preferred to forget his father-in-law's theme on the Caudill lineage. Had Steven not been a Zonnheiser, Henry Caudill would have never agreed to Steven's marrying his daughter. Henry hadn't given a rip whether Steven loved Caroline. His parental concerns had been devoted to Steven's social status and income potential.

"I hadn't noticed that Marshall was overly fond of kids. While he loves our kids, I never thought he was attached to any of his girlfriend's children."

Caroline paused. "Maybe that's not it either. I hate the fact that we don't know her. She doesn't run in our circle of friends and isn't a member of any of the things we are. This is moving too fast to suit me."

"When we see them together tonight, I'm sure that'll answer some of the questions." Steven heard his wife sigh as he continued. "I can't remember Marshall ever inviting us to dinner at his home before. Restaurants and clubs, yes. But a home meal and he's grilling? I think we might consider that dried up, old, hardworking Lily may be the best thing that's ever happened to Marshall. She may be causing him actually to work to keep up with her."

Marshall envisioned the menu being fairly simple. Steak, baked potatoes, green salad. Upon Lily's arrival, he quickly realized that nothing could be farther from the truth. Lily didn't understand the concept of a simple meal. Everything food related was a showcase of her abilities.

The simple barbecue dinner consisted of a mixed grill of lamb skewers threaded through rosemary stems marinated in garlic, herbs and olive oil, turkey basil sausage stuffed in sweet onions crowns, shrimp, and steak. Marshall hoped he was up to the grilling task.

In addition, there was a pesto, tomato and fresh mozzarella salad, garlic mashed potatoes, sugar snap peas and bread pudding with a cinnamon crème anglais. Marshall considered teasing her about the quantity of food but decided against it. If the grilling didn't work, at least they would still have plenty of food. The shaped dough was going into the oven for fresh baked bread when Steven and Caroline arrived.

Steven and Caroline were easy people to entertain. Marshall opened the wine.

"How's your grilling?" Marshall asked Steven when Lily and Caroline were out of earshot.

He could have sworn his brother-in-law

looked happy at his situation. "Do you need help?"

Marshall rolled his eyes. *How had he gotten into this?* "Probably. Lily's standards are pretty high."

Steven did laugh this time. "So it'll be two of us getting into trouble, not just one? I don't know that I'm up to a professional critique."

Marshall poured the wine. "Me, either."

He and Steven studiously placed the meat on the grill. Marshall couldn't remember being under such a burden from another woman.

Steven stared at the horizon. "Lily's a lot of fun. Different from other women you've dated." His voice was thoughtful and held that far-away quality he had when he discussed a point of law.

Marshall glanced at his boyish-faced brother-in-law to see if he was joking. Apparently, Steven wasn't feeling the pressure Marshall was under.

"Yeah," Marshall said struggling with the lamb. "These skewers are so flimsy. I'm afraid they're going to fall apart over the flame."

"Not a skewer, that's rosemary. These should taste great, I can't wait to try them."

Marshall looked at his brother-in-law. "You're such a Renaissance man, Steven. How do you know about everything? Lawyers are supposed to have tunnel-vision."

Steven chuckled, turning his attention to the grill. "You, two, are hitting it off."

Marshall watched the flames leap up around the oil drippings. "Okay, I think we need to move the lamb over. She warned me this would happen."

Both men worked with tongs shifting the meat to the outside edge of the grill. Marshall stopped for a moment and stared over the balcony at the city skyline. "What's with you and Caroline?" he asked. "Every time I turn around you're making plans for me."

"No, we're not. Lily's different from the numerous women you've dated in the past. We're curious. That's all."

"No. You may only be curious, but Caroline believes there is more going on. Marriage is not on the agenda."

Steven's head popped up as his face turned thoughtful. "Marriage? You're thinking of marrying her?"

Marshall slapped his forehead. "I'm not. Are you this dogmatic during a cross-examination?"

His brother-in-law shrugged. "I don't do trial work. There's an investigator in my office. We could run a background check on her if you'd like."

"On Lily? Why? What do you think she's after? Everything I give her, she returns," Marshall groused. "If I asked her to marry me, she'd probably refuse."

If he'd thought the other man was intense before, the look he received was truly that of a lawyer at work. "Why?"

Why? He shook his head. "She's not the marrying type."

"Meaning?"

"Her career comes first. She loves her house and her yard. She works every weekend. She doesn't even have time for a dog, much less me."

"If you're serious about asking her, let me draw up a prenup."

Marshall had been lost in his thoughts. He laughed harshly at the lawyer's words. "That'll encourage her. Particularly when I add, I'm not prepared to share all my worldly goods. Did you and Caroline sign a prenup?"

Steven's laugh sounded more embarrassed than mirthful. "Caroline was furious at me and had started dating someone else. I was terrified I was going to lose her." He exhaled.

Marshall waited. He'd never seen the other man even anxious. This was new territory.

"I refused to consider it. Both sets of parents wanted it. But, Marshall, if Caroline left me tomorrow, she could take everything because my life wouldn't be worth living without her. She and the kids are so much more important to me than anything we own."

Marshall almost swallowed his tongue. He had no idea, Steven felt that way about his sister. How had his sister managed to marry a man who adored her and met the Caudill qualifications? Lucky, lucky her. But as joyous as it made him, he also realized another truth.

"I wish I felt like that about Lily, but I don't."

Steven chuckled. "When I married Caroline I didn't feel that way either. I only knew living without her was impossible. But after Brandon and Michael were born, I looked up one day and realized if she left me, I'd cease to exist. Love grows. You're dating a gardener, I'll bet she knows how to nurture people as well as plants."

Marshall added the shrimp to the grill and moved the meat.

Steven had long since given up any pretense of caring about the food and lounged against the wall with his arms folded. "What are you going to do?"

Marshall said nothing. *What was there to do?*

His brother-in-law had a few more words of advice. "It's been my experience that indecisiveness rarely wins the day. If this is what you want, you need to go get it. And let me assure you, marriage is going to mean some compromises on your part as well as hers. She alone is not going to give up her career, her house, and her life to work with your plan."

Marshall removed the meat from the grill. "Yeah, well that's easier said than done."

Caroline helped in the kitchen although Lily was so efficient there wasn't much to do. Lily asked a lot of questions about Caroline's children. While Caroline was forthcoming with answers, she knew they were skirting the real issue.

The oven timer dinged. Lily removed the bread.

Caroline cautioned herself to go easy. "Marshall seems happy, don't you think?"

Lily's attention was on the potatoes. "I think so. He loves being challenged, and his career is certainly providing that."

A smile she couldn't hold back had her grinning. Lily might as well know now that Caroline was no fool. "I think he finds you a challenge, too."

Lily laughed. "Perhaps." She disappeared through the door with the potatoes.

When she returned, Caroline tried another direction. "I heard about Muffy and the library."

Lily simply shrugged. "Muffy was drunk. I doubt if sober she would have even said anything. She's an attractive woman who'll find another man soon and Marshall will be completely forgotten."

"Do you think that's how it works?" Caroline considered her divorced friends who were frustrated in their search for a second or third husband.

"When the time is right, fate takes a hand.

What's supposed to happen, will."

Well, that was an interesting take on it. "Do you think fate is the reason you and Marshall are together?"

Lily shrugged. "I don't know, but we didn't plan it. We're probably close enough that we can slice the bread. Why don't you go ahead? I don't think it'll make any difference." Lily selected a serrated knife and handed it to Caroline.

"Thick slices will be easier since it's still warm."

Caroline didn't want to be direct, but she wasn't getting the answers she wanted. In her frustration, she hacked at the bread. "Just between us, how do you feel about him?"

Lily shook her head. "I'm torn between being crazy about him," she admitted, "and wanting to run the other way as fast as I can."

Caroline said nothing.

The glass door opened. The men's voices could be heard in the distance as they triumphantly returned with the meat.

Leather covered books lined the shelves of the lawyer's office. Oversized, framed degrees hung on the wall behind the massive desk. Two armchairs sat in front of the desk. Muffy positioned herself in one facing the young lawyer. According to the wall behind him, he was barely three years out of law school.

Books always gave Muffy a comfortable feeling, as though the person in charge of those books was also blessed with all the knowledge contained within.

The young lawyer, named Bryce, smiled encouragingly.

She remembered it all quite distinctly as she related the details to him. The late night accident in her car had been caused by food poisoning from the Library event. She'd been sick all weekend.

Luscious Foods had poisoned her and caused her vehicle insurance to increase. It was only right that she file a lawsuit against such a negligent company.

Bryce was just starting his practice. Muffy had taken great care in picking him, and he proved to be quite malleable.

By the end of the meeting, her new lawyer was suitably outraged. Not only by her pain and suffering, but by the caterer's callous disregard for their clients' safety.

The fact that Luscious Foods was a big-name catering company with more than adequate insurance didn't hurt either.

Bryce's open, appreciative appraisal of her renewed her confidence. Marshall had been a fool to let her go.

And that witch, Lily Carmichael, would see

just how fast Marshall would leave her, once she had legal troubles. The accident had prevented any late night drive-byes, so maybe Marshall was already seeing someone else. Several weeks had passed since the auction. Marshall's relationships had never included longevity.

And once he'd dumped Lily, she would devote herself to seeing that no one used her catering company again.

Chapter Eighteen

Marshall couldn't believe she's joined him at the coast. The past few weeks with her had been some of the most satisfying he could remember. Tonight, he'd wined and dined her. And in a show of gallantry, aided by sufficient alcohol, he carried her up the stairs to his bedroom.

He would not be rushed. Savoring every inch of her starting with her toes, he sucked and bit and nuzzled his way to her knee and then began on the other leg. Lily's hips bucked in invitation as she gasped and panted. She begged and pleaded, but he ignored her, wanting to explore all of her. Their natures were so similar that each drove the other higher until both were insane.

Finally, his mouth reached the adjunct of her legs. His tongue licked the swollen outer folds. Lily squirmed and trembled unable to control her response. As his tongue found her most sensitive spot, he could feel the ripple of electric passion wash over her.

Even though he was rock hard and his demons were pleading for release, he was determined to take his time.

But with Lily there was no slow and easy. It was all hard and fast. Even this fight, he lost. Tying and blindfolding her had only made her wilder. While she'd always been responsive, she'd never begged or demanded like she did now.

"Please, Marshall, help me," her voice verged on hysteria, her actions uncoordinated and frantic.

"Okay, baby, hang on, just a little longer." He could hold back no longer. Rising above her, he stroked her juicy mound. So wet. So hot. So welcoming. All for him. No one else. His.

His voiced rumbled low in her ears. "I can't stand not being inside you."

"Now," she demanded as she raised her knees to cushion him. Her head tossed from side to side. Her hips thrust continually against his hand, demanding action.

"What do you want, Lily. Tell me," he commanded her, managing to hold back a little longer.

"You. I want you," she pleaded.

"You've got me. Feel me." He pressed against her. "You've got me here, now."

"No. More. Inside me. Now." She was wild, untamed, and needy. "More. More. More. Now."

"Like this?" He entered her in one long push. Both moaned with a pleasure so intense that it edged on pain as he filled her. Her velvet sheath enclosed him like a warm mitten.

"Again," she insisted when she could speak.

"Tell me what you want." He pushed at her, overwhelming her with his urgency as he plunged into her again. "Tell me."

"You. Only you." Her carnal response thrilled him, but he needed her completely. Not just her body. He needed…

"Tell me what I want to hear." He pumped into her, driving her hard, making her as crazed as he was. "You know what I need, baby, give it to me. Tell me."

"Harder. Faster. Now." She garbled incoherently.

"Tell me. Come on, sweetheart. Tell me, now." Sweat rolled down his back. The jackhammer motion of his body was met stroke after stroke by hers moving in tandem with him.

They were so close. He could feel her unravel. He pushed again. "Lily. Now. Tell me."

"I love you," she screamed.

"Again. Tell me again," he demanded knowing she was beyond comprehension.

"I love you." She burst into tears and came apart in his arms. Unable to hold back, he followed her into oblivion.

The next morning, Lily slept late. Stretching she found herself to be sore in places she'd never imagined. Marshall's side of the bed was cold, indicating his long absence.

Naked, she crawled out of the bed and wobbled to the door. The morning breath and unsteady feet were the least of her problems.

Her eyes burned with each blink, either from too much alcohol or lack of sleep. But all of her body's complaints were negligible because for the first time in her life, her heart zinged with a happiness that if she'd had any energy at all would have had her dancing across the floor. Opening the door to yell down for coffee service, she stopped when male voices drifted up to her from the kitchen below.

He was not alone. Quietly, she stood in the open doorway. Cool air rushed into the room as the muffled voices drifted up to her. The words eluded her.

Josh had arrived sometime earlier. Easing the door shut, she headed for the bathroom. With her eyes closed the hot running water washed away the exhaustion of the previous night's activities.

As life returned to her weary limbs her mind lingered on her last night's exploits. Blindfolded sex exhilarated her. The wave of fire Marshall's touch created left her trembling. Who knew kinky would turn her on? In forty-four years, she'd finally let herself go into a free fall – no control, no safety net and it was the most intense moment of her life. For the first time, she felt free and unafraid. For the first time, she was confident someone was there to catch her.

Climbing out of the shower, the floor length

mirror reflected a body she scarcely recognized. Her breasts and neck had bite marks; red lines from his fingernails marked her thighs and back. Lily wasn't fooled, Marshall had a good as tattooed her, marking her, making sure that everyone who saw her knew she belonged to him. At least until he tired of her.

Josh and Marshall looked up expectantly as she entered the kitchen. No one mentioned her choice of long pants and a high neck shirt. Instead, Marshall offered her a mug of coffee and a warm smile.

Josh could hardly wait for her to sit before he announced his news. "MIT wants us to test the next generation of AUVs in Australia's Great Barrier Reef. Isn't that great?" He could hardly remain seated his excitement was so overwhelming.

Marshall's dignity was under control, but his dancing eyes and barely suppressed grin told how he truly felt. Whatever this meant, it was a big deal.

Lily swallowed as realization dawned on her. Marshall was going to Australia. Her heart skipped a beat as she felt a moment of panic. Forcing a smile, she agreed. "Fabulous. What are AUVs?"

"A motorized underwater vehicle. Small, compact, economical. They've been around since the 90s, but each generation brings revolutionary changes. No cables, tethers or remote controls, but able to reach areas we've been unable to explore." Josh began to sketch a drawing for her on a piece of paper as Lily watched over his shoulder. As she snuck a peek at Marshall, he appeared lost in thought jotting notes on a legal pad.

Josh continued. "We've got to be there by Wednesday."

"How long will you be gone?" she asked, afraid of the answer.

"About six weeks," Josh said. "It's the break we've been needing. If everything works, we'll be frontrunners in deep water exploration. And the Great Barrier Reef will add international exposure."

How could Lily not be happy for them? Perhaps happy wasn't the first emotion she felt, but even above her petty selfishness, she truly wanted Marshall's happiness.

"I've got to call my folks," Josh said, jumping off the barstool. "Great to see you, Lily."

"You, too, Josh."

Marshall puttered at the kitchen counter. Not trusting her voice, Lily didn't feel she could offer heartfelt congratulations when what she wanted was to scream in frustration. Never had she kidded herself into thinking their relationship was long term, but she hadn't expected it to be ripped out from under her so soon. Six weeks was as good as forever with a man like Marshall. By the time he returned there would probably be a little Down Under Sheila on his arm.

He might even call her for a quick toss in the hay if he was particularly horny. But that would be worse than anything she could imagine. Sort of a marine biologist/rock star groupie thing. "Got an itch, babe, you wanna scratch it? No? Not a problem, there are others waiting. Catch you later." Okay, Marshall wouldn't be so flippant, but the result would be the same. The relationship was over.

Marshall handed her a travel mug. "Let's go for a walk along the beach."

Coming out of her musing she took the mug. He hadn't left her yet. Lily focused her attention on the drink. Letting him see how his leaving affected her would not be good.

A walk on the beach sounded great, but she wasn't as sure her sore body would agree. And the thought of climbing back up that rocky incline made her shudder. Maybe she should suggest a less aerobic activity, but she kept her mouth closed and followed him out the door. Instead of going toward the coastline he headed for his car. Opening the passenger's side door, he helped her inside.

Lily watched the compound fade away as he drove down the beach highway. She concentrated on remaining calm, so he wouldn't know how dejected she felt about his leaving. But she shouldn't have worried, Marshall's mind was thousands of miles away. No doubt on a sandy Australian beach.

He turned onto another road that headed west. "Easier place to walk," he said as he parked the car. She nodded and offered him a half smile. She could control her emotions. She could.

The sweet hot beverage, she expected to be coffee, wasn't. "What's this?" she asked.

"Coffee," he said, but before she could question him, added, "And Baileys. We were out of cocoa."

The sand was smooth on the isolated beach. They walked in silence for quite a distance passing only a few other early morning walkers and dogs out for a run. Occasionally, Lily would stop to pick at a rough spot in the sand to discover a perfect sand dollar or an unusual stone.

Delighted with her find, she showed Marshall, who merely said, "We'll dry it out when we get back," and returned to his own musing.

'Australia's going to be great, isn't it?" she asked in an attempt to start a conversation.

When Marshall failed to respond, she called

his name.

"I'm sorry, what did you say? I was thinking about something else."

"That's okay. It wasn't important."

A short time later, she darted closer to the water to discover a starfish. When she returned to show Marshall, he was staring off into the distance, waiting in a distracted manner.

Together they ambled and watched the waves surge foaming whitecaps onto the sand. No further conversation passed between them. Every so often, Lily would find another treasure and add it to her growing collection crowding the pockets of her jacket.

The closer they came to returning to the car, the more she tried not to think about what his behavior meant.

She loved him. He was moving on.

"Where does this leave us, Marshall?" Lily threw her bag into the car. She couldn't go without knowing.

"This is work. Did you think I wouldn't go?"

Lily forced a smile. "No. I knew you'd leave."

"It'll only be a few weeks. I'll email you." Marshall kissed her forehead. His preoccupied manner shook her up.

Lily groped for words. Nothing came. She had to leave before she started crying. "Okay." She climbed into the driver's seat.

In her rearview mirror, she could see him

standing on the porch watching her as she drove out of the compound.

Lily tried not to think about the fact that loving Marshall was one-sided. His response to her had never changed. What had she expected? For him, she remained only a pleasant diversion. There was no way to avoid heartbreak now.

Marshall sat strapped into the seat on the small jet staring out the window. There was nothing to see; the sky was black. His reflection in the glass looked back at him, providing a certain tranquility he didn't feel.

Josh watched a movie next to him, wearing earphones and occasionally laughing out loud. Other than that the jet was quiet. Usually, he preferred to sit in the cockpit with the other pilot, but tonight he'd requested a co-pilot other than himself.

Over and over Marshall replayed his and Lily's last weekend together.

I love you, Marshall.

Would she have said it if he hadn't pushed her? Was it the truth? Or simply a moment of uncontrolled passion? Why had he pushed her so? Why had he needed to hear it?

I love you, Marshall.

Then the next day the distance between them was palpable. What had happened? Maybe she hadn't known how to retract her words? Certainly their parting had been tepid.

"I'll email you from Australia."

"Okay."

Okay?

What kind of response was okay? It certainly wasn't the passionate 'I love you, Marshall' or even 'expect to hear back from me'. Just 'okay'. If she'd been younger, it would have ranked right up there with 'whatever'.

Maybe going to Australia was what he needed. A little distance to gain some perspective, but he refused to accept that.

No, what he wanted was to see her and work this out. Not be separated by an entire ocean.

Closing his eyes, he began to drift off to sleep with Lily still on his mind.

I love you, Marshall, she whispered.

Chapter Nineteen

"You're the only person I know who consistently comes back from a vacation looking like hell," Dori commented as she sat down at Lily's worktable the following Monday morning.

Lily felt worse than her appearance indicated, which was saying something. Her mirror had shown her pale cheeks and listless eyes. "I think I'm coming down with the flu. This morning I was dizzy and nauseated. I'm so tired I can hardly see straight. And what is that dreadful stench coming from the kitchen?" Lily leaned back in her chair.

Dori sniffed the air. "You are sick if the smell of caramelized onions is bothering you."

Lily felt Dori's cool fingers on her forehead testing for fever.

"I need to make a doctor's appointment. I can't get the flu now."

"Mid-summer's hardly flu season, so it might be something else. Lots of things start out feeling like the flu. Are you up to working this morning or do you want to go home?"

"I've had too much time off. Let's work, but shut the damn door. The odors coming from the kitchen are churning my stomach."

Dori did as requested. On the way back to her seat, she asked. "How was the beach?"

"I don't know." Lily frowned into her cup of coffee.

"You don't know? Should I call someone else for this information? What happened?"

Lily was still working out the details for herself. "Everything was going great until yesterday morning. Josh showed up with the news they'd been selected to test some equipment in Australia for six weeks. Suddenly, Marshall couldn't wait to get rid of me. We took a last walk on the beach, but Marshall might as well have already left town for as little conversation as he managed to dredge up."

Lily sighed. "It was just so weird. You know how a goodnight kiss can be awkward after a first date, especially when you know you'll never see that person again. It was kind of like that. So, it's over. He'll email me a couple of times out of politeness or duty or something, and that'll be it. The whole thing was like a fireworks display, burning fast and bright and then nothing, but it was great when the sparks were flying."

"I'm sorry."

"For what? That it's over? We all knew it was short term. Marshall got me out of the rut I'd been in since Charlie's death. That was the point, wasn't it? He was great. Now it's time to get back to work."

Dori hesitated, then said, "Well, aren't you lucky that we're jam-packed for the next few weeks. By the time he gets back you'll probably already have forgotten him."

The lie was designed to comfort her and meant nothing. But both nodded their heads in agreement to avoid acknowledging Lily's broken heart.

Lily threw herself into work, taking on more clients. The schedule had already been tight before she added new jobs each day. The kitchen staff groused under the workload, but no one challenged her. She was short-tempered with those who crossed her. Before long everyone backed off and left her alone.

Each morning began early and ended at midnight or later. Too exhausted to go home, Lily spent one night on the office couch. Sunday had managed to slip under her radar, and they had a day without any events scheduled combined with a light Monday and Tuesday, allowing her staff to breathe a collective sigh of relief.

Dori forced Lily to stay home on Sunday to give everyone a break. But instead of sleeping late, Lily sat in her kitchen sipping tea and nibbling dry toast. Her stomach felt better, but this was the third day in a row she'd been sick. She'd hidden it at work, but it worried her. Her doctor's appointment wasn't until Tuesday.

Oh, Lord! Don't let this be what she thought it was. The previous evening on her way home from a late evening, she forced herself to stop at a 24-hour pharmacy. Now she waited for the test results to develop. Maybe it was just a light touch of food poisoning. If her breasts hadn't been so tender, she might even have believed it.

The timer above her stove dinged. Lily shut it off as she walked down the hall to the bathroom. Death row inmates moved more eagerly than she did.

The details turning over in her mind refused to form an acceptable solution. Pregnancy wasn't an option. True, they hadn't used birth control, but at forty-four, a woman who had hot flashes and night sweats was beyond the age of conception. Wasn't she?

Fifteen years with Charlie hadn't produced any children. But Marshall operated with an entirely different gene structure. Everything else about him was potent, why wouldn't his sperm be?

The testing wand's answer was definitive. Pregnant. With that knowledge her legs gave way, her head spun and her heart raced. To avoid falling, she staggered to the toilet to plop down on the closed seat. Resting her forehead on her knees she grunted in misery.

Why now? Why me? How would she tell Marshall?

"I know you didn't want to see me again, but guess what? You're going to be a father. Choosing what was behind door number two was to be a mistake. You should have just taken my heart and run."

No good. She gave her heart away. Letting him see it would just cause her more misery. She staggered down the hall and stretching out on her bed.

What if she didn't tell Marshall? If he didn't call when he returned, it wouldn't even be an issue. Women had babies alone all the time. She could do this.

Dori's reaction, however, would not be so easy. Her pregnancy could be the proverbial straw. Dori would want to sell for sure now.

But even if Dori had changed her mind and wanted to keep the business, having a partner too fat and slow to help wouldn't delight her. Lily did the nine-month math on her fingers. She wouldn't be too fat until after Christmas when they were slow anyway. Maybe if she had the baby in March and was back to work by next May or June when Luscious Foods started getting busy again, it could work. She'd just have to put the baby on a strict schedule.

Marshall probably wouldn't call her anyway if his emails were any indication. It wasn't as if she was looking for X-rated, but his sounded more like they were from a polite stranger. He was definitely moving on.

She closed her eyes and drifted off to hide in sleep.

Australia was a whirlwind of activity. From the moment, the plane set down in Brisbane, Marshall and Josh were thrown into the busy routine.

The Aussie group was young and eager, but inexperienced and unprepared for a project of this scale, which was even greater than Marshall had envisioned. In addition to The Great Barrier Reef, testing was scheduled for the Bass Strait and the deep ports of Western Australia.

MIT's equipment was still in transit. Marshall inwardly seethed. Josh's information had been that the testing was ready now -- not in a week or a month. MIT should have been arriving at the same time.

But the delay was needed to set up the additional testing sites and formulate the data for each dive. The Aussies bubbled over with enthusiasm leaving no room for apathy or loneliness.

The temporary aspect of the project was drawn out on a daily basis. This was not a six-week project. Marshall could envision four to six months of work ahead of him. Keeping busy had always challenged him before. Now Lily slid into second place while his expertise was required each day, but each night she returned in the starring role of his night-time dreams.

His attempts at email were dismal, but hers were just as bad. In fact, Lily's were so damn boring if he hadn't known her he wouldn't have believed it. If a Portland weather report had been his only desire, he could have looked online for it.

Her descriptions of her catering events read like an itinerary - no spark, no interest. Who cared what the menu was? Or about the fact the three different varieties of eggplants and six different kinds of chilies were sprouting nicely in her garden.

He wanted to know if she missed him. If she missed him as much as he missed her. He wanted to know how she truly felt and what she wasn't saying. He wanted to see her. Touch her. Taste her.

Why wasn't she with him instead of serving lunch to some business group? If he emailed her now, would she come?

The answer was all too apparent. Marshall kept his thoughts to himself. Complaining would not solve his problems.

After three weeks, an unexpected break came. MIT announced a ten-day delay giving the scientists some breathing room. Marshall and Josh opted for a quick trip home. Rather than wait for the private jet, Marshall booked them on a commercial flight leaving that afternoon.

✦

Lily leaned by the window in her office, her arms wrapped around her waist, staring unseeing at the gravel parking lot and the chain link fence that separated them from their neighbors.

"You're pensive. What're you thinking?" Dori asked, coming into the office.

"Wishing I had the power to roll back time," Lily said without turning around.

"Oh? Do you have a date in mind you'd like to revisit?"

"About three months ago, I think, sometime before the bachelor auction. I'd like to go back to a time when I wouldn't be standing here missing Marshall. A time when being alone didn't seem lonely to me like it does now. Ignorance is funny, isn't it? I'm not so sure knowledge is power. In my ignorance, I managed to be happy-go-lucky never knowing what I was missing. Now I'm just lonely and sad. And really, if I continue this way, sort of pathetic."

Dori said nothing but came to the window and put her arm around her friend. "Maybe it would have been better if he'd left you slowly, gotten you used to the idea. But if you got your wish and went back in time, you'd also have missed the thrill of the ride. What's that Garth Brooks' song about the dance?"

"If you quote Garth Brooks' lyrics to me, we are finished as partners," Lily declared, making Dori laugh.

Josh flirted with the first class flight attendants on the plane -- women who were closer to Marshall's age than Josh's. His age didn't hurt him with the women. They were more than willing to flirt back. Marshall closed his eyes and pretended to sleep.

The plane landed in LA. Marshall and Josh were hustled down to customs where they waited to gather their bags. German Shepherds and armed guards patrolled in and around the luggage. Few of their fellow passengers waiting in line looked American born, considering that it was summer and high travel time.

The inspectors were thorough, going through bags, looking at articles of clothing and jewelry. Some of his fellow passengers were removing belts and shoes. Finally, they came to the front of the line.

"Your trip was work-related?" one of the armed guards asked Josh. Marshall watched as the second guard rifled through their suitcases.

"Yes," Josh answered.

The inspector let them pass without further incident. The men carried their baggage through another door and just as they were about to throw it onto the conveyor belt to be re-sorted to their next flight, Marshall noticed a man holding a placard with their names. He nodded in the man's direction and headed toward him with Josh close on his heels.

Relieved that he'd found his charges, the man's face broke into a smile. "I have a message for you." The messenger handed Marshall an envelope. "You have no idea what it took to get me in here," he said. "Had this not been an emergency we wouldn't have been able to contact you at all."

Tearing open the envelope, Marshall read the note quickly and handed it to Josh. "Do you know where we're supposed to go?"

"Follow me." The man led them through an exit door and hailed a passing taxi. "The cab will take you to an adjacent landing strip where your jet's waiting to take you to Dead Man's Cove."

Josh reread the note that the quick-thinking Sara had sent. "Another oil spill." He shook his head in disbelief. "Oh, man. This could affect us for years. I suppose we can get research money for this, but environmental disasters are not my first choice of jobs."

"Nor mine. Is your cell phone working?"

Marshall asked as he checked his own.

"No. I never recharged the battery."

"Maybe there'll be a phone where I can call Lily and have her meet us at the coast."

"Does she know you're coming home?"

"No. I'm surprising her."

The weariness seeped into Lily's bones. Summer was in full swing with long days and lonely nights. Everything ached.

The one day there were no events, Lily still worked.

At four, she was able to slip away. Another evening alone did not excite her, but she was too exhausted to think about going out.

The baby worried her. The roller coaster of her emotions had her constantly on edge. Some days she was ecstatic. Others, like today, she worried about a miscarriage or Downs Syndrome.

Other days she found her attitude had changed with the knowledge of her pregnancy. A baby might not have been planned, but even without Marshall's participation, it wasn't unwelcome. Of all the gifts she'd ever received, this was the best.

Her imagination ran wild. She hoped for a girl. A little dark-haired, blue-eyed sweetheart that she could name Cayenne after the spicy time she and Marshall had spent together. The heat of a habanero or a scotch bonnet was probably more descriptive, but having a daughter with either of those names wasn't cute.

Habanera Carmichael sounded like a woman who'd enjoyed too many margaritas. Telling the staid Marshall that she opted for such an unusual name might have yanked his chain, but it wouldn't have produced a joyous response. With a name like Cayenne, Pepper would make a cute nickname.

Marshall's emails were strained. Lily hadn't even bothered to answer the last one. Just let him go, she cautioned herself. If he called when he came home, she'd play it by ear.

Lily curled up on the recliner with a glass of orange juice to watch the evening news. It wasn't her first choice, not being a big TV watcher, but she was too tired to do anything else.

Another oil spill on the Oregon Coast dominated the news. Harried reporters stood on cliffs above the water and in frantic voices pointed out the destruction.

This one was bad. Helicopters flew overhead providing shots of the massive tanker that had run aground. An aerial view of the water darkened by the extensive area of the oil was repeatedly shown along with computer-generated images of potential future problems.

Seabirds, covered with oil endangering their lives, were rescued as volunteers pulled them from the slick water. The helplessness of the wild animals trapped by their greasy coats gave the environmental devastation a more visual pull on the emotions.

The reporters interviewed residents who discussed the impact to their lives and businesses, before calling on experts, like scientists, to discuss the future of Oregon's coast. From the hundreds of Marine Biologists located in Oregon, the one interviewed was none other than Marshall Caudill. Apparently, he was back from Down Under.

The phone rang. Lily sat straighter in her chair, torn between answering and knowing there was no one she wanted to talk to at this moment. Eventually, on the fourth ring she answered the phone dreading the conversation.

"You watching the news?" Dori asked without identifying herself.

Lily attempted levity. "He photographs well, doesn't he?" She listened to Dori's hollow laugh. "I can't talk about this, now. We'll talk tomorrow." Lily hung up the phone.

Unable to watch any more, she switched off the television and went to bed. Just before she snuggled under the covers, she turned off her phone. For the first time since the night Charlie had died, she wasn't going to lie at-the-ready for a middle-of-the-night disaster phone call or a doorbell being rung in the twilight hours by the police. And if Marshall needed to call her … well, that was his problem. As it was, he'd probably haunt her dreams.

Instead, she tossed and turned. Sleep eluded her as her mind replayed the night her husband had died. Funny how all the details seemed so clear after so many years --the brittle chill in the air, the grass frosted over from the rains and sudden drop in temperature. Nothing about the scene had lost its impact in the intervening time since that stormy January night.

Midnight had come and gone. Keyed up from work, too exhausted to sleep, they sprawled in the hot tub unwinding. A bottle of Merlot consumed between them.

Too much time had passed for her to recount the conversation. She only remembered that nothing earth-shaking had been said. It had simply been another day. What her memory was clear about was that there had been no Ben and Jerry's Cherry Garcia ice cream in the house -- Charlie's favorite.

At the time, she'd thought it was funny. Her husband, like a lot of chefs, ate all day long, and yet he never consumed a meal. Sitting down for dinner was a rarity. When quizzed about his last meal, he couldn't remember eating a thing, yet maintaining his weight had been a constant problem.

His desire for ice cream had been strong enough for Charlie to leave the warmth of the hot tub and the potential comfort of his bed to make a last run to the store. As with so many of his midnight rides, he took Jackson with him.

The fact he did not come immediately home could have been attributed to any number of things. Had she called the restaurant she might have found him there tackling whatever problem kept him from sleeping. Her dream even included Jackson, laying in the dining room waiting for Charlie's whistle that it was time to go.

Instead, she was jarred awake by the persistent doorbell. Four forty-four a.m. The clock's red numbers burned into her brain. A time when the angels are closest to the earth. A protected time for others, but not for her. For Lily, four forty-four a.m. was the time to receive bad news.

Two polite young police officers had stood at her door on that cold January night to tell her that Charlie's truck had left the Marquam Bridge about twenty minutes after he had left home. Gravely the police informed her that neither he nor the dog ever got out and, in fact, had a passing motorist not seen the accident, he might have disappeared without a clue.

The official manner used by the officers assigned to this unpleasant duty was designed to avoid messy emotions spilling out. Lily had politely obliged. Too stunned for conversation, she nodded after they had finished, mumbled something about phone calls she had to make and latched the door before she burst into tears. She cried for her husband, for herself and their life together.

Chapter Twenty

The coast was a mess and getting progressively worse as the oil carried by the movement of water brought it closer to the shoreline, expanding its area of damage. Volunteers and rescue crews, from Oregon and neighboring states, swarmed into the area like ants at a picnic. Some to help, some to photograph, many to merely gawk.

Every bed at CMI was filled. Marshall hadn't spent fifteen minutes alone in the four days they'd been here. Everyone insisted on just a little piece of him, tugging and pulling him in as many directions as a piece of salt water taffy. Through it all, Lily's silence frustrated him. He'd tried to call her half-dozen times and in a rare moment of solitude, he'd managed to email her twice to no response.

MIT listened as he described his coastal problems, but insisted he and Josh return to Australia in three days.

Early Friday morning, Ginger sat behind the tall receptionist desk. Lily stood on the other side, issuing the day's assignments.

"You need to be at home in bed," Ginger announced as she shifted her chair backward as far as the desk would allow.

Lily clutched her stomach. "I thought I was over this. It must be some sort of relapse of the flu I had a couple of weeks ago." The morning sickness hadn't bothered her for several days, but this morning it had hit her with a vengeance. A line of sweat broke out on her forehead. She lowered her head to rest on the counter of Ginger's workstation turning only when the door opened.

The man who entered appeared to be out of place. His brown suit and stuffy expression eliminated him as a candidate for a catered party. Lily raised her head and gave him a brief perusal before she dismissed him. A lot of people sought directions. Her major concern focused on whether or not she could make it to the restroom if needed.

"May I help you?" Ginger asked.

Lily swallowed hard as a wave of nausea washed over her immobilizing her from making any move.

"Is Lilith Carmichael or Doralene Conners here?" The man asked ignoring Lily slightly bent over the desk holding her stomach. His tone smacked of official duty.

"I'm Lilith Carmichael," she admitted.

As though seeing her for the first time, the

man stepped over to her and removed a folded paper from his jacket pocket. "You're served," he announced slapping the paper on the desk in front of Lily. The noise reverberated in the quiet room.

His immediate presence was close enough for his cologne to overpower her, and suddenly her stomach heaved forward, spewing its contents over his pant legs and shoes.

"Christ! Lady! I'm just doing my job here."

Holding a hand over her mouth she ran down the hallway to the bathroom. By the time Lily re-emerged, the reception area had been cleaned up, and the process server had departed. The faint odor lingered, but the front door was propped open to help air it out.

Dori stood at the desk with the folded paper in her hand. A damp washcloth held to her face, Lily slowly entered the reception area.

"Let's talk," Dori gestured toward her office.

Lily collapsed on the couch while Dori shut the door. "What's wrong with you? You're never sick. And, at least, if you're going to throw up on someone, a process server was a good choice, but frankly, this might be a problem in the future if you continue this way."

"I'm not sick. I'm pregnant." Her weak voice was filled with disgust.

Dori studied her partner sprawled on the

couch and commented. "I thought as much. How far along are you?"

"According to the doctor, two months," Lily admitted.

Dori grimaced. "Marshall Caudill's brought nothing but joy into my life. He got my partner pregnant and in the process broke her heart. And his ex-girlfriend has slapped us with a food-borne illness lawsuit. Do you think he's done improving our lives or will this continue?"

"Muffy's suing us?"

"Uh-huh. Apparently we used unsafe food methods in our preparation for the library event. After eating, she became ill and three days later had a car accident, as a result," Dori summarized from the papers she held in her hands.

"She didn't eat any of our food," Lily pointed out. "And she was drunk."

"I think, in this case, that is merely a technically. What I can tell you for sure is this will cause our insurance rates to go through the roof. It'll be cheaper to settle with her than to file another claim."

"Shall we talk seriously about selling?" Lily asked trying not to display any emotion on her face.

"Are you ready to have this discussion?"

"Not really, but it seems life is conspiring against us. It's probably time," Lily admitted.

`"Yes, and we will eventually sell, but not

today. I'm not letting some Barbie-doll bimbo run us out of business. We have thirty days to respond. Let's think about our best course of action."

Lily gave her partner a weak smile.

"You know as well as I do that if we're going to be in Perth by Monday evening, we'll need to leave early Sunday," Josh said. "Your plane's on the East Coast, so I've booked a commercial flight for us.

Josh and Marshall sat at CMI's large kitchen table. For the first time since their arrival, the two men were alone. Dinner consisted of mismatched leftovers. Josh rose to place their dishes in the dishwasher and give the kitchen one final cleaning.

"We're finished here anyway. At least there's nothing more we can do at this point. Peter's cutting short his stay in the San Juan's to be here in your absence."

Marshall was torn between his responsibilities to stay or go. The coastal cleanup? Or Australia? If MIT wasn't insisting, would Marshall return? Josh doubted it. Australia was their opportunity for the big time, but Dead Man's Cove was their special piece of the earth to protect.

"I haven't reached Lily. I want to drive to Portland in the morning and see her." Marshall's reply caught Josh off guard. He hadn't even considered a third possibility. Josh hesitated. Marshall had been antsy all week, but it had eluded Josh that Lily was the cause.

"It's Saturday," he pointed out, "You know she'll be working. Obviously, she's busy, or she'd have called you back."

"No. There's something about this that doesn't feel right." Marshall rose from the table and picked up the stack of work papers. A couple slipped from the stack and floated to the floor. Marshall didn't notice.

"I thought she wasn't expecting you?"

"She knows I'm here. I've been on the news every night. Her assistant assures me she's getting my messages." Marshall growled. "I don't have time to play these damn games with her. She knows how I feel. If she doesn't feel the same, she should say so, not just avoid me."

Josh smothered a chuckle, which would only serve to inflame the situation. He glanced at the man he admired most in the world and wondered how such a smart man could be so stupid. "I wonder who she learned that from. Wait! Isn't that how you broke up with Muffy?"

Marshall's annoyance was conveyed in his tone. "Muffy and I didn't have a committed relationship. Lily and I do." He grabbed the banister of the stairs and sighed before he began the climb to the top.

"A committed relationship?" Since this was the first time Josh had heard of it, he was betting Lily hadn't heard of it at all.

Marshall harrumphed. "Committed enough."

"So you've told Lily how you feel?" Josh asked, sensing that Marshall was committed in a way only convenient to Marshall. Josh had spent ten years watching the older man dance his way out of situations with women. He had tried more women than Judge Judy. Never in that length of time had Marshall ever indicated a woman meant more to him than a convenient passage of time.

"She understands how I feel."

Josh raised an eyebrow, wisely saying nothing, but called up the stairs after him. "Our plane reservations are for eleven o'clock Sunday morning. I'll meet you at the airport at nine."

Marshall left at midnight, his packed bags in the trunk. If he hurried, he'd have twenty-four hours to be with her. A lot could happen in twenty-four hours, especially with a woman as hot-blooded as Lily. All he needed was to be with her long enough, and she'd go back to caring about him the way she had.

In his mind he could see her dark eyes

clouded with desire staring up at him, her short dark curly hair spread in a complete disarray on his pillow, her lips pink and puffy. Wanting him. Needing him while he drove into her so deeply she'd never want another. She would be his before the sun rose.

Something was wrong.

At four-thirty in the morning, her driveway was empty. No one was home. Where could she be? Was she seeing someone else? On the off chance he was wrong, he rang the doorbell. Six, maybe seven times.

No response.

His weariness from the arduous week, on top of these frustrations over Lily, hit him hard. Where was she? Who could she be seeing? At least it wasn't Josh. This time.

At the freeway, Marshall maneuvered his car in the direction of her kitchen rather than his loft. Could she be at work? Right. Who went to work at this hour of the morning?

Apparently, caterers did. Her kitchen was ablaze with lights. Several vehicles were parked in the lot. The place was jumping.

The front door was locked, but the kitchen door was slightly ajar. Marshall slipped in and stood in the shadows watching the beehive of activity. Both Dori and Lily were cooking. And they weren't alone. At least half a dozen other employees ran from the store room to the van, carrying equipment.

A timer rang. Lily whirled and opened the bottom oven. "Oven door," she shouted. Shaking a pan, she announced, "we've got a good twenty more minutes on this frittata," as she pushed the rack back into place and checked the one below it.

"Let's load everything else into the vans. Bring the frittatas later," Dori said.

Lily closed the oven door and straightened. Her eyes met Marshall's. He tried to read her expression but wasn't sure whether her look of surprise was a good thing or not.

"You're up early," he said. The room, which had been pulsing with life, froze as everyone's attention focused in his direction. He was pretty sure Dori swore under her breath.

Lily ignored her. "We're doing breakfast for four hundred in about an hour."

That statement shook Dori into action as she gestured for the staff to load the vans. Lily busied herself wiping down stainless steel tables.

Marshall crossed the room watching her with each step. "Is there a reason you haven't returned my calls or emails?"

"Look at the schedule, Marshall," she

pointed to a well-marked calendar of events on the wall. "We've been swamped. Today started two hours ago, and we'll be lucky if it turns out to be a twelve-hour day. I'm too tired to correspond."

"I see."

She bit her lower lip, as though ashamed her answer smacked of haughtiness. "How was Australia? You weren't gone as long as you expected."

"We have to return tomorrow. Josh and I had a break in the schedule. But oil spill extended our stay. All of CMI is working to avoid an environmental catastrophe. If MIT weren't insisting on their return the Australia trip would be put on hold."

Lily nodded but avoided looking him in the eye as she wiped the spotless work surface for the third time.

"We're ready," Dori yelled from the loading dock.

Lily rechecked the egg dish in the oven. "You're going to have to go on. I'll bring these in the next load. They're still several minutes away from being ready."

Marshall surveyed the kitchen while he waited. Tables had been cleaned, but trashcans needed emptying and a large pile of dishes was randomly stacked in front of the dishwasher, both on the dish table and the floor.

Lily strode to the loading dock. While she

and Dori discussed the logistics of the food, equipment, invoice and map, Marshall sorted dishes.

One of the staff hurried by him to grab something from the back room. As she passed him a second time on the way back to the van, she pointed toward a black plastic apron hanging from the wire shelf. "Use that."

He nodded and slipped the apron over his head.

"What do you think you're doing?" Lily demanded a few minutes later.

"Helping out," Marshall said. "This is rocket science I can figure out how to load a dish rack and use the sprayer."

"I don't need your help."

"I'm not doing it because you need my help. I'm doing it because we're spending the day together. And if you have to work, then I'll work with you."

"I don't have time to argue with you," she declared and stomped off across the room to leave him alone.

Apparently he'd done something wrong because she was madder than he'd ever seen her, but he was hesitant to delve too deeply into his behavior or what he might have done to piss her off.

After several minutes of fussing, Lily finally

pulled the frittatas from the oven. Marshall admired her efficiency as she threw diced tomatoes and grated cheese across the top before covering them with film wrap, followed by tin foil, then slid each pan into the large hard plastic boxes. As rolled them to the loading dock, Marshall hurried to her side to lift the heavy boxes into the van.

"If I wasn't here, how would you do this?" he asked, amazed by the weight of the equipment.

"The same way you're doing it. One at a time."

Marshall didn't comment. When they'd finished, Lily added, "Get in the van. I'll lock up and get you an apron. I need a clean jacket."

"I've got an apron."

"That's a dishwashing apron. You'll be serving."

The van pulled away from the curb. He understood why it always smelled of food. The egg smell permeated the vehicle. Despite the fact the hot boxes were locked into place, Lily drove carefully, concentrating on the road as though rush-hour traffic would erupt at any moment even though it was five am. Neither spoke for several blocks.

He wanted to touch her, but he knew she wouldn't tolerate it. Not yet. Within a few hours, he planned to wear her down further, to let her vent her anger so that they could get past it. He had no idea why she was so mad at him, but he felt if he tormented her now, the results would be on the same level as batting a wasp nest with a stick.

The day whizzed by. One event followed another. Breakfast for four hundred, followed by box lunches for two different locations and a hot buffet lunch for fifty in a downtown office building. Staff rotated in and out the door with each event. The only constant employees were Lily and Dori. By mid-afternoon, Marshall's lack of sleep caught up with him. He stretched out on Lily's couch while waiting for his next assignment and fell asleep in seconds.

Whispered voices filled the room where he slept. It took him a moment to recall his location.

"Go home and take him with you."

"We've still got another event."

"It's a drop-off and I can handle it. And you're about to keel over yourself."

"Okay, I'll go. You just want him out of here."

"Don't be ridiculous. His presence today was truly helpful. It's you I want out of here. You ran out of steam about two hours ago."

Marshall laughed quietly to himself, pleased that his help had been valued. He got up from the couch refreshed and ready to go.

"Let's go." He captured Lily by the upper

arm and practically dragging her out the door. Dori grinned. Lily's back was to him as he was pulling her along, but judging by Dori's expression, he'd bet money that Lily's look was promising serious retribution. He smiled in return. For once Dori's ass was on the line, not his.

Lily protested when he forced her into his car rather than allowing her to drive, but he wasn't letting her out of his sight. And if she drove to her house, he was pretty sure the welcome mat would be withdrawn before he could arrive at the door.

"We're not going to your house," she declared.

"I haven't been home in weeks. I need to check the mail and make sure the place hasn't burned to the ground."

Grumpily, Lily sat stewing in her seat. Complaining wasn't getting her anywhere. Just because he was dragging her home with him didn't mean she was going to stay and they damn sure weren't going to have sex. No matter what.

He parked at the far end of the underground lot and once again held her upper arm firmly as he escorted her to the elevator. She didn't resist. There was no purpose to it. While he did things like check his mail, go to the bathroom or water the plants she'd simply take the elevator to the first floor, hail a cab and go home. Alone.

Her plans changed when Marshall failed to release the arm he held captive. He marched her out of the elevator and straight through the various rooms until she stood before the sliding glasses doors leading to the deck.

"Take off your clothes."

"No."

"Do it, or I'll do it for you. You're so tired you can hardly stand up. You need to soak some of the soreness from your body. The water temperature is only at about one-hundred degrees, but that'll be warm enough to make you feel better."

Not too warm for her pregnancy.

He tapped his foot. Finally, the lure of the hot tub won out, and she reached for the top button of her uniform. But even naked she would not be swayed into more. He would not seduce her. Of this, she was certain.

Naked hot tub bathing in the late afternoon in downtown Portland was going to be a daring experience. She hesitated as she viewed her surroundings. There were taller residential buildings close enough that she could be easily seen.

"Once you're in the tub no one can see you. And I'll bring you a robe when you're ready to get out," he assured her as though reading her mind.

She finally removed her jacket, and he held out his hand to take it. By the time she'd reached for the zipper on her pants, her fingers were trembling.

"Go on," he demanded when he held her pants as well. The bra followed by her panties was next. His stare was immediately disapproving when she stood naked before him. Glancing down, she realized she had not maintained her spa treatments for him. So what? Once she told him she was pregnant, it'll be all over anyway.

He led the way to the tub, concealing her with his body, and flung back the lid. Carefully, she climbed in and sank into the luxuriousness of the warm water and the unique position of bathing in public with a view.

Marshall left her to soak. Within a few moments, he reappeared with a tempting glass of red wine and disappeared again.

A drink would be perfect. She hadn't had a drink since the last time they'd been together -- before she'd known she was pregnant. But despite her desire, she couldn't drink now.

By the time, Marshall returned with the promised robe, Lily's muscles had dissolved into overcooked noodles.

"You didn't drink your wine," he said.

"Hmmm," she mumbled unable to form words and unwilling to share her reasons.

"Do you have enough energy to stand or do

I need to carry you?"

"I'll stand." She struggled to her feet.

"Good, let's have dinner and go to bed. We both need to sleep."

Lily opened her mouth to argue, but Marshall placed his fingers over her lips. "Tonight is about sleep –- not sex, so don't even bother to get worked up."

Chapter Twenty-One

Dawn streaked through the vertical blinds leaving pink stripes on his cream walls. She'd planned to sneak out before the morning sickness began. Her traitorous stomach already trembled with early warning signs.

But with his warm body curled around hers, it felt much too good to rise. From the minute he'd tucked her in next to him, she'd felt her anger drain away. Lying next to him erased the time they'd spent apart. Never had she felt as safe and protected and, dammit, loved as when he was with her. Why couldn't he have just stayed away?

Forcing herself, she slid out from under his arm and eased out of bed. Guilt bit at her ankles like a bad dog. If only the circumstances had been different…

Marshall deserved to know about the pregnancy, and she planned to tell him, just not this morning. After the Australia trip, if he called when he returned home, she'd tell him then.

Where was her willpower? All she wanted to do was crawl back into bed with him. He cared for her. Yesterday had proved that. But if she stayed, she had to tell him about the baby.

Instead, she crept down the stairs. The coffee

pot stood ready to go. Without thought, she plugged it in. Bending to the floor to pick up a piece of trash, she caught a whiff of last night's pizza in the garbage.

A thump from the floor above her had her jerking to attention. The blood rushed to her head as she inhaled the lethal combination of coffee fumes and food garbage. Her stomach lurched. With no time to spare, she sprinted down the hall to the bathroom.

Morning sickness hit her hard. Kneeling on the floor in front of the commode, she rested her head on the seat and tried to recover her zapped energy. If she didn't get out of here now, Marshall would wake for sure.

As Lily struggled to her feet, her stomach gave her just enough warning to raise the lid a second time before she was hunched again emptying any final remains.

This was good. She'd continue to be sick, but it'd be dry heaves. Not pleasant, but not as messy.

Gingerly, she struggled to her feet. Much better. She leaned over the sink intending to rinse her mouth when she saw Marshall's naked torso reflected in the mirror.

"Here's a washcloth. Was it the pizza? It didn't set very well with me either."

Lily shook her head and took the cloth from

his hand. She rinsed her face to avoid conversation.

"Your toothbrush's still in the cabinet if you want to use it."

She nodded as her mind raced. What could she tell him? Nothing appeared except the truth.

She bent to clean up the toilet seat, but Marshall stopped her.

"I'll get this, you go lie down. Are you feeling better? Why are you dressed? It's still dark out." Marshall's warm, naked body weakened her resolve to leave.

"I've got to go to work early today." She gathered her car keys and cell phone and pushed the elevator button.

"You can't go to work, you're sick. Stay here and let me nurse you until I have to leave for the airport. I'll call and catch a later flight." Marshall stroked her arms, attempting to pull her away from the door.

"I'm fine. You need to get ready to go. Have a great time in Australia and email me when you can." She stepped onto the elevator and smiled encouraging to assure him she was okay. An adult, mature parting.

"But you're sick," he said confusion in his voice.

Just as the elevator door was closing, she held out her hand and stopped it. "I'm not sick, Marshall. I'm pregnant." She released the door.

Marshall stared at her completely speechless

as the door closed, and she disappeared from view.

Jack Raulerson slouched against the doorframe of Steven Zonnheiser's office. His smug expression irritated Steven. He despised interruptions, but particularly from Raulerson. There was something about him that rubbed Steven the wrong way.

Not bothering to acknowledge him with an invitation to enter, Steven asked, "Yes?"

Raulerson studied his fingernails. "Guess who's getting sued again?" he asked in a lazy drawl.

"Who?"

"Luscious Foods." Raulerson refrained from smirking, but with an obvious effort. "That's your caterer, isn't it?"

"Cause of action?" Steven demanded, refusing to be drawn into the by-play.

"A guest got sick at an event. Although, they may have lucked out again because the complainant alleges that she had a vehicular accident as a result, only the accident didn't happen until three days later."

"Three days? That sounds screwy. Who's the plaintiff?"

"Muffin Avril Parsons. Here's a copy of the pleadings." Jack tossed them onto the desk.

Steven's fingers drummed a rhythm on the imported mahogany desk as he scanned the filings. Finally, he said, "Thanks," and laid the paperwork on a stack of files. He resumed working, dismissing Raulerson without giving an opinion on the lawsuit.

Patty, his assistant, stuck her head in the door a few minutes later. "I'm grabbing a sandwich from the deli downstairs. Can I get you anything?"

"No, but could you close my door?" Steven asked looking up. As soon as the door clicked, he picked up the phone and dialed his wife's number. The downtown Portland skyline failed to hold his interest as he stared out of the floor to ceiling windows.

"Caroline, why does the name Muffin Avril Parsons sound familiar to me?" he asked without going into detail.

"She dated Marshall just before he met Lily."

"I thought so. A tall blonde?" He only remembered her from the bachelor auction because she and Caroline had spoken at the end. Muffy's behavior at that point had stopped just short of rudeness to his wife. "Do you know anything about an incident at the Library Gala event? It took place while we were in Pebble Beach."

Steven listened carefully to his wife's

summary occasionally jotting notes. After he had hung up the phone, he stood and paced the terrazzo tile floor, trying to decide on the appropriate course of action.

Across town, Lily was wearing a hole in the carpeting with her constant crisscrossing of the room. Dori sat on the couch holding the file the women were supposed to be discussing. "So what did he say when you told him."

"Nothing."

"How could he say nothing, even if it was 'have a nice life,' he must have said something," Dori's tone indicated her patience was near the end.

"The elevator closed before he could say anything."

"Oh." A wealth of understanding came from that word. Lily finally looked at her partner for the first time -- guilt written all over her face.

Dori's lips pulled together in a tight line. "How did he look when you told him?"

"Like I'd just pulled out a gun and shot him between the eyes."

"What did you want him to say?" Dori asked, her voice gentle.

"I don't know. I rehearsed the scene a hundred times and never once did I envision how it would really happen."

"Lily, you've got to come to grips with this.

What do you want from this man?" Lily shrugged. "Has he told you he loves you?"

"No."

"Have you told him?"

Lily gritted her teeth. "I don't know. When you say it in the heat of passion, does that count?"

Dori looked at her partner, knowing her worst fears had come to pass. Gently, she nodded her head. "Sometimes that's when it counts the most."

Once the plane was airborne, Marshall found it impossible to remain seated. He strode the long aisles of the 747 missing the privacy of his jet. Nervous flight attendants offered assistance, but he just shook them off with a weak medical excuse about sitting too long.

Pregnant. Of all the manipulative tricks.

All his life he'd kept clear of scheming women to avoid this exact issue. Probably it'd been her plan from the beginning. And she'd told him so matter-of-factly! No coming to him to discuss solutions. No, it was simply. *By the way, I'm knocked up.* His hand still hurt from punching the door after it had closed.

She'd either want money or his name. He'd give her neither. Boy, had she set him up. Refusing his gifts, she'd been saving up for the grand prize. She wasn't planning on buying a vowel; she wanted the whole alphabet.

He surveyed the passengers as he paced. Families with small children surrounded him on the plane. Discontented wailing little rug rats. He'd never wanted that. Or everything else that came with them. He might love and admire his sister, but her lifestyle had no appeal.

A young boy caught Marshall's stare and waved his toy plane. Marshall stepped away not wanting to entertain a small child. The dark-haired child with large brown eyes gestured to the windows and said, "Plane."

Marshall nodded. "Yes, we're on the plane, aren't we?"

The child bobbed his head in agreement, then frowned and pointed to his ears. Reluctantly Marshall knelt beside the young boy to determine if his ears hurt from the changes in altitude or the noise of the jet engines. The reward for his concern was a huge toothless grin and the excited chatter of a toddler, not one word of which he understood.

Unable to think of an appropriate response, Marshall pursed his lips together and sputtered an engine noise, which was immediately imitated. The boy's entire face glowed with happiness. From between the seats, the child produced a book on planes. Marshall imitated the sounds of the motors of many of the planes as both man and boy studied the book. When Marshall spurted like a motor failing followed by the sound of a plane making a crash dive and ended with a loud boom, the boy laughed. Maybe having a son wouldn't be so bad.

The child's mother had been concentrating on a baby in her arms looked over to smile at the man willing to talk her son.

"Have many kids do you have?" she asked.

"None." Her question brought Marshall's kneeling position to his attention. He stood, giving the young boy a grin. "Yet," he added. Briefly, he pictured Lily growing pregnant with his child and found he wasn't as angry as he wanted to be.

⚙

Muffy lounged on her deck slathering lotion onto her legs. She peered closely at her legs. Her tan was fading. Certainly her joints were stiff from her inactivity.

She'd hoped the lawsuit would be more satisfying. The legal system worked too slowly. The caterers must be panicking by now. It annoyed her that she couldn't observe it first-hand.

The telephone rang. Finally on the persistent third ring she picked it up expecting a telemarketer to blotch her name before offering to save her money. There was no one she was expecting to call.

"Muffin Parsons?" A woman asked, her voice crisp and authoritative. "I'm Carly Thompson with *The News Report* on Channel 9. I'm doing a story about foodborne illness and food poisoning. I understand that you recently filed a lawsuit against a caterer because you became ill and had a car accident as a result. Is that true?"

Muffy's demeanor picked up instantly. "Will I be on television?"

The reporter laughed. "If you agree to an interview."

"Absolutely."

"My camera crew and I can come out this afternoon if that's okay with you. Are you still in pain from the accident?"

"Uh-huh. What color should I wear for the camera?"

"Any color besides blue will be fine. Try to harmonize with your living room."

A few hours later, Muffy answered her door on crutches and ushered the news team inside. There was the familiar face of the female reporter and two cameramen burdened down with equipment.

The cameramen surveyed the white-on-white room and hunkered down to set up their equipment while the female reporter did the introductions.

"Do you want her here?" Carly asked one of the men indicating a location on the couch.

"That's good," he said while Muffy sat and arranged herself on the couch. Her posture perfect. Her smile immaculate.

"Jim, turn on your camera, so she can see how the red lights work," Carly suggested. The red light on the camera came on.

"As you talk to the cameras watch the red lights. Try to speak to the camera with the light on." Carly advised as she took a seat on a chair facing the couch. The other cameraman moved his camera into position at Muffy's left.

Jim the first cameraman spoke. "No good, Carly. The room's too light. She needs some color behind her or she'll be washed out."

"Would plants work?" Muffy asked.

"Yeah, they'd be great."

Muffy left her crutches leaning against the couch and walked around the house gathering plants, which she arranged on the table behind the couch.

"Better," Jim said, looking through his lens. "What about that rust colored vase by the fireplace? Could we move that in closer?"

Muffy hurried over to retrieve the heavy vase and arranged it in position.

"Hey, this is looking good. I think if we added a touch of green to the couch, it'd bring out your eyes."

Muffy smiled at the man behind the camera, letting her cheeks dimple. "I've got a throw in the bedroom."

"Perfect."

Finally, Muffy settled on the couch, and the

interview began. She told her tale of woe without interruption. She described the library gala in detail, smiling for the camera. She'd always been photogenic and knew without a doubt she presented a lovely picture of wronged innocence. Like her lawyer, the audience would be outraged by her misfortune.

Carly asked. "What exactly did you eat that made you sick?"

"They had a wide selection of food," she avoided being pinned down.

"Did you know there were eleven other caterers at that event? How did you know it was something from Luscious Foods that caused your illness?"

"I didn't eat anything else."

"Did you have anything to drink?"

Muffy hesitated. Martini's had been flowing freely. "Maybe, I don't remember, but I could've had a drink."

"Then you were sick all weekend?" The other woman looked concerned as she continued. "So sick you couldn't even leave the house?"

"Yes."

The reporter was asking all the right questions. This was going better than Muffy expected.

Carly flipped open her notebook and

consulted her notes. "Except to go for a drive, Monday night, well actually early Tuesday morning? What time was that?"

Good. Establish a timeline for the viewers. "After midnight. My stomach was upset. I couldn't sleep. Sometimes a drive will calm me down."

"I see. So you've had this experience before?" The reporter tilted her head, eyes wide.

Muffy stopped. Her brain whirled. She knew that look, she'd used it herself. For the first time, a shiver of alarm ran up her spine. She looked at the cameras and forced another smile. "Of course, everyone's had times when they couldn't sleep."

Carly's questioning became more detailed, but Muffy stuck closely to her facts. Finally, the reporter snapped her notebook closed, and Muffy exhaled a breath she didn't know she'd been holding. The interview was finished. It had gone well. She placed a hand on the arm of the couch to rise and noticed the reporter did not do the same.

Carly leaned closer. "Do you know a man named Marshall Caudill?"

Muffy's stomach churned. She'd been set up. A ball of fury caught in her throat. Had the camera light been off, she might have demanded the reporter leave. She thought about how to answer. Did she know Marshall? There was simply no denying she did.

Carly didn't wait for the answer. Instead, she asked her next question. "According to the hospital report, he came to drive you home. Is that correct?"

"Yes." Muffy breathed a little easier and strained with the effort the smile cost her. Of course, that information was available from the hospital. She twisted her head, trying to ease the tension in her shoulders without appearing nervous. What else could this damn woman ask?

"Were you dating exclusively at that time?"

The sucker punch left her breathless. This wasn't the way this interview was supposed to go. Clutching the arm of the couch for support, Muffy rose shakily to her feet, rolled her eyes back in her head and gracefully swooned to the floor.

Explain that to the news audience, you bitch.

Chapter Twenty-Two

Sleep once again eluded Lily, but this time erotic dreams weren't the problem. Except for the occasional morning sickness, her pregnancy was going smoothly. Instead, guilt rode her hard. Marshall had once accused her of being afraid and she'd denied it, but it was true.

Each night she lay awake with questions chasing each other in circles. Why hadn't she faced him like an adult and explained she wasn't holding him accountable? His shocked look followed by his silence made sleep impossible. Every time she thought about how she'd avoided him when they had time to talk gave rise to her self-loathing. Talking now with him halfway around the world was an insurmountable option.

Emailing him wasn't the answer either. There was nothing she could say in an email that would make it right. But it was a start. It took her only three hours to compose a three-sentence email.

"I'm sorry. Telling you the way I did was wrong, but I'd already made a decision and I wanted you to know I expected nothing from you. I should have handled the whole thing differently."

Three days later her email bounced back as undeliverable.

Dori wanted to throttle her partner for mishandling telling Marshall about her pregnancy. Instead she worried. Did Lily truly want the baby? How did Marshall feel? What if Lily worked so hard she had a miscarriage? Would she ever forgive herself? These and a thousand similar questions crossed Dori's mind. Finally unable to help herself, she took matters into her own hands.

"I'm making plane reservations for you."

"Where am I going?" Lily asked hardly caring.

"Australia. You and Marshall have got to resolve this thing."

"I don't even know where he is. Unless you're thinking, I'm going to tour the entire continent, going there isn't the answer."

"Why don't you know where he is?"

"He didn't tell me and I haven't heard from him."

Once again, Dori found herself cursing Marshall under her breath as she stormed out of the office and slammed the door behind her.

Testing had been moved back to the original site – the Great Barrier Reef. Local newspapers covered the international team of Scientists lowering MIT's equipment into the water.

Hours later Marshall poured over the oceanic maps, charting the testing patterns for the upcoming days. Josh tapped him slightly on the shoulder.

"Do you have a moment?"

Marshall looked up into the worried eyes of the younger man. "Sure." Josh led the way to the equipment monitors. The multitude of cameras brought back clear photos of the ocean floor.

"Look at this," Josh said pointing to some bright green algae. Marshall leaned forward until he was almost pressed his nose to the monitor. "Can you get closer?"

Josh maneuvered the camera within inches of the plant.

"Caulerpa taxifolia." Marshall murmured. "Good eye. We need samples. Don't make an announcement until we're sure." Australia had already battled the toxic algae, also known as killer algae in New South Wales, but to find an outbreak of it in less temperate waters was a disaster in the making. To allow the fast-spreading, impossible-to-irradiate algae into the barrier reef would ruin the ecosystem of the water and all the marine life as those living around the Mediterranean Sea had already discovered.

The samples arrived and within hours the identification had been confirmed and his world exploded. The government dry docked MIT's AUVs, refusing to allow them back in the water without industrial cleaning. Keeping the algae contained was their number one priority.

Scientists from every discipline on the continent camped on the doorstep of the testing site. Between the media, the gawkers and those with a genuine need to know, Marshall struggled to complete reports to MIT on the possibility of continued testing.

CMI and Dead Man's Cove were faring no better.

"Have you heard from Sara?" he asked Josh for the third time that week.

"Not only is your email down," Josh blurted out frustrated by the continuous problems. "But a virus has spread to CMI's computer system. Sara arranged for a computer specialist to come out and revamp the system, but he can't get there until Monday. So the system's shut down."

"She can't get anyone sooner than that?" Marshall was ready to explode.

"Marshall," Josh said through gritted teeth. "The technician's coming from Portland. Sara's working night and day on the shore clean up. Give her a break."

By the end of the following week, most of Marshall's immediate duties had been put on hold. He slept well for the first time in days; the ever-tightening band around his heart eased.

Josh banged on his door early Saturday

morning. "I've got to pick up something for my mother. Let's pick up something touristy and see a bit of the area."

In a rented car, Josh practiced driving on the left-hand side of the road causing Marshall no end of stress. If there had been a brake on the passenger's side Marshall would have certainly used it.

"Stop stomping on the floorboard."

Marshall gritted his teeth and aspired to be a better passenger, but Josh's driving had him so on edge he couldn't help himself. "You're driving too close to the curb."

"A few minutes ago, I was hugging the center lane," Josh groused. "Look, there's a shopping area."

"You can't turn here. It's one way."

Several horns sounded behind them.

"You're making a U? In front of the no U-turn sign?"

Several minutes later Josh located the entrance to the shopping center and parked in front of a party store.

"I'll just be a minute." He scowled at Marshall.

"No problem, I need the time to restart my heart and build up my endurance."

When Josh didn't immediately reappear, Marshall got out to stretch his legs and window gaze. The party store featured life-size cardboard cutouts in the window. Mel Gibson was featured in three different poses. The only one Marshall recognized was Braveheart. The same held true for Russell Crowe, Hugh Jackman, and Nicole Kidman. Animated characters that followed were easier

But the one that caught his eye was Betty Boop in a classic Marilyn Monroe pose. Her skirt was blowing up over a grate and a silly little dog appeared beside her. Betty Boop's eyes were green rather than dark chocolate brown. But short of that, Lily stood before him with a sexy, yet innocent come-and-get-me grin.

He stood transfixed by the poster.

"Wow. Except for the size of her head, Lily looks like Betty Boop," a voice commented over his shoulder. Marshall faced Josh.

"I've got to go home. I've left things a mess. MIT doesn't need me. Lily does. God, I've completely mishandled this situation."

"What situation?"

"Lily's pregnant."

Josh stood mouth agape staring at his friend. "I'll drive you back to the hotel. There's a flight out this evening. You'd better find a way to be on it."

Marshall nodded as they headed toward the car.

"Wait," Marshall said. "I need that poster."

"No, you don't." Josh admonished. "You

need the real thing."

◈

"Are you going through with the report?" the station manager asked as he watched the sound technician adjust Carly's microphone.

"Of course. Our journalistic integrity depends on it."

"Her lawyer's threatening a lawsuit if we show it," he said.

"I'll mention that in my report if you think it will help," she offered.

"No. I think the report will stand on its own. It's a good story."

"Thanks for letting me do this my way." Pleased he was willing to trust her judgment.

"I'd feel better about it if you told me who gave you the tip." He nudged her harder. Carly knew he hoped going out on a limb for her hadn't cost him his job.

"I promised confidentiality, and he'd do the same for me."

"It's good work, Carly. The kind of work that makes a reporter's reputation."

Carly sat in the anchor's chair and waited for her co-anchor to introduce the story. It was good work. Proud that she'd done the job well in addition to repaying a favor at the same time. Steven Zonnheiser had kept her kid brother out of juvenile detention over a hair-brained childish stunt. Investigating and reporting a questionable situation was the least she could do in return.

And what a story she'd discovered.

The red light on the camera flashed giving her the cue. Carly faced the camera and delivered the news.

"Love, loss, and revenge. It's an age-old story that rarely goes out of style. In a recent investigation of a lawsuit involving a woman suing a caterer over a supposed food-borne illness, Channel Nine News uncovered an entirely different set of facts. A fraudulent lawsuit with the intent to ruin a local businesswoman simply because that woman accepted a date with a man whose former girlfriend was angry."

As the story unwound, the camera showed a clip of Muffy stating she'd eaten no one's food but the caterer in question. Random interviews with half dozen people followed stating Muffy been drunk, but she hadn't eaten the food. She attempted to throw it before the caterers intervened.

In another interview snippet, Muffy stated she was so sick she couldn't leave her house all weekend followed by the tennis club administrator displaying his scheduling book. According to the written record, she'd played tennis from noon to three the following day with

Suzanna Gerland, who, when interviewed, remembered that Muffy had won all three sets.

A clip of Muffy whirled as she discussed her on-going injuries and her need to use crutches to walk even the shortest of distances. While Muffy smiled in a beguiling manner at the camera, an inset of her moving back and forth across the living room moving plants, a vase and a throw without aid or pain painted a different picture.

When Marshall's name surfaced. Muffy's swoon had been omitted, but others interviewed talked about the bachelor auction. Liv Shelton discussed the breakup between Muffy and Marshall, weeks before the library incident.

At the end of the news report, Muffy, looking as perfect as ever, stated simply "I had no other choice but to file a lawsuit. I couldn't allow my reputation to be ruined."

As the news moved on to other stories, Steven leaned back in the recliner and smiled. Carly had done a superb job. Helping her had been very beneficial to him. Caroline rose from the couch, leaned over and kissed him.

"Thank you," she whispered in his ear.

Briefly, he wondered how Caroline always knew. Maybe his sons were right. Maybe she did have eyes in the back of her head.

Chapter Twenty-Three

Marshall grabbed a cab at the Portland airport and headed straight to Luscious Food's kitchen. Even though it was late afternoon, the chances of Lily being at work were good. He scanned the parking lot for her missing van. Maybe she was making a delivery.

Inside, Ginger was closing up the office for the day. As soon as Marshall entered, Ginger fidgeted.

Marshall noted her nervousness. "Is Lily here?"

"She and Dori are out celebrating. I don't know where," she added defensively before Marshall could quiz her.

"Celebrating?" Marshall asked half afraid his name would be involved in the answer. Could they be celebrating her pregnancy? Or were they celebrating that she was no longer pregnant? What could she have done in the month or so he'd been gone? Perhaps this was why she hadn't wanted an opinion from him. Why hadn't he come home sooner?

"The lawsuit against them got dropped," Ginger said.

"Lawsuit? What lawsuit?" Marshall wasn't

sure if relief or panic were on the horizon

"The one your ex-girlfriend initiated because she was mad at you."

"Oh, hell," Marshall exclaimed. "What happened?"

Ginger detailed the facts making Marshall wanted to bang his head on her counter. No wonder Lily had been so angry the last time she'd seen him. Leaving her for a month had been a big mistake. He'd have sooner left his wallet on a street corner than leave her alone again. She was much more precious to him than his money or possessions, and yet he treated her more callously. There was no time left, he had to find her now.

"Ginger, I've bungled this whole thing. Do you not know where they are?"

Ginger hesitated twisting her fingers. Finally she asked, "Do you love her?"

Marshall tented his fingers and stared at the receptionist. This was not the woman he wanted to confess to, but if it got him to Lily sooner, so be it. "Yeah, but it took me a long time to figure it out."

Ginger frowned. "You don't deserve her, you know."

"That's probably true, but she loves me, too. Even if she's angry enough to spit nails at me, we need each other."

Ginger pursed her lips. "They're around the corner at the Lickity Split. Since they're not drinking, they may have already gone home by now."

"They're not drinking?" Marshall asked.

"Of course not. Lily's pregnant."

Marshall nodded. She hadn't done anything foolish. Relief washed over him in waves as he hurried to the restaurant where happy hour was in full swing.

Marshall searched the restaurant and the parking lot carefully to satisfy himself that the two women had already departed. Marshall's cab dropped him by the loft to pick up his car. He drove by Lily's house and saw that she hadn't gone straight home either.

Rather than waiting, he drove to Caroline's house. Both she and Steven were home along with their three children, two large dogs, and Princess.

The family was delighted to see him, but Princess was overjoyed. If Lily's reaction were half as enthusiastic, Marshall would be the luckiest man on the planet.

"We didn't expect you back this soon," Steven commented as he ushered the boys and the animals outside to roughhouse in the back yard.

"I'm going to ask Lily to marry me," Marshall announced without preamble.

Caroline stopped searching the refrigerator

and stared at her brother.

Steven grinned and slapped Marshall on the back. "Congratulations. This calls for a drink. Caroline, what would you like?"

Caroline's expression hadn't changed, but the sound of her name brought her attention back to her husband. "A glass of red wine. Thanks."

The bar was located in an alcove adjacent to the kitchen. As Steven opened the cabinet doors for glasses, he asked Marshall, "Bourbon?"

"Fine," Marshall agreed. "You don't seem overjoyed, Caroline."

"I'm surprised that's all. You've spent weeks telling me that Lily was a short-term relationship. Out-of-the-blue you've done an about face. What changed your mind?"

"I love her."

Caroline smiled. "It's about time. Are you thinking next summer?"

"Next summer? That's a year away. Lily's not a blushing debutante. She doesn't need a yearlong engagement. If I can convince her to marry me, it's going to be as soon as I can arrange it. This week, if possible," Marshall declared.

Steven placed a glass of red wine in front of his wife and handed his brother-in-law a low-ball of bourbon on the rocks before returning to the bar for his glass.

Caroline eyed her brother carefully and

asked. "What do you mean 'if I can convince her'? Why do you think she wouldn't want to marry you?"

Marshall shrugged and lifted his glass in a mock salute to his family. "My timing is off. Lily's pregnant."

Steven choked on his drink and Caroline set her untouched wine back on the granite counter with such force that both men looked to see if she'd snapped the stem of the wineglass.

"Are you the father?" she demanded.

Marshall raised an eyebrow designed to convince Caroline she'd better not cross over the line between concern and nosy.

"Yes," he said. His voice allowed no doubt.

Despite Marshall's subtle warning, Caroline couldn't help herself. She had to ask, "You're sure? You've been away for over a month."

"Caroline," Steven and Marshall both voiced together.

Marshall's lips formed a tight line. "I'm sure. Before Lily hooked up with me, she could've qualified for a convent. Her whole life revolves around work."

"How could you get a woman pregnant at your age?" The high-pitched quality of Caroline's voice reflected her appalled state.

"Age doesn't affect the mechanics of how it happens," Marshall said dryly.

Steven snorted, earning a look from his wife who continued quizzing her brother. "Marshall, do you mean to tell me you were so overcome by passion you couldn't take thirty seconds to open the bedroom drawer and put on a …" Caroline sputtered finding it impossible to say condom. "…to protect yourself."

"No, what I mean to tell you is that we were 'so overcome by passion' that we were seldom in the bedroom when it happened. Personally I think doing it in your laundry room was what did the trick."

As Caroline gasped, her husband, unable to contain himself burst into laughter.

"My laundry room is hardly conducive to such behavior," she declared.

Marshall shrugged. "Conducive or not, when hormones run amok, things happen where they happen." When his sister didn't respond, he added. "Regardless of age. I'm just hoping that Lily understands that the pregnancy isn't the only reason I want to marry her."

Caroline's expression shifted from defiance to concern. "I'll be right back," she said as she left the room.

Steven had stopped laughing at the interplay between brother and sister and asked Marshall, "Do you really think she'll refuse you?"

"She's angry about a number of things. Muffy sued her," Marshall said slumping into a chair.

A sly grin crossed his brother-in-law's face. "After that report on TV last night, if the lawsuit hasn't been dropped, it will be."

Marshall's instincts told him Steven knew more than was said, but this wasn't the time for that discussion. "So I heard. I'm hoping that helps."

Caroline reentered the kitchen holding a small box. "Exquisite jewelry sometimes helps when you need a sure thing. This was our mother's ring." She opened the box and showed her brother the ring their father had given their mother. The cluster of diamonds after fifty years was still breathtaking.

"Are you sure?" Marshall asked knowing the ring had been a special bequest to Caroline from their mother.

"She'd be delighted you're finally getting married. If she were still alive, she'd have offered it to you herself."

Marshall gave Caroline a fierce hug. As they pulled back, tears glistened in her eyes.

"I'm thrilled for you," Caroline whispered.

"I am, too," Steven said. "Now go find Lily. Caroline and I have important business in the laundry room."

"Steven," Caroline gasped.

But the surprise was on Marshall when

Caroline giggled and didn't seem the least embarrassed.

Marshall's mission to convince the independent Lily to marry him gave him trepidation as he anticipated an uphill battle.

Her van was parked in the driveway. Even though it was almost eight o'clock, the sun hadn't set yet. From over the top of the privacy fence he could see the sprinkler sweeping her back yard garden. Without too much thought, Marshall walked toward the rear of the house and opened the gate.

With the advent of summer, her backyard had changed. The garden was filled with a profusion of plants. He stood slightly awed by the sight of corn stalks and fruit trees preceded by rippling rows of greenery almost up to the patio and realized he'd never really looked at her yard before.

He thought of her as being tidy and organized, but her garden was an explosion of shapes and colors. Tentatively he stepped away from the gate when a movement caught his eye. Against the far side of the yard where it curved into a narrow side yard, Lily harvested beans from a large trellis.

"Hello, Lily."

Lily lurched back and dropped her fist full

of beans, missing the tub at her feet. Turning, she faced the voice she knew as well as her own since it had been keeping her awake at night for weeks.

Lily fought to hold herself back. Her body wanted to greet him in a way that would make the neighbors call the vice squad. Her heart raced. She could hear it pounding against her chest. He could probably hear it, too.

Had she not been so focused on her body's reaction, she might have thought of a clever comment. As it was unable to think of anything intelligent, she went for the obvious. "So you're back from Australia or is this just a brief vacation?"

"For good. I'm through traveling for a while. There's a book in the back of my mind, I want to write and now is as good a time as any."

Lily stared at the man in front of her. His lips might have been moving, but for as little sense as he was making, Swahili could have been the chosen language.

Finally, Lily asked. "What about CMI?"

"CMI can function without me. We've lost sight of the fact it's a team effort, not a one-man show. Lots of my colleagues have held back from the spotlight because they preferred me handling the publicity segment. As a result, I've become more sought after because I was the face of the Institute. No more. Now that responsibility's going to be shared."

"Why are you doing this?" Lily finally managed to croak out.

"Because a father needs to be at home with his family."

"Don't even go there, Marshall," Lily warned, shaking her head trying to head off the inevitable turn in the conversation.

"Sooner or later, Lily, it's gotta be discussed. I'm not going to wait forever for you to make an honest man of me."

Lily laughed. This was not good. She was supposed to be angry with him. If he made her laugh, how could she maintain her distance? "Are you attempting the World's Worst Proposal?"

"Hell, no," Marshall said. "If I proposed to you, you'd refuse."

"Yeah. And why is that, Marshall?" She knelt by the tub and replaced the beans that had fallen to the ground. It was dark enough that continuing to work in the garden would be futile. Picking up the tub, she headed for the back door.

"Because you'd think the only reason I'm asking is because you're pregnant." Marshall reached the door before her and held it open, allowing her to enter first.

There was little point in not inviting him inside. He was determined to come in regardless of what she wanted.

"I assume you're here to talk." She put the beans on the kitchen table. "Can I get you something to drink?"

"No. And I don't want to talk right now, either."

"Well, what do you want?" As soon as the words were out of her mouth, she realized her mistake as he closed the distance between them with one short step and wrapped his arms around her.

Lily considered struggling, but her body welcomed the man just as it always had, and she lacked the energy to fight both of them. Besides she missed him. To admit anything else would have been a lie.

He kissed her. His fingers framed her face. Her lips were open, but his tongue only brushed across her bottom lip a time or two, it didn't take possession of her mouth. The kiss wasn't carnal, but rather tender and loving.

Lily could handle his indifference and even his anger, but a tender emotion, suspiciously feeling like love or something very close to it, was impossible for her to comprehend. Large tears filled her eyes and rolled down her cheeks onto his hands.

He kissed her tears away and murmured, "You haven't cried since the first night we made love when you were worried about disappointing me. I don't think these are the same tears. Why are you crying now?"

Lily shook her head unable to form any coherent words and unable to understand her own emotions.

"You missed me, didn't you? I think you and Little David or Little Julia needed me to be here for you and I wasn't."

The caressing sound of his voice swept her along, cradling her emotionally until he chose to name their child.

Her head popped up. "David or Julia? I don't think so. Cayenne or Basil."

Marshall snorted. "Cayenne, maybe. Basil sounds like a boy we're condemning to a life as an English fop. I don't think so."

"I'm not locked into Basil, but I don't want something as plain and ordinary as David. That sounds like a first-grade reader. 'See, David, run. Run, David, run. "

"That was Dick, not David," he informed her. "And I'm so bloody sorry that I want a normal name for my son."

"'Bloody sorry.' Jeez, you've been down under waaay too long. And what's so *bloody* important about an average name or in your case *normal*?"

"Well, let's go with the fact we're already saddling him with the world's oldest parents. When he's ready for college, I'll be sixty-five."

"What are you worried about? Women will still be falling all over you," Lily retorted.

"Maybe," he said. "But I'll only have eyes for young Alex's mother."

"You're such a liar," she said, voicing her doubt about his declaration. "But Alex isn't a bad name." She tried it out. "Alistar Carmichael. Alexi Carmichael."

"Not Alistar. Not Alexi. Alexander. *Alexander Caudill.*" His stance did not encourage defiance, but she couldn't help herself.

"Alexander James Caudill," she declared.

Cautiously, Marshall nodded his agreement.

"That way, if he turns out to be a cool little kid, we can call him AJ," she said pleased with the decision.

"I should probably mention my family isn't big on nicknames," he said. "Maybe I should hope for a girl."

Both stood there looking at each other.

The guilt Lily had been feeling for the past two weeks surfaced. It just bubbled up out of her as she declared, "I'm sorry about the way I told you. I can well imagine that you're not delighted."

Marshall wrapped his arm around Lily and

guided her down the long hallway to her bedroom. "You didn't give me many opportunities to be delighted or anything else for that matter." His voice was low. Not angry, but hurt. "I was furious at first. Partially, because of the pregnancy, but partially, because you didn't trust me to help solve the problem. By the time you'd told me, you'd already made your decision. I finally realized that it wasn't so much a lack of trust, but more that you saw me as just one more problem to solve."

Lily and Marshall sat on the edge of the bed. "I never thought you wanted the commitment of a child. I tried to keep you from feeling trapped."

Marshall stroked her arms and pulled her to him. "When are you going to learn you don't always have to be the one in charge?"

"I'm sorry about the pregnancy." Could she sound more pathetic? Even to her own ears, she was disgusting.

Marshall didn't respond. He just continued to hold her.

She began a second time. "I hadn't planned to get pregnant. I'm too old. But once it happened, giving the baby up was impossible. It just seemed like this was my only opportunity. That's selfish, I know and didn't take you into consideration at all, but I'm not expecting anything from you. I'm okay with taking care of the baby alone. Nobody even has to know you're the father."

"Lily, fathers take care of their children. I'm not sorry that you're pregnant. And I'm not interested in marrying you just because you're pregnant."

"You're not?"

"Hell, no. I love you. I can't conceive of living my life without you," Marshall declared. "The pregnancy's just an unexpected gift."

"You love me?" Lily asked surprised.

"Tell me what you want. Do you want me to give up working entirely? Should we move into this house? My loft? Some place new? The coast? New York City? Tell me. I'm willing to do whatever you want with a few caveats."

"Caveats?"

"Conditions," he clarified.

"I know what caveat means. What're yours?" she asked.

"We have to live together -- in the same town. In the same house and sleep in the same bed," he stated, not wanting to be unclear. "Both of us have to commit to working fewer hours. Marriage and family have to become our number one priority."

"You love me?" she repeated, stunned by the direction of the entire conversation.

Marshall laughed. "Yeah, Betty Boop, I do."

Lily frowned.

"Frown all you want, but it was a Betty Boop poster that made me realize how much I missed you. Loving you snuck up on me. Somehow I thought love would be different than this. Something with a more definite sign –- like a club to the head, but I never expected I'd have trouble breathing because being without you hurt so much."

Lily stared open mouthed at the man she'd known she loved for weeks, the man she'd missed so much it'd hurt and wanted to tell him, but couldn't find the words.

Marshall watched her eyes and seemed to follow the emotional conflict as it flickered across her face.

"I know you love me, too."

Lily finally found her voice. "Marry me, Marshall," she said. Sucking in a deep breath, she attempted levity. "Let me make an honest man out of you."

"You're not going down on one knee? I've always hoped for a romantic proposal." Marshall feigned hurt.

Lily raised an eyebrow but lowered herself to one knee. "Will you marry me and be a father to our child?" She asked.

"This is so sudden." Marshall fluttered his hands around his chest in a parody of distress making Lily snicker. But his lips curled upward in a grin as he leaned over and kissed her lightly. "Yes, I'll marry you."

Lily broke off the kiss. "About your caveats…" She struggled off her knee so she could sit on the bed. Marshall's smile faded.

"Dori and I have discussed selling Luscious Foods. If it were to sell, we could sell or rent out my house and move to the coast. I think we should keep the loft, so we have a place in town. But you can't give up CMI for me. However, a book would be cool. Will it bother you if I don't work?"

Marshall listened with interest, surprised that such a compromise was possible but more astonished at the multitude of directions her mind took when she was problem-solving. "The guys at the coast are going to love you. I'm all in favor of your solutions. However, if we move to the coast and you become bored, there's a lot less opportunity for you to start another career."

"Marshall, we're young. We have the rest of our lives ahead of us. In my twenties, my career options were limited by my narrow interests. In my forties, I have a lot more ideas to investigate. Now that I've had a successful career I have nothing to prove, so in some ways I'm freer than I've ever been."

"Will you miss working?"

"No. In the past few weeks, I've come to realize that I am not just a caterer. I'll miss Dori. But I won't miss the work itself. And if you're worried, every so often we can invite a fussy mother of the bride down to the coast to discuss the intricacies of selecting corresponding hues of lavender to create the perfect wedding ambiance."

Marshall had no trouble imagining such a guest. "Where do you want to go on a honeymoon?"

"Tuscany. I've always wanted to go to Italy, but Tuscany in particular."

"That can be arranged, my family has a villa in Tuscany." Then he laughed and hugged her. "You and I are going to be very happy," he added as he removed the ring from his pocket. "My father gave this ring to my mother for their engagement. Now that you've said yes, there's no returning it."

Lily took a deep breath and stared at the stunning ring. "It's too perfect."

Marshall slipped it on her finger pleased to see it fit. He leaned over to kiss her, but she raised her hand to stop him.

"Before I marry you, there's one thing I have to know."

Marshall waited.

"What is the name of our song?"

Releasing his breath, Marshall chuckled. "*At Last*."

"*At Last*?" Lily searched her memory trying to put lyrics with that title.

Marshall elaborated. "It's the perfect song

for us. The first line is '*at last, my love has come along*'."

THANK YOU!

Thanks for reading The Wrong Lover, book 3.5 in the Wrong Series where Wrong Never Felt So Right. I truly hoped you enjoyed it.

If you liked this book, tell a friend, write a review, or send an email. If you hated this book, tell me why. Let me know where I failed to value your time. I welcome any comments you would like to make.

If you would like to be notified of the next book in this series. Please go to my website at: www.Nancybrophy.com and sign up for my newsletter. Or you can email me at: Nancybrophy@gmail.com. I appreciate hearing from readers.

About the Author:

Nancy Brophy lives in Portland, Oregon. She, her husband, her two dogs, PB and J, and forty chickens own a house that was destroyed by fire. Fourteen hair-pulling months later they've moved back into the house. One day she'll be able to laugh about it. Then she'll use it in a story.

Stories don't get written by themselves.

The following people played a major role in bringing this story to life: Cassiel Knight, Darla Luke, Su Lute, Linda Mercury, Jessie Smith, Linda Kearney, Theresa Patrick and Millie Lee.

A special thanks to my good friends, Marshall and Lily, who took the time to tell me their story.

Nancy would love to hear from you.

www.nancybrophy.com
Nancybrophy@gmail.com